CHAPTER 1

L aura Smith was twenty-four and still single when her friend, flatmate and fellow primary school teacher Julie, dragged her along to a family birthday party insisting Laura was never going to find the man of her dreams if she sat at home every evening marking exercise books! The party was in honour of Julie's mother's fiftieth birthday and although it crossed Laura's mind such an occasion would be severely lacking in eligible young bachelors, to humour Julie, she had nonetheless donned her best party dress and added her latest purchase - a stunning pair of stilettos!

The party was as Laura had imagined, full of aunties, uncles, cousins and friends of the family, the average age group being around the fifty mark. She had been introduced to numerous guests as Julie's colleague and flatmate, resulting in the majority of conversations being a discussion on how she felt about the current programme for education.

After helping herself to a large drink and equally large slice of birthday cake, Laura found an empty sofa at the far end of the enormous lounge and was enjoying being alone for five minutes. She had just taken a large bite of cake when a tall, rather dishy guy gestured towards the empty seat beside her and she nodded gesturing she had a mouthful of cake. He smiled and as he sat down next to her the air around them was immediately filled with the heavenly waft of woody aftershave.

When she was able to speak, Laura apologised and was rewarded with another grin. The 'dish' held out his hand and squeezed hers gently as he introduced himself. "I'm Peter and I'm delighted to have found someone around my own age to speak to!" Instantly realising she might be offended by his comment, he immediately added, "Oh I'm sorry, you're not a relative are you?" The look of horror on his face was a picture!

Laura laughed, "No it's okay, no offence taken, especially as I escaped over here for more or less the same reason! My flatmate insisted I come along and I have barely seen her all evening!"

"Ah, it seems we might be in the same boat as I was also invited along, however in my case it was more of a summons! The birthday girl is married to my boss and it would be more than my job is worth not to show face!" he gave a wry smile.

Laura grinned," That would make your boss my flatmate's father! Does that lead me to assume you are in accountancy?"

"It's a small world!" he laughed. "Yes I play with numbers for a living. Am I allowed to know your name?"

"Oh I'm sorry, how rude of me! I'm Laura Smith and I'm a primary teacher at the same school as Julie, the boss's daughter."

"Well Laura Smith, do you think we have done our duty and could leave now without offending our hosts? I'm not really keen on the whole buffet thing and could do with a light supper somewhere a bit more peaceful. I don't wish to appear forward but would you care to join me?"

"I'd like that very much," she rewarded him with her best smile, her sparkling deep blue eyes drawing him in until he felt his stomach tighten.

They had a candlelit supper at a lovely quaint little bistro and chatted easily for hours. The other guests gradually left until they were eventually alone, the waiters discreetly going about their work until Laura looked around and realised there was just one waiter left behind the bar. "Peter it must be very late, what time is it? We've stayed far too long and I think the waiter needs to close up. I've thoroughly enjoyed myself tonight and would like to thank you for rescuing me from a very dull party!"

Peter glanced at his watch and as he pushed back his chair to get up from the table the waiter immediately came over to ask if they would like anything else. Peter refused saying he couldn't eat another thing, complimented him on the delicious food and apologised for staying so late. The waiter shook Peter's hand insisting it was a pleasure for him when his customers chose to spend their whole evening at his bistro. He introduced himself as Carlos the proprietor and Peter thanked him, paid the bill and assured him he would recommend the bistro to his colleagues and friends. After many goodnights and shaking of hands, they finally left the bistro just after 2am.

"You have a friend for life there Peter!" Laura laughed. "The food was excellent and it's such a lovely little place."

"We accountants seem to have a reputation for being boring, but if I haven't bored you senseless, we can come back again sometime!" They laughed and chatted happily as they walked towards the High Street to flag down a taxi and when Peter asked for Laura's phone number she only hesitated for a split second!

The next day Peter phoned and invited Laura out to dinner the following weekend and she readily accepted. They had another great evening, this time Peter choosing his favourite Italian restaurant. The food was excellent as was the company and they talked non-stop about their families, jobs, ambitions, hopes and dreams.

After dinner they went to a small wine bar for a few drinks and both were equally sorry when the evening came to an end. Laura didn't hesitate to invite Peter to come along to her school fundraiser the following Saturday afternoon.

"We are holding it in the gardens in Princess Street and everyone has to bring their own picnic. There will be stalls; races; a talent contest and entertainment - you know the usual thing," she smiled up at him. "Don't feel as though you have to come, it might not be your scene?"

Peter had not been on a picnic since he was a child, nor had he spent much time around children, but if it meant spending time with Laura he was more than happy to go along. "Well it's not how I usually spend my Saturday afternoons," he smiled, "but I would love to come and support your fund-raiser - it will be a nice change for me!" he replied with his usual wide grin.

Peter always said he knew on the day of the picnic that he would marry Laura. Her vitality, endless enthusiasm and ability to make every child feel involved and important were awe-inspiring!

On Saturday they were blessed with glorious sunshine and the children sat on large rugs with their families to have their picnics. One by one, each child in Laura's class came up to say hello and show her a new dress, sandals or favourite toy. Some brought a cake or a home-baked treat and in return she showered each child with praise and thanks, all of them leaving with their choice of treat from a large box of home-baked goodies she had brought with her.

Surprisingly, Peter really enjoyed the picnic as Laura laid out quite a spread. He brought along a basket of fruit, a bottle of wine and just in case Laura wasn't able to drink 'on duty', some small bottles of ginger ale. When they finished their picnic they wandered round the various stalls, cheered and clapped at all those who took part in the races and made a great fuss of the children who ran up to them to show off their winning badges and ribbons.

The day was a great success and after an enjoyable afternoon they rewarded themselves with another visit to the bistro. They were just having a nightcap before leaving when Peter asked Laura if she would like to make his day complete and agree to be his girl. Laura fought hard to suppress a giggle at the old fashioned wording, but at the same time found it quite endearing and said she would love to be his girl!

A year later they were again at the bistro, by which time they were on first name terms with all the waiters who always made a great fuss of them, seating them at 'their' table. They had a lovely meal and although they didn't usually have a dessert, Peter persuaded her to have one for a special treat.

When their plates arrived, all that was on Laura's plate was a small square red velvet box. She nervously looked up at Peter. "If you open it you will be saying yes, making me the happiest man in the world by becoming my wife, but if you leave it closed…" Laura quickly put her fingers to his lips to stop him saying anything more and slowly opened the box to reveal a beautiful engagement ring. Peter leaned across took the solid gold band, set with an oval ruby and smaller diamonds either side, and placed it on her finger. "I love you Laura Smith and I promise to make you happy till the day I die," he lifted her hand to his mouth and kissed her ring finger.

Laura was so overwhelmed and emotional she could barely speak but managed to whisper back, "I love you too Peter, with all my heart and soul." Peter leaned across and they kissed to a huge round of applause from the waiters and other diners. Carlos was at the table in an instant with two long-stemmed glasses and a bottle of champagne.

"Congratulations, please accept my best wishes, I will order a special highchair for the bambinos!" Everyone laughed and the other diners raised their glasses to toast them. Laura's head was spinning, she loved and adored Peter and never had she been so happy! Since meeting him, she felt her life was perfect!

Neither of them wanted to wait very long to get married so over the next few months they made wedding plans. Peter already owned a large, beautiful ground floor apartment on the outskirts of Edinburgh with three bedrooms, a lounge with patio doors leading onto a terraced garden and a large kitchen/dining-room so they didn't need to find somewhere to live.

A week before the wedding, Laura and Julie packed up the majority of her belongings and moved them to the apartment. Julie couldn't believe how fast Laura and Peter's relationship had grown and took all the credit for their chance meeting on the night of her mother's birthday party. She was delighted when Laura asked if she would be her bridesmaid and now it was so close, she was very excited about the wedding!

Their wedding day was just perfect and they shared it with their families and close friends. There was only one place they wanted to have their reception and for them Carlos closed the bistro for the day and provided a huge buffet with many choices, all absolutely delicious! As Laura and Peter cut the cake the waiters broke into song and everyone clapped along! When they finished eating, the tables were pushed back and they all enjoyed an evening of music and dancing. At the end of a perfect day, Peter and Laura stood at the bistro door hugging and thanking their guests, all congratulating them and saying how much they enjoyed their special day!

After the last guest left, Laura and Peter thanked Carlos for a brilliant reception and, after the usual hugs and kisses, the newlyweds headed home to the apartment to start married life. When they reached their front door Peter scooped Laura up in his arms and carried her across the threshold in traditional fashion then whirled her round and round until they collapsed onto the sofa, both dizzy and laughing! It had been a wonderful day and they felt it was impossible to feel any happier than they did at that moment!

CHAPTER 2

Marlene Ross stared out of the office window and her stomach churned as she thought about the conversation she was about to have with her boss Johnathan. Although she had attempted to speak to him many times over the past couple of weeks, she repeatedly lost her nerve and left the office feeling both annoyed and upset with herself.

She started work as a junior secretary for Mason & Cook Solicitors ten years ago and slowly climbed the office ladder. Two years ago she was delighted when she was promoted to Johnathan Mason's secretary, one of the younger partners in the firm with a reputation for being difficult, demanding and generally rude!

At that time she hoped her long-term boyfriend Paul would soon propose as now they were both earning a good wage they could afford to rent a flat together. However, when Paul came home on leave from the Navy a few months later, her world fell apart when he told her he had no intention of getting married. After a huge row, Marlene realised it had been very convenient for Paul to have a girl readily waiting at home for him when he was on shore leave. Paul had given her an ultimatum, either carry on as they were or they were over and she chose the latter, firmly slamming the door behind him!

After the break up, Marlene chose not to date anyone until about eight months ago, when one evening Johnathan asked her to work late and type up a deposition for a court case the following morning. Marlene and Johnathan had a friendly, easy working relationship and she had not found him to be as bad as his reputation, although he had his moments!

They worked until about ten o'clock that evening, happily chatting now and then whilst getting the documents ready. Johnathan was much more informal and more relaxed than usual, allowing her to see a softer side to him. Although she couldn't quite put her finger on why, their relationship definitely changed that night.

Over the next couple of weeks they became very aware of each other, the tension between them almost tangible and it was obvious they were attracted to each other. Marlene couldn't believe it as she had always liked him more than she should, but not for one minute did she ever think he even noticed her other than on a professional basis.

It wasn't long before another similar situation arose requiring them both to stay late to complete urgent paperwork. They were standing side by side at a desk collating papers and Marlene could feel the electricity between them. A quick glance up at Johnathan was all it took for him to turn, take her in his arms and kiss her with a passion she had never experienced before. She felt her knees give and he scooped her up in his arms and carried her across to the sofa in the corner of his office where they spent over an hour having wild sex! As they lay together dishevelled and completely spent, Marlene could not believe what had just happened! How could Johnathan fancy her when his fiancé was like a model? As long as he wanted her she didn't care about Avril and the last hour proved he found her sexy and attractive!

That night was the start of their affair and gradually they stayed back at the office until they were seeing each other at least a couple of nights a week. When she asked Johnathan why they couldn't see more of each other, he said it was because he didn't want to raise suspicion amongst the other staff, so Marlene suggested he came to her flat instead which he was more than happy to agree to.

After a couple of month's Marlene confessed her love for Johnathan and although he professed to love her too, he still made excuses as to why he hadn't called off his engagement to Avril. Marlene continued with the affair, totally head over heels in love with Johnathan and hoping his relationship with Avril would soon end to allow them to be open about theirs.

They had been together for about four months when Marlene had a pregnancy scare and after a week of pure panic, she was very relieved when her period finally arrived. However, the scare didn't stop her continuing the affair with her boss and they carried on as before.

One evening, almost seven months into their 'relationship', Johnathan told Marlene he would be away for the weekend with friends, which of course included Avril. Knowing about the weekend only made Marlene feel totally miserable so in an attempt to cheer up her flatmate, Lisa persuaded her to go along to a dance on the Saturday night.

They were getting ready when Marlene found she couldn't zip up her dress. "You must have put weight on Marl!" exclaimed Lisa who was trying with all her might to get the zip past Marlene's waist, "I'm going to break it if I pull any harder!" Marlene couldn't understand it and chose another dress, which also felt too tight but still looked really good on her and they headed out for the evening. They had a brilliant night, dancing so much they walked home barefoot carrying their shoes, singing and dancing all the way!

The next day the dress episode was still on Marlene's mind as over the past two weeks her skirts had also felt a bit tighter than usual. Trying on a couple of her 'tighter' skirts, she was shocked to find she had no chance of zipping them up and alarm bells began ringing in her head! She also recalled a conversation the previous week when Johnathan said he could swear her breasts were getting larger!

As she left the doctor's surgery the following week, Marlene was in shock as the doctor confirmed she was indeed around four and a half months pregnant, maybe slightly more. When she told him she couldn't be that pregnant as she had some bleeding, he told her that could sometimes happen and she was definitely more than four months. "I agree you are very slim, even at this point, but I don't think you will be able to hide your pregnancy for much longer, your baby grows much faster from now on," smiled the doctor who didn't appear to notice the shock and disappointment on Marlene's face.

There was no point in standing staring out the window, she had put it off long enough - it was time to talk to Johnathan. As she walked towards his office she was shaking, so scared of how he was going to react to the news that they were going to have a baby. He was sitting at his desk reading some paperwork and she stole a few seconds to study his handsome, chiselled face before dropping her bombshell.

When her flatmate arrived home later that evening she found Marlene huddled on the sofa, very red eyed and looking deathly pale. Dropping everything, she rushed over and wrapped her arms around her friend. "What on earth is the matter Marl? You look dreadful sweetheart!" Marlene started sobbing and Lisa held her tightly, rocking gently to comfort her. They stayed like that for ages until finally Marlene stopped crying.

"Right, we are going to have a long talk about whatever has got you into this state but first I am going to put the kettle on because I have a feeling we are going to need tea and a packet of biscuits!" Lisa went into the kitchen and Marlene fetched her blanket from the bedroom. Once they were cosy on the sofa under the blanket with their tea in one hand, chocolate biscuit in the other, Lisa turned to Marlene. "Now, would I be correct in guessing all these tears are something to do with the boss?" Marlene nodded, still not quite trusting herself to speak. "Okay, in your own time Marl and don't leave anything out!" A few minutes passed whilst Marlene sipped her tea and tried hard to compose herself.

"It's over between us Lisa, he doesn't want anything to do with me."

"Why Marl? Did you have a fight?"

Fresh tears streamed down Marlene's face. "No, I told him I had been to the doctor and he said I am nearly five months pregnant."

"Oh dear lord! I thought you were putting on a bit of weight, but it never crossed my mind you could be expecting! How did you not know Marl?"

"I had a bit of a scare a while back, but I got my period and thought I was okay! The doctor said it's not uncommon for that to happen during pregnancy."

"What are you going to do? What did Johnathan say?"

"I told him calmly about the baby and his face turned to stone Lisa, there was no expression, no happiness, no anger, absolutely nothing! Then he leant back in his chair and asked me how I could have been so stupid. Me stupid! What about him? It takes two! I tried to talk him round by telling him he was just shocked and that I had been the same to start with, but now all I could think about was the tiny person growing inside me! I said to him he would be a dad in a few months and he would feel differently when he saw our baby!"

"And he said?"

"He gave me a cold stare and said if I thought I was going to ruin his life then to think again. He said he wanted nothing to do with any baby and couldn't I get rid of it somehow! He was like a stranger Lisa, I couldn't believe how angry he was! When I told him I would be having the baby and I would need him to help me, he actually accused me of getting pregnant just to get him to split from Avril! He said it would ruin his career if such a scandal came out at work and told me to make sure I left before anyone noticed anything!"

"You could tell Avril Marl, tell her just what her precious fiancé has been doing behind her back! You can't let him fire you, you need your job now more than ever!" Lisa was pacing around the room at this point and Marlene thought she was going to explode with rage! "Right, we need to calmly talk this through and come up with a plan to make sure Johnathan Mason does not shirk his responsibilities. Get the kettle on again Marl, I'll get a pen and some paper and we are going to work out a way to make sure you are not left to cope with this alone!"

After hours of talking they decided the best plan was to make sure Johnathan looked after Marlene and the baby financially. There would be no point in trying to change his mind as he had made it perfectly clear he wanted nothing more to do with her. The plan was to make two copies of an agreement between Marlene and Johnathan stating he would make an initial payment to cover her wages from now until the baby arrived and thereafter he would pay a set sum each week to support them. If he did not agree to this arrangement, Marlene would have no option but to tell the senior partners at the firm, one being his father Alex, and of course they would inform the delightful Avril! It had taken a great deal of persuasion from Lisa to get Marlene to agree to this, however she was very worried about how she would manage without any money and had already considered leaving Glasgow to live with her parents - the problem was she didn't think her dad would accept her situation.

Over the weekend they wrote and rewrote the agreement and first thing on Monday morning Marlene and Lisa stood together in front of Johnathan's desk watching as he read through the agreement. When he finished, he threw it down on the desk, shaking his head. "You can't prove a thing and if you tell anyone, I will say you made a pass at me a few months ago, I turned you down and now you find yourself pregnant to some random one night stand, you and your friend here are trying to lay the blame at my door!"

"Look Johnathan, you might think you're some high and mighty smart arse solicitor but you forget Marlene and I share a flat, I've been there when you have stayed overnight with her!"

"Again, you can't prove it and anyway who is going to take your word over mine?" he said arrogantly. "Now ladies, if you are quite finished, I believe Marlene here needs to pack up her things as she no longer has a job here. Oh and before you think of saying anything as you leave, I will say you made all this up to spite me as I caught you stealing from my wallet!" he leant back in his chair with an arrogant smirk on his face. "If you go quietly, it will save your reputation on two counts, as a slut and a thief, and, as I'm not quite a total bastard, I will make sure you are paid to the end of the month and tell everyone you had to leave to look after your sick father."

Marlene couldn't believe he could be so callous. How could she ever have believed he loved her? To think he would actually say those things about her...

Marlene turned to walk away but Lisa leaned across Johnathan's desk until she was within a few inches from his face. "You are one evil pig of a man and I swear, one way or another, you will pay for what you have just done, believe me you will not get away with this!" and with that she swiped everything off his desk onto the floor before she stormed out of his office, slamming the door behind her!

There were a few questioning looks from other employees as a red-eyed Marlene left with Lisa a few minutes later but Johnathan later told them Marlene's father was very ill and she was upset because she had no alternative but to leave Glasgow and return home to look after him.

As Marlene and Lisa walked away from the building, Marlene became more distraught with every step....

CHAPTER 3

Bryan Carson was sitting in a bar after work with his best mate Liam. They had been friends since junior school and considered themselves to be more like brothers than friends. As they chatted over their pints of lager, a group of girls arrived laughing and chatting and the boys winked at each other!

"Mine is the blonde with the cute little dimples," joked Liam as Bryan stood up to go to the bar for refills. As he leant against the bar, he smiled to himself as one of the girls recalled how she had put one of the junior doctors in his place on the ward earlier that day and the girls erupted in laughter again. As Bryan headed back to his seat with the drinks, one of the girls stood up pushing her chair back into his path and he fell back with such force that he was winded.

When he got his breath back and opened his eyes, both Liam and a girl with cascading red curls were leaning over him, the redhead insisting he watched as she moved her finger from left to right and back again. He suddenly realised the spilt lager was seeping through his clothes and insisted he was fine but wet, at which point the redhead grabbed her scarf and started dabbing at his clothes to mop up some of the liquid. Suddenly Liam started to laugh, then Bryan joined in and before they knew it they had been introduced to all the girls and joined them at their table.

The redhead introduced herself to Bryan as Angela Johnson a trainee doctor at Willow Hospital just a few hundred yards along the road. They chatted for over an hour and Bryan was impressed at how determined Angela was to study hard and qualify as a doctor. He told her his uncle owned a plumbing business and when he left school he started work as his uncle's apprentice. He too had worked hard and his uncle was so impressed he gave him shares in the business two years after he completed his apprenticeship - they were now equal partners. By the end of the evening Bryan was brave enough to ask Angela out on a date and to his surprise she agreed, gave him a peck on the cheek and ran off to catch up with the other girls as they headed home.

Bryan later learned Angela flat-shared with three other girls, all of whom were qualified nurses. Their dates had to be arranged around Angela's long shifts and sometimes they didn't see each other for a couple of weeks. However, their relationship seemed to work really well and they continued to see each other whenever Angela could take some time out from studying and working.

They had been dating for around a year and a half when problems arose with Angela's flat-share which resulted in their relationship moving up a step. One of the girls got married and a few weeks later another took a position at a hospital nearer her family, which only left herself and Joe. After a couple of weeks trying to find two new flatmates, Joe told Angela she was moving in with her boyfriend and when Bryan met her later that week the conversation was all about Angela's hunt for a new flat-share.

Although Bryan suggested she move in with him, Angela fought against that idea right up until two days before she had to move out of the flat when she was left with no other option but to take him up on his offer. Bryan was absolutely delighted, although it was purely a desperate move on Angela's part. However things went smoothly and they adapted to living together very well. Bryan was extremely happy and couldn't see their relationship was very one-sided as Angela was completely focussed on her career and nothing got in the way of her goals.

Bryan worked very hard, the plumbing business growing successfully and he felt his life was near enough perfect. He and Angela had been together for just over two years and he was hoping, after she qualified next year, to get married and in time have a family.

However, a few months later, Angela arrived home one evening, threw her bag on the floor, kicked off her shoes and stormed into the bathroom shouting her career was over! Bryan, thinking she obviously had a bad day at work, went to put the kettle on and took their dinner out of the oven – she would feel better after something to eat.

Eventually Angela came out of the bathroom and Bryan tried to put his arms around her but she pushed him away, thumped past him and threw herself down on the settee. Bryan sat down in the chair opposite, leant forward and placed his hands on her knees, gently rubbing them in an affectionate and comforting manner. "Things can't be that bad my love? Did you do something wrong at work?"

"You would think that!" she snarled, hitting his hands away, "I am good at what I do and so no, I bloody well did not do anything wrong! It's you, this is your fault!"

"Whoa! Calm down Ange! How on earth can I be to blame for ruining your career?"

"Because YOU got me bloody pregnant!" she yelled in his face.

Bryan stared at Angela as she stomped around the flat slinging accusations and insults at him. He thought the best option was to let her calm down and try and talk to her later. It took quite a while but once she sat down again he moved closer and reached over to take her hand, which she quickly snatched away folding her arms with a loud grunt.

"Look Ange we will manage somehow, you can take a year off and by then we can have a plan in place, get a babysitter for the days we both have to work and…"

"You don't get it!" she screamed at him, "I don't want to take a year out! I'm not going to take time off work - all I need is to get rid of this thing inside me, don't you get it?" The excitement bubbling up inside Bryan died instantly and he stood up and turned to face her.

"NO! There is no way! You can't do that! I will not let you KILL my child just so you can have a career, no way!"

"WATCH ME!"

Angela stormed off to the bedroom and Bryan never went near her that night, sleeping on the settee, or rather not sleeping. There was no way she was going to get rid of his baby. He thought back to the night his mother dragged him round to his aunt Jen's house. His mum and aunt had a blazing row and then his mum stormed off without a backward glance and without him. He could clearly remember Jen sitting him on her knee, cuddling him tightly and singing to him as he sobbed. He was only six years old and never heard from his mother again, not even a birthday card.

Thank god for aunt Jen, she had treated him like her own child and although he might not have had much, he had a happy, loving home where there was always food on the table, a warm bed and laughter, always laughter! He smiled to himself - somehow he would change Angela's mind because his child was going to have the best dad ever, no matter what it took!

Over the next few days Bryan tried everything to turn Angela around, even proposing to her, but she wouldn't change her mind. However, after putting Bryan through the week from hell, Angela arrived home one evening and announced she was too far along in her pregnancy to have a termination, said she was going for a bath and would speak to him later.

Bryan was ecstatic! He didn't care that she would have gone through with the termination - she was going to have their baby! He was so happy and very relieved – everything was going to be okay and Ange would soon grow to love the baby growing inside her!

When she came out of the bathroom, Angela seemed very calm but Bryan could see the tension in her face. She sat down opposite him on the settee and looked straight into his eyes with a steely glare.

"As I told you earlier, it is too late to have a termination so I have no option but to have this child, but before you get all hopeful, you need to know I still have no intention of keeping it and will be making arrangements for it to be adopted."

"No! You can't do that! This is my baby too and as his or her father, I will not let you give our baby away! It's not happening Angela – not happening!!"

Angela lost her cool and started shouting, "I have my career to think of – it's all I've ever wanted and I don't want a kid, never have, never will. Have I ever said I wanted one? No! I don't want it!!"

She lowered her voice slightly and launched into a long speech about how medicine had been her lifelong dream and as she talked, Bryan's mind was working overtime, trying to come up with a solution to stop her doing this. Surely once she actually held her baby in her arms she would fall instantly in love? Somehow he needed to persuade her not to make any arrangements until after the baby was born. He would have to keep the peace between them whilst trying to find a way to make sure Angela could not give their baby away.

Once she finished talking, he nodded, calmly got up and headed towards the kitchen asking whether she would like a tea or coffee. He was relieved when she answered him asking for a hot chocolate, at least she was talking – he had to keep things between them normal and stay in her good books until he could come up with something she would agree to.

As the weeks passed Angela dressed carefully to hide her changing shape although at work her white coat made it relatively easy. Bryan saw no change in her attitude towards having a baby, in fact she regularly complained about the changes to her body and always referred to their baby as 'it' or 'this thing' and he gradually began to realise Angela was not going to change her mind about the adoption. He knew if he wanted to keep his baby the responsibility of caring for him or her would lie solely with him.

Bryan had spoken to his uncle Matt when Angela first told him she was going to have a termination and he had been very upset for Bryan. When he then heard it was too late to have a termination but Angela was giving the baby up for adoption he agreed with Bryan that she had to be stopped. Bryan assured Matt he was not going to let it happen, he would somehow keep his baby and Matt told him to take as much time off work as he needed once the baby was born. He would manage the business himself and they had enough lads to cover the workload. That was the moment Bryan decided he would take care of his baby and when he found a babysitter, who he could trust, he would be able to go back to work.

When Angela could not hide her pregnancy any longer she had to inform the hospital and they were not at all happy about it, nor that she had hidden it from them for so long. She assured them she would not be taking any leave other than for the birth plus a week or so afterwards and on that basis they agreed she would not have to repeat the year. However, if her circumstances changed and she required more leave, the agreement would no longer apply.

As Angela walked away from the meeting, she prayed everything would go smoothly - this child would not disrupt her training! She only had about four weeks left until her due date and up until now she had successfully managed to hide the evidence by wearing a larger coat at work. Unfortunately her colleagues had begun to realise she was pregnant and for her it was extremely embarrassing! She couldn't wait to get it over and done with and get her life back to normal!

That night she told Bryan about the meeting at the hospital and their agreement to allow her to continue the year. She looked delighted, the happiest he had seen her since she found out she was pregnant, but that soon changed when Bryan told her there would be no adoption and he would be taking the responsibility for their baby's care. She told him he was mad! Had he no idea how hard it would be to look after a baby? How would he manage with work? She even accused him of trying to trap her into looking after the child but he simply held his hand up telling her it was all taken care of and she wouldn't need to do anything for the baby. To his dismay, she simply replied, "Great because once it's born I want nothing to do with it". How could she be so callous, cold and unfeeling? Where was the girl he met in the pub?

CHAPTER 4

Maggie Roberts is an extremely likeable and popular sixteen year old in her last year at high school. Many people comment on her looks, 'striking' being the most popular comment, although Maggie is completely oblivious. She has stunning light brown hair with natural red tints, which light up her hair in the sunshine. Her eyes are a distinctive green, which sparkle when she is happy, but when feeling sad they turn several shades darker. Add to that the fact that she is a very gifted student, gaining straight A's in every subject, Maggie's lot is pretty well perfect. Her parents fully expect Maggie and her two younger brothers to go to university as they themselves have very successful careers, her father a highly respected surgeon and her mother a pharmacist, therefore university fees will be no object. Maggie's dream is to follow in her parents' footsteps by entering into the world of medicine.

There is however a downside to her perfect world. Maggie studies very hard and apart from a Saturday has no social life to speak of. This way of life was instilled by her parents from a young age and only once she turned fourteen did she successfully managed to convince them she needed to have one day a week to meet with her friends and be a normal teenager.

Allie had been Maggie's best friend since year one and had stood by her, even although they were only ever able to spend time together out of school on a Saturday. Allie's sixteenth birthday was coming up soon and her parents agreed to her having a party at their house. Allie chose the Saturday night for her party although her birthday was actually the day before, as she knew Maggie's strict parents would not break their rules and let her come on the Friday. It was unknown for them to allow Maggie to stay over at Allie's house but for once, as it was a special occasion and only after speaking to Allie's mum to confirm there was indeed a party, they had relented and allowed Maggie to stay overnight.

On the day of the party, Maggie felt on top of the world, very excited about spending the evening away from home and she could stay up as late as she wanted as Abbie's mum said it was a special night! She was also quite nervous as Simon Fisher, a pupil in her year, had also been invited to the party. Maggie had first taken a shine to him almost two years ago and she had secretly prayed for him to notice her, but the attraction had been very one-sided. Maggie's feelings for him had grown over time and her stomach flipped over every time she saw him in the corridors at school but her never looked her way.

Maggie could not believe it when only ten minutes after arriving at the party, Simon came over and started chatting to her. She had made a huge effort with her appearance and Abbie lent her a mini skirt and cute short top, which really suited her - she looked amazing! Maggie's mother would have said it made her look cheap, but it was what all the teenagers were wearing and it completely changed how she looked!

Simon and Maggie chatted easily, danced for ages and then sat at the bottom of the stairs to have something to drink and share a plate of food. Maggie was laughing at one of Simon's jokes and as she turned to smile at him, he kissed her and it felt as though a box of fireworks were exploding through her body!

Later as she lay in bed watching the dawn break, Maggie relived every second over and over again. After the kiss, Simon led her up to Abbie's bedroom, telling her he wanted to be alone with her. They just kissed to start with but Simon slowly worked his way down her body, waking senses and emotions Maggie could never have imagined! She felt light headed and out of control and before she realised what was happening his full weight was on top of her and he was thrusting into her over and over, finally collapsing down at her side.

Maggie lay still for a few seconds, shocked and dazed and then got up off the bed and made for the bathroom. She locked the door, slumped down and cried into a towel. What on earth had she done? Why didn't she have the strength to push him off her? She felt so ashamed and hid in the bathroom, watching out the window until she saw Simon leave with his mates. She felt light headed and nauseous so after washing herself she went straight to bed, pretending to be asleep when she heard Abbie coming into the room.

Gradually she began to feel more alert and she suspected Simon had laced her drinks. She felt stupid and sad he'd done that to her. Did he even really like her or had it been his intention to try and get her into bed? As she lay watching the sunrise she promised herself no boy would ever use her like that again...

CHAPTER 5

Sara and James Andrews married when she was eighteen and he was twenty-two. There were those who thought Sara was too young but they knew everything there was to know about each other. Their mums were best friends and so they grew up around each other and as they progressed through their teens, their close friendship turned into deep love. Sara loved her job as a trainee nurse and James completed his apprenticeship as an electrician and was now working for a small local firm. He was determined to start up his own business and worked all the hours he could to get the experience and the money to set up on his own.

They began married life in a small rented cottage in a little village just outside Perth and for the first few years they both worked very hard to succeed in their chosen careers. Sara passed all her exams and became a staff nurse in charge of a children's ward. She loved being around the children and longed for the day when she would hold her own baby in her arms. James fulfilled his dream of starting his own business and with hard work built it up to be very successful, employing two qualified electricians and recently taking on a young apprentice.

They had just celebrated their fourth wedding anniversary when they bought an old run-down farmhouse and gradually over the past few years turned it into a beautiful home of which they were extremely proud. They loved their lives but they loved children and longed to start a family - then their lives would be complete.

Not long after their eighth anniversary, Sara realised she might at last be pregnant and couldn't wait to get into work to get one of the doctors to give her a check over and hopefully confirm her suspicions. That evening she made a special effort with dinner and placed a little box tied with a ribbon on the table. When James sat down he immediately asked what was in the box and Sara handed it to him telling him it was a surprise for him to open!

James untied the ribbon, opened the lid of the box and inside he found a tiny pair of knitted baby bootees. "Really?" he exclaimed!

"Yes James, absolutely yes!" she squealed grinning widely. "I can't believe it myself but I got one of the doctors at the hospital to check me over today and I, Mr Andrews, am about ten weeks pregnant with little baby Andrews!" James got up and engulfed Sara in a huge bear hug!

"I can't believe it Sara! We are very happy and have everything we need but this baby will make our lives complete. I am so happy and you my love will start taking things easier at work, no more extra shifts!"

Sara enjoyed being pregnant, the only downside was the tiredness and sometimes on her day off she spent a good part of it sleeping. She had the appetite of an elephant, so James told her, and it was not unusual for her to eat dinner and feel hungry half an hour later! The baby was growing well and right from month five she had quite a good size bump. She secretly hoped she didn't get too big as she was only just over five feet tall and had already lost sight of her feet!

From the day she found out she was pregnant she had been knitting baby clothes and the girls at the hospital were doing the same. When she left work to have her baby the girls had a party for her and she was showered with gifts from nurses, doctors and even parents of children who had previously been patients in her care. She was overwhelmed at their kindness and generosity and it was a very emotional day!

James couldn't believe the amount of gifts she came home with that evening and as they sat looking through them all they could feel how close they were to having their dream! James recently finished decorating the baby's room and everything was now ready. Sara had plans to spend the next couple of days giving the house a good clean and tidy up and then concentrate on getting the baby clothes washed. She also wanted to put all the other baby items she had bought and the gifts they had received, into the nursery.

Everything went to plan and although tired carrying her huge bump around, Sara did all the jobs on her list. Today she had given the nursery a final clean and as it was a lovely warm, windy day the washing line was laden with baby clothes. Sara couldn't believe how much pleasure she got from looking at the tiny garments pegged to the line. She was just glowing with pride already and her baby hadn't even arrived!

Sara lay in bed that evening listening to James breathing deeply and gently rubbed her swollen belly. She suddenly realised her baby wasn't doing the usual night aerobics and thinking back through her day she couldn't remember feeling any movement. It could be that there just wasn't much room left for such antics as she only had three weeks before her due date. After a poor night's sleep, Sara phoned the doctor who told her to come in and he would check to see what baby was up to.

However, her doctor was not very happy when he examined her and she was admitted to hospital "To be on the safe side," he had said, but Sara knew something was wrong and prayed that no matter what happened to her, the baby would be okay.

When James arrived at the hospital, Sara was in a dreadful state. The doctors had just told her they could no longer find a heartbeat and they would have to induce the birth. The idea of giving birth to a dead baby horrified her and she didn't know how she was going to find the inner strength to get through such an ordeal. James was visibly upset but he was more concerned for Sara and could not imagine how she must be feeling. Sara was put on a drip, which induced her labour, and after a seven-hour ordeal she gave birth to her stillborn daughter.

The sadness they both felt was overwhelming as their baby was perfect, however the chord had been tightly wrapped round her neck and had been responsible for her death.

The midwife wrapped their daughter in a blanket, handed her to Sara and discreetly left the room. James and Sara spent a couple of hours with their baby, finding it hard to come to terms with how perfect she was as, although not breathing, she looked like she was simply asleep. She was a beautiful wee soul and they loved her instantly, so sad they would only have a moment in time with her.

"Grace," whispered James, "what do you think sweetheart?" Sara looked down at her precious baby daughter thinking James couldn't have chosen a better name and nodded her agreement as she fought back fresh tears.

It was absolutely heart breaking as, after kissing her goodbye, they watched their tiny daughter being wheeled out of the room, knowing they would never see or hold her again...

CHAPTER 6

After a sleepless night, Marlene and Lisa discussed options over an extended breakfast. Staying at the flat with Lisa in Glasgow was not an option as Marlene would now have no income and Lisa could not afford to pay the rent and bills herself. The flat wasn't large enough to take in another lodger and even if it was, who would pay to flat-share with a new baby? After exhausting every possible idea, they were left with the family option, which meant Marlene had to call her parents and ask if she could stay with them until she had her baby. It was the last thing Marlene wanted, but it would give her time to work out what she was going to do after the birth.

However, the call to her parents was much worse than she anticipated. Her mother burst into tears and handed the phone to her father who slated her for bringing disgrace on the family!

"Do you know how it will feel for us to bear the shame of having an illegitimate child in the family, a child who will carry our family name?" raged her father. Before slamming the receiver down he added that she was not to show her face in their village or anywhere close by in case anyone they knew should find out what sort of daughter they had raised!

After more tears, tea and biscuits, Marlene could only think of one last option and if that failed she would have to do the unthinkable and give her baby away...

She told Lisa about her father's sister Christine who was a lovely person, extremely kind and caring. Marlene loved staying with her for holidays when she was younger and they had kept in touch regularly - she was Marlene's last hope!

"Aunt Chris, it's Marlene."

"Hello love, what a lovely surprise! How are things in Glasgow?"

"Well that's why I'm calling you, things are not good at all and I'm hoping you can help me?"

"Of course love, if I can, I will. Tell me what's wrong."

"I am in a real mess! I was seeing a guy at work, well my boss actually, for months and I found out I am pregnant and he wants nothing to do with me or the baby, in fact he's blackmailing me and has fired me..." Marlene trailed off as a sob escaped and fresh tears streamed down her face.

"Slow down Marlene love, have you called your mum and dad?"

"Yes, they have disowned me aunt Chris and dad said some horrible things! I'm at my wits end and don't know what to do now!"

"Give me half an hour pet and I will call you back. Don't be upsetting yourself as it's not good for you or the baby. We will sort something out, leave it with me."

Aunt Chris was as good as her word, calling back within half an hour with not only a plan but to confirm arrangements. Marlene would go and live with Chris until the baby was born and for as long after as she needed to. She was to stop worrying and get packing as her cousin Jamie, (Christine's eldest son), was coming to collect her on Saturday, which gave her two full days to get organised. After several reassuring comments from her aunt, they said their goodbyes and Marlene sat down to relay the plan to Lisa who gave her a tight hug and went to make more tea.

Between the two of them, all the packing was finished by the following afternoon and Marlene had also telephoned work to ensure her final pay cheque would be sent to the flat - that way Lisa could then forward it to Marlene and prevent Johnathan knowing her whereabouts.

Marlene and Lisa had a lovely last dinner together and managed to laugh at some of the antics they got up to when times had been better. Marlene found that despite the desperate situation she was in, she was enjoying herself and felt relaxed for the first time since finding out she was expecting a baby. She also felt relieved to be leaving Glasgow as there would be no chance of bumping into anyone from the office, which would have been sure to spark rumours, or rather add to the rumours, surrounding her sudden departure! She wondered what lies Johnathan told to cover up the truth and the disgusting way in which he had treated her?

CHAPTER 7

Three weeks after disclosing her pregnancy to the hospital management, Angela delivered a baby girl after a ten hour labour, only showing enough attention to her child so as not to arouse the attention of the nursing staff. The minute Bryan visited she totally switched off, usually heading to have a peaceful bath.

Bryan was over the moon! His daughter was gorgeous with big eyes and dainty features - he couldn't take his eyes off her! He secretly hoped Angela's maternal instincts would kick in when their baby arrived but so far this was not the case, in fact she was totally disinterested. When Bryan saw his daughter for the first time he asked Angela if there was a name she liked but she shook her head saying, "She's yours, call her what you want".

Bryan named his daughter after his grandmother and his aunt Jen. When he told Angela he had chosen the name Anna Jenifer Carson there wasn't even a flicker of interest, never mind the tiniest spark of emotion.

Angela and Anna had been home from hospital for three days when Angela announced she was going back to work the following day. She had spent her three days at home studying, three days without once looking at her baby daughter, three days and nights where she let Bryan do everything for Anna, three days and nights where she slept or studied as her baby cried for attention.

Bryan and Matt agreed he would take a month off work to get into a routine and organise a babysitter for Anna whilst he was at work during the day. Bryan had hoped something deep down in Angela would trigger her love for Anna, but she acted like she wasn't there, in fact she didn't spend any time in the same room as her baby.

Once she returned to work, Angela began going out with friends for a couple of hours after her shift, which meant it was late before she came home and then she would sleep on the settee. When she was on night duty, she stayed at the hospital, which meant she didn't come home at all for three days at a time, maybe more.

Bryan was managing really well although Anna was waking up two or three times a night and it was very tiring but he managed to get a couple of hours sleep most afternoons while Anna slept. With only a week to go before he was due to go back to work he still hadn't found a babysitter but luckily, with only a couple of days to go, he found Mrs Hughes who looked after two other young children at her home less than a five minute walk away. Although his aunt Jen offered to look after Anna, she was crippled with arthritis and her hands became very painful. Bryan told her he would like nothing more than for her to look after Anna but he could not be responsible for causing her further discomfort and pain.

On the eve of his return to work, Bryan tried to get as organised as possible to make his first day as a working daddy run smoothly. He packed a little bag for Anna with everything she would need for Mrs Hughes; laid out Anna's clothes for the morning; organised everything he would need for her bath, nightclothes etc for when they got home in the evening; made a pan of mince for his tea, which would do two nights; laid everything out for a quick breakfast and made a couple of sandwiches to take to work just in case he didn't have time for the 'quick breakfast'. Matt insisted Bryan start an hour later in the morning and finish an hour earlier in the evening, while Anna was still so young, which would give him plenty of time to drop her off and collect her from Mrs Hughes.

On his first day back at work, Bryan spent the whole day worrying about his baby girl and couldn't wait to finish and collect Anna from Mrs Hughes. He was relieved when she assured him Anna had been as good as gold and he headed home, glad the first day was over. Only another four this week and himself and Anna would have the whole weekend together!

When he arrived home he set about bathing and feeding his little princess and once she was asleep in her cot, Bryan got organised for the following morning before having the mince he was glad he had made. He was feeling very tired as he had been up quite a bit during the night with Anna, but he was confident he would get into a routine and things would improve as Anna grew older.

It wasn't until he went to have a bath that he noticed all Angela's toiletries were missing from the bathroom shelves. He looked in the wardrobe and chest of drawers to find all her clothes were gone and as he looked around the flat he couldn't find anything to show Angela had lived there. It wasn't until he was sitting beside the fire with a hot drink that he noticed a folded note behind the clock.

> 'Bryan, I told you I didn't want a baby but you wouldn't listen and

now you have chosen her over me.
We probably wouldn't have stayed
together for much longer anyway
as I will be taking up a residency in
another hospital once I am qualified. I
will have to work very hard over the
next year and will need peace and
quiet to study and I can't get that
here anymore.

Angela'

Bryan read the note several times in total disbelief
that Angela could be so callous and unfeeling, but then
his mother had been the same. She couldn't even use their
daughter's name! He wasn't going to waste any more energy
thinking about Angela, he had to concentrate on looking
after Anna - she was his number one priority!

After a month of working, looking after Anna and
getting up several times every night, Bryan began to feel
the effects of sleep deprivation. He fell asleep at every tea
break and lunchtime and there were days when he found
it hard to concentrate. He knew his uncle would have said
something to any of their employees who did the same and
was very aware that since Anna was born he hadn't been
pulling his weight at work - Matt was making allowances
for him because he was family.

He struggled on for another month until one night he
fell asleep in the armchair cuddling Anna whilst waiting
for her milk to warm up on the stove. Suddenly Bryan woke
up and opened his eyes to see the room full of smoke. He
quickly jumped up, ran out of his flat and banged on his
neighbours' door. Luckily Jim and Rita were at home and
Jim helped him sort out the flat while Rita looked after

Anna. The pan he used to heat up the bottle of milk had dried up and burnt through but they managed to clear the smoke by opening windows and doors. Luckily there wasn't any damage other than the ruined pan and a few burn marks on the cooker. Once he finished cleaning up Bryan fetched Anna from Rita, fed her, settled her in her cot and then lay on top of the bed watching her sleep.

He lay awake for hours until Anna woke for her next bottle and as he fed her, he studied her beautiful little face and realised he was lucky not to have killed her. Things were going to have to change, as no matter how hard he thought it would be, he had been a fool to think he would be able to work and at the same time look after a young baby. He lay back down after settling Anna in her cot and thought about how he could ensure his little girl would be safe from now on.

Bryan phoned Matt the next morning, explained what happened the previous evening and told him he would have to take a few days off work to sort everything out. Matt told him to take as much time as he needed and not to worry about work, Anna was more important.

Over the next couple of days, Bryan came up with plan after plan, only to realise that other than giving up work, which was not an option, or getting a live in nanny, which he couldn't afford, he was left with the option he said he would never do and felt devastated.

Bryan took Anna for a long walk around the park in her pram having finally made the decision he knew would be right for his daughter. He loved her more than words could say but he had to be responsible and do what was right for her, she could have died of smoke inhalation on the night of the fire if he had not woken up.

Bryan stood opposite the hospital entrance and waited for Angela after leaving an urgent message at the reception desk asking her to meet him. He smiled down at Anna tucked up cosily in her pram, sound asleep. If only she could have done that more during the night he thought ruefully!

Twenty minutes later Bryan watched as Angela made her way across the car park to where they waited and for the first time he noticed how she had changed compared to the first night they met. Her body language warned everyone not to get in her way, her face stony and hard looking. Had she always been like that? Had he just not seen it before now or had she gradually become like this?

Without opening her mouth, Bryan could tell from Angela's body language that she was irritated by this interruption to her day and knew whatever she was about to say wouldn't be in any way friendly. "Whatever it is you want Bryan, you need to make it quick because I'm really busy."

"And I'm not? Are you not going to ask how your daughter is or at least look at her?"

"I'm quite sure she is fine or you wouldn't be here with her!" Angela said sarcastically, still not looking in the direction of the pram.

"Okay, I get the message that you really don't care about her so no doubt you will be delighted to hear that although I have tried, I cannot work and look after Anna in the way she needs and deserves. I am going to have her adopted and I need you to attend a meeting with social services to sign the papers." Bryan watched Angela's face closely and even after hearing what he said, she showed not a flicker of concern!

"Okay, no problem, give me a call and I'll be there. Is that all? I need to get back!"

Bryan shook his head, "You are unbelievable!" He turned the pram round and steered his baby girl away from her mother for the last time, not that she gave a damn!

It had been the hardest day of Bryan's life and he was in pieces, absolutely distraught by the memory of cuddling his daughter for the very last time. He felt as though someone had ripped his heart out and he was finding it hard to breathe properly. Never again did he want to go through a day such as this, never again would he let someone like Angela ruin his life - he hoped he never set eyes on her again as long as he lived! She signed the adoption papers last week as he had asked, but as he couldn't bear the thought of seeing her, he made a separate appointment for himself yesterday.

Early this morning, he packed a bag full of Anna's clothes, some nappies and a few of her soft toys. He dressed her so she looked very pretty in a little pink dress and wrapped her in a knitted lacy white shawl, a gift from one of his neighbours.

He had taken lots of photographs since making the decision to give his daughter to someone who could care and look after her safely. He bought a small wooden box in which he could keep the photos along with some of Anna's things. He carefully cut off a tiny curl of her hair and put it in the box along with her little hairbrush; first teddy; first tiny pair of bootees and her first little nightgown.

At lunchtime he gave Anna a last bottle, all the time fighting back the urge to change his mind and keep her here with him. As he changed her nappy she was gurgling and smiling up at him and as hard as he tried he couldn't stop the tears – his heart was breaking! As he settled Anna in her pram her big eyes watched him intently and he wondered if she could sense something was wrong. It suddenly occurred to him that he would have to push an empty pram home again and that would be unbearable, so he decided to ask the social worker to give to a family who needed it.

He took Anna for a last walk around the park before heading to his appointment at the social work office where he had to hand over his precious daughter to a young social worker named Rosie who assured him Anna would be placed with loving parents who would provide her with a good home and look after her for him.

He asked for just one more cuddle and Rosie told him to take as long as he needed and handed Anna back to him. For a few seconds he thought of changing his mind and leaving with her, but deep down he knew it was impossible for him to raise a child on his own without any help. He cuddled her as tightly as he dared, closed his eyes and sniffed her skin, then kissed her tiny forehead for the very last time and handed her back to Rosie. He quickly turned away and left so Rosie couldn't see the tears streaming down his face...

Hours later, Bryan still sat on the chair by Anna's cot holding her blanket, breathing in the scent of 'just bathed and powdered baby'. For twelve weeks his world revolved around his baby girl and giving her up was the hardest thing he would ever do. He knew he would never get over the trauma of giving her away - nor would he ever forget the heartbreak Angela had caused, destroying both his own and his daughter's lives...

CHAPTER 8

Lesley and Steve Thomas are a very happy, loving couple, always ready to help others and always welcoming with bright cheerful smiles. They live in a small village on the east coast of Scotland and love the friendliness and great community spirit surrounding them.

Steve is the village policeman, a fair man, respected and liked by the majority of the villagers. He met Lesley three years ago when she moved to the village to take up her post as the teacher at the small school, which consists of one large classroom attached to the local church. Lesley teaches the village children within the age range of five to eleven years and therefore quite a mixed bunch. She adores every one of them, even young Johnny with his spiky red hair, missing front teeth and a large spread of freckles across the bridge of his nose! Johnny spent more time at the naughty desk than all the other children put together, but he wasn't a bad child, just full of mischief and Lesley secretly had a soft spot for him!

Always making a point of introducing himself to any newcomer to the village, Steve had popped into the school on Lesley's second day to say a quick hello and they instantly hit it off. In fact, he would tell anyone who asked, that the minute he saw her he fell in love! After having quite a long chat with Steve, Lesley watched as he walked through the playground. He was about six foot with broad shoulders, big brown eyes and light brown hair. When he smiled his mouth turned up at the corners and his laugh was infectious. She instantly liked him and hoped she would see much more of Steve the policeman!

As Steve left the classroom there was an extra spring in his step, that girl was stunning with her long brown hair curling down her back and a glint in those brown eyes which hinted at a wicked sense of humour. Yes, today he was feeling at one with the world and he was going to make a point of seeing the new teacher again very soon!

The very next day Steve asked Lesley if she would like to go along to the village dance with him on the following Saturday and the rest, as they say, is history!

Lesley had only been in the village eight months when Steve proposed and Lesley accepted. Four months later, on the twenty-third of December, they were married in the little village church. It was a lovely bright day although cold and frosty! Just about everyone in the village squeezed into the church and the children sang 'All Things Bright and Beautiful', Lesley's favourite hymn. They had planned to leave on honeymoon straight from the church but the villagers had other ideas! They secretly organised a wedding breakfast in the church hall, everyone contributing some food and drink, which resulted in a very large and impressive buffet!

Lizzie, one of the church elders, made and decorated a wedding cake complete with a bride and groom ornament on top, the groom dressed in a policeman's uniform! Three of the local lads played music and it turned into a brilliant afternoon party with Steve and Lesley escaping just after 7pm under a shower of rice, which the children took great delight in throwing at them! They later found out the party continued on until just after midnight, the villagers enjoying a reason to celebrate!

They had a short but enjoyable honeymoon, spending a couple of days with each set of parents over Christmas where other relatives and friends joined them to celebrate their marriage. They returned to the police house a couple of days before Hogmanay, wanting to start the New Year together in their own home as newlyweds.

They were deeply in love and extremely happy, more than they could ever have thought possible. Around the time of their second wedding anniversary, Lesley suspected she might be pregnant and on Christmas Day one of the presents she gave Steve was a bib with 'Daddy' written on it. He was absolutely ecstatic, whooping and laughing as he whirled her around the room until they had to sit down, out of breath and both giggling like youngsters! Everything was perfect and they were very excited to be starting a family!

All went well during the pregnancy, they were now into May and Lesley was glowing with health, her bump quite large now! The children at school had been working hard to help with ideas for their sports day the following month, when the parents could also visit the classroom to see the children's work on display. They had been working on a project about food, where it comes from and how it is grown. The classroom walls were covered in pictures of fruit; vegetables; trees; tractors and people in fields picking tatties - the children making an excellent job of painting every one. Lesley was really pleased at how hard they had all been working, even little Johnny who now had a lovely set of front teeth!

Lesley was packing up after a busy day when she felt an unusual twinge low down under her bump. She put it down to the baby stretching or kicking her and carried on home to make dinner for herself and Steve. Later that evening as she got ready for bed, she felt another sharp pain in the same place, but this time it lasted a couple of minutes and she began to feel a bit uneasy. She mentioned it to Steve and he suggested she had probably overdone things at school that day.

However, when the same happened again shortly afterwards, Steve decided to call the doctor just to be on the safe side and went down to his office to call Dr Harris. He went back up to Lesley and told her the doctor said it would probably be nothing to worry about but he would pop along and give her a quick check to see if baby was behaving.

As they waited for the doctor to arrive, Lesley couldn't remember feeling the baby move since she arrived home and told Dr Harris when he arrived at the house.

"Now don't be getting yourself all worried, let's have a listen and find out what this wee one is up to!" he gave her a reassuring smile and patted her hand. He was a lovely friendly man with a great bedside manner and he knew every single one of his patients by their first names. Unfortunately he was close to retirement and would be sorely missed by the villagers.

He felt around the baby first and then put the trumpet to her bump to listen to the baby's heartbeat. He moved it around carefully, listening intently. He prodded her bump and listened again with the trumpet. "The little devil is playing hide and seek tonight so to be on the safe side I think we will pop you along to the cottage hospital and we can keep an eye on things there," he said patting her hand again.

They decided Steve would drive Lesley to the hospital to be checked over and as it was so late they took a small bag in case she was admitted overnight. Steve gave her a reassuring smile, a quick hug and helped her into the car. They set off for the hospital, Dr Harris following behind in his own car. Steve was overly bright, although Lesley knew he was having the same worrying thoughts as she was, but they both acted as relaxed as possible for the sake of the other.

Steve waited outside in the corridor as a midwife, Dr Harris and another doctor examined Lesley in a small room at the hospital. They had been in there for some time and Steve was wandering back and forth, too worried to sit still. Eventually the door opened and Dr Harris came towards Steve, "I'm sorry lad, I'm afraid the baby's heartbeat is very weak and there is obviously a serious problem so we are going to get Lesley into theatre and see if we can get the little one out and give him a helping hand. It's a few weeks too soon but we will do everything we can," he squeezed Steve's shoulder. "You can pop in quickly and see your wife, but then we have to get things moving."

Steve nodded unable to speak and walked towards the door. Taking a few deep breaths he gave a quick tap on the door and went in to find the midwife busy fastening the tabs on a gown she had put on Lesley. He waited until she was finished and left saying she would be back in a couple of minutes to take Lesley to theatre.

"Now don't you be worrying my love," Lesley said giving him a reassuring smile. "They know what they are doing and I'm sure they will do the best to save our baby." Her eyes were bright and glistened with unshed tears but she needed to stay strong and believe everything would turn out just fine. Steve smiled at his very brave wife, gave her a tight hug and whispered in her ear that he loved her and would be here when she woke up after the surgery.

He watched as they wheeled Lesley down to theatre, then sat weeping into his hands - Lesley didn't deserve this! She was such a good person and would be such a brilliant mother.

"Please God," he pleaded looking to the heavens, "please let both of them come out of this okay!"

It was the longest two hours of his life and he thought he was going to lose his mind. Eventually, Lesley's bed was wheeled back to her room and he could see she was still asleep. As the porters manoeuvred her bed into the room, the nurse told Steve she would let him have a couple of minutes with his wife once she checked Lesley was comfortable.

"What about the baby?"

"The doctor will be along shortly to talk to you Mr Thomas," she smiled and headed in to see to Lesley as the porters left. After a few minutes the nurse reappeared and nodded to him, signalling that he could now go in and see his wife.

He crept into the room and it tore at his heart to see his precious wife lying there looking so pale. He didn't even know how their baby was so he couldn't tell her anything if she should wake up. He kissed her forehead and stood holding her hand until Dr Harris arrived and beckoned him out of the room. He was fond of this couple, had known Steve for a few years and wanted to do everything in his power to help their baby to survive.

"Your wife is going to be fine Steve. Congratulations! You have a son, but I'm afraid he has a very weak and irregular heartbeat and although my colleagues are doing what they can, I'll be honest with you and say he's got a fight ahead of him. I'm so sorry, sometimes babies are born with heart defects but until we find out exactly what the problem is I can't tell you any more just now. Once they get him more stable you will be able to see him," he gave Steve's arm a pat. "Best not say too much to Lesley until she recovers from the anaesthetic. I have to go now but I'll be back in the morning to check on them both," he smiled at Steve and then headed off back down the corridor.

When Steve got home in the early hours he stoked up the fire and spent the remainder of the night staring into the flames, silently praying for his son's life…

CHAPTER 9

Lucy and Patrick met when he came into the florist shop, where Lucy worked, to buy his mother flowers for her birthday.

There was an instant attraction between them as Patrick chatted away to her, asking her personal questions as she made up his mother's bouquet. She laughed at his fast moves and turned him down when he asked her to go to the pictures with him and again when he said they could start slowly and go for a coffee instead! As he was leaving the shop he cocked his head to the side, put on a 'little boy lost' look and pleaded with her one last time, but she shook her head laughing and said she hoped his mother liked her flowers.

When he had gone, Lucy's boss Rhona asked her what on earth she was playing at? Had she lost her mind? The boy was very good looking, a real charmer and deserved extra points for buying his mum a huge bouquet of flowers which showed he was caring and kind! Lucy shook her head and smiled, "He probably chats up a girl in every shop he visits!" she laughed.

Rhona shook her head, "You will never get a lad that way Lucy, you need to start giving them a chance – you are too picky! The next time you get asked out, you need to say yes!" Lucy just laughed and went to hold the door open for a customer who was struggling to get into the shop with a pram.

The following day Lucy was serving an elderly gentleman when she noticed a card stuck to the outside of the shop window, which read 'PLEASE COME OUT WITH ME'. She felt herself blush and busied herself in choosing some foliage to complete the bouquet she was putting together.

That evening as they were locking up the shop Patrick appeared, obviously having come straight from work as he was dressed in dungarees and work boots. Rhona winked at her and left quickly.

"Hello again," Patrick grinned at Lucy.

"Hello," she gave him a small smile, "do you need to buy more flowers?"

"No, I'm here to beg you to come for a coffee with me," he raised his eyebrows. "Please!!"

"I don't go out with men I don't know."

"Well let's remedy that straight away then. My name is Patrick Edwards; I am a carpenter; I am not seeing any other girls; I have a brother and a sister; I live at home with my brother and parents and I can't think about anything else but you!" He held up his thumb, which was bandaged, "I even burst my thumb open today because I was too busy thinking about how I could get you to come out with me!"

Lucy studied the gorgeous guy standing in front of her looking very sheepish, holding up his bandaged thumb and giving her the puppy dog eyes again. "Okay Patrick Edwards, just because I caused you to hurt your thumb, I will let you take me for a coffee but I have to catch my bus in an hour!"

Patrick nodded eagerly and they went to the small café round the corner from the florist shop. They chatted easily over their coffee and before they knew it Lucy realised she had missed her bus and after having a second coffee she also missed the next bus, so Patrick insisted on walking her home. They went to get Patrick's bike, which he had locked up beside Lucy's work, and although they started walking, it wasn't long before Patrick persuaded Lucy to sit on the handlebars of his bike and they laughed and chatted as he gave her a lift home!

They never looked back from that first date and saw each other as much as possible. They had been going out together for eighteen months when Patrick surprised Lucy by taking her out for dinner one Saturday evening to a small restaurant overlooking the river. As they waited for their deserts, Patrick got up and crouched down beside Lucy. In his hand was a green velvet heart-shaped box and he opened it to reveal a beautiful Emerald ring. "I love you and want us to be together forever! Will you make me the happiest man on this earth and agree to marry me?"

Lucy didn't hesitate for a second and nodded, her eyes glistening as they filled with tears. Patrick took the ring from the box, slid it onto her finger and then raised her hand to his lips to kiss it. They were deeply in love and Lucy could not believe how this cheeky guy, who walked into the shop to buy his mum flowers, had changed her life - she couldn't have been happier!

The following Monday morning Lucy took great delight in walking into the florists, grinning from ear to ear, and wagging her finger at Rhona to show off her ring. Rhona was delighted, hugging and congratulating her before rushing round to the bakers shop to buy some cakes to celebrate and have with their morning tea!

Both Lucy and Patrick were good with money and saved hard for their wedding but as it drew closer Lucy's parents surprised them and said they would pay for the wedding as their gift, leaving the money they had saved to set up home together.

They had been lucky to rent a small cottage from a family friend and chose not to go away on honeymoon, but spend the money on making the cottage cosy and a home of which they were very proud!

Their wedding in February was magical! The air was crisp with winter sunshine and a sprinkling of snow lay like a lace blanket on the ground. Lucy looked stunning in a long white dress and a cape with a hood, everyone saying she looked just like a princess! The service in the small church was enjoyed by all, as not only was it emotional but as the minister knew them both quite well and had a good sense of humour, there were also a few laughs, mainly at Patrick's expense! They had a lovely wedding breakfast in a small hotel and some of Patrick's friends, who all played musical instruments, got together for the evening as their wedding gift and had everyone dancing all night!

Lucy and Patrick slipped away unnoticed just before midnight and when they safely reached the cottage, they laughed at their cleverness in fooling their friends and sneaking away! However, when they pulled the bed covers back they realised they had not been so smart after all! There was confetti and rice everywhere and they laughed even more as they tried their best to clean up the bed! It had been a wonderful day!

CHAPTER 10

As the years passed, Laura and Peter's love continued to grow deeper and they settled into married life very easily. They both worked hard but spent any spare time together and the attraction between them was just as strong as when they first met.

Laura's love of teaching continued to grow and she found it more rewarding as time passed. Each year she said goodbye to the children who were moving up to the next year and looked forward to meeting a class of new children after the summer holidays. She could always tell on day one which child would visit the naughty corner the most, who would be the chatterbox and she usually managed to pick out the clever one in the group.

Peter worked incredibly hard and slowly but surely worked his way up the ladder, taking charge of some of their most important customers who earned unthinkable amounts of money! Four years ago, on his thirty-fourth birthday, he was made a junior partner in the firm and was highly thought of by 'the old man' – his nickname for his boss!

They had a close group of friends, three other couples, and they called themselves 'the gang'. They took turn about going to each other's house for dinner or they all went to the bistro on special occasions. The group were all in their thirties and gradually babies began to arrive leaving Peter and Laura the only couple without children. They had always expected to fall pregnant at some point, but thought it would have happened before now as Laura was almost thirty-three. They talked about it and agreed if it was meant to be it would happen when the time was right. However, Laura had now secretly accepted she would not be lucky enough to have a child of her own and must be content with being part of her pupils' lives.

A month before Christmas some of the children went down with a sickness bug and Laura eventually succumbed too. She had been very ill for just over a week, the bug hitting her so hard she had to take time off work to recover, which was very rare for Laura. Thankfully, she began to feel slightly better in time for Christmas, which was lovely that year as all the gang and their children came over for dinner.

They didn't go out to an arranged Hogmanay party as Laura just couldn't shake off the bug and was still feeling under the weather. Although she returned to work at the beginning of the new term, she still felt unwell and fell asleep most evenings after dinner, which again was very rare for Laura. Peter began to worry there might be something more sinister causing her fatigue and suggested she visit the doctor but Laura shrugged off his concern saying it was simply the bug she had picked up from the kids at school and she would be okay soon.

By mid-January she was finding it hard to get out of bed in the mornings and began to think that Peter might be right and maybe there was something wrong with her. This time Peter insisted she go and see the doctor who gave her a thorough check-up and told her she was not suffering from an illness but from the usual tiredness most women experience in early pregnancy. Laura burst into tears and the doctor passed her a tissue. "Do you not want a baby Mrs Cameron?"

"Oh yes, more than anything, it's just I thought it wasn't going to happen for me!"

"Well that's good news then!" he smiled. "Now you get yourself home and get plenty of rest. The sickness and tiredness are due to increased hormones and shouldn't last too much longer. On your way out make an appointment at the reception desk for four weeks time and we will see how you are getting along then."

Laura was in a daze as she made her way home. She had a bath and put on her dressing gown - it would have to be supper on a tray tonight for her and Peter.

"Hey sweetheart! Still not feeling well?" Peter came over to the cooker where Laura was making their supper and gave her a kiss and cuddle. "What's for dinner? I had a meeting with the old man and missed lunch today - I'm starving!" Peter referred to his boss as the old man for years as they had a good relationship and it was a pet name rather than an insult. "I have some good news for you but just let me nip and get changed and I'll tell you all about it over dinner," and with that he rushed off to the bedroom. Laura smiled to herself as he was not the only one with some news and no matter what Peter was about to tell her, she reckoned her news would beat his!

Laura served up dinner and Peter appeared with a bottle of champagne, which he placed on a tray with two glasses. "I thought we could have a little celebration tonight," he winked at her. He was grinning from ear to ear and looked as though he would burst with excitement!

"Actually, you are not the only one with some news my love, but as you look fit to burst, I think you should go first!" she said laughing.

They got settled on the sofa and Peter popped the cork and filled their glasses. They loved having supper on a tray now and again but she felt a bit guilty, thinking dinner should have been a bit more exciting and the table set to celebrate their good news. He handed her a glass and chinked his against it, "You, my dear wife are looking at the new senior partner at Lloyd and Young! I can't believe the old man made me a senior partner so soon Laura!"

"Oh Peter that's fantastic news! I'm so proud of you - you deserve it! You work your socks off for the firm and it's about time you were rewarded for it! Congratulations!"

"I was thinking, why don't we get away somewhere for a holiday during your summer break?" Laura looked down at the table shaking her head.

"I'm sorry Peter, I won't be able to go anywhere in the summer this year." She looked up at him and saw how disappointed he looked. "It's to do with the news I received today." Laura was trying hard to keep a serious look on her face but could not stop a smile creeping back. "I will be too busy in the summer because I will be busy nursing our baby!" For a split second Peter didn't react as he processed what Laura had said and then in a flash he was picking her up off the sofa and twirling her round, kissing every part of her face!

"I can't believe it! I thought it wasn't going to happen for us, oh Laura I am the happiest man alive!" He gave Laura a long and loving kiss and carried her back to the sofa.

Over supper they chatted excitedly about the baby, chose a room for the nursery, decided what colour to paint it and discussed what furniture they needed to buy. They also chatted about Peter's promotion at work and how perfect the timing was as he was now going to be providing for a family! They were so excited and Peter kept saying, "Is this really happening?" Laura was pleased to see Peter so happy and felt that now their lives were complete!

As promised by the doctor, Laura soon begun to feel better and as the pregnancy progressed she blossomed. Peter decorated the nursery and by May it was fully furnished with a cot, chest of drawers, blanket box and a beautiful rocking chair that Peter bought as a surprise for Laura. When she was alone she would sometimes sit in the chair gently rocking back and forth, trying to imagine how it would feel to rock her precious baby to sleep. On a couple of occasions, Peter came home to find Laura dozing in the chair and thought she had never looked more beautiful!

The school closed for summer at the end of June and Laura was looking forward to having a whole month to potter around the house and get ready for the new arrival. However, only a week later she went into labour in the middle of the night and Peter drove her to hospital, very concerned their baby was coming too early.

After fourteen hours in labour Laura was completely exhausted. She had earlier complained of a headache, which had become unbearable and her blood pressure was now dangerously high. The doctor was called and he decided, for the safety of both mother and baby, they would need to deliver Laura immediately by caesarean section. As Laura was wheeled out of the room Peter squeezed her hand and kissed her, reassuring her that everything would be fine and he would be there waiting for her and their baby. When the door closed behind them leaving Peter alone, he fought back the tears as he worried for his wife and baby…

CHAPTER 11

Jean was an unexpected baby for her mother and father who were shopkeepers in the small village of Beauly, a few miles outside Inverness. Chrissie realised she was pregnant with her first child at the age of forty-two which was a shock but everything went well and they enjoyed being older parents. However, sadly just after Jean turned twelve, her father died suddenly of a heart attack leaving Chrissie and Jean alone.

Running the shop was hard work and Chrissie relied heavily on her young daughter to help, which meant Jean rarely had time to go out with her friends after school or at the weekends as she was always working. She left school at fifteen to work full-time in the shop, get more involved and learn everything she needed to know about running a busy shop. Over the next few years she made some changes to the layout, introduced some new stock and gradually relieved her mother of her workload.

On Saturdays the shop shut at six o'clock and so Jean had the night free. She and her pal Daisy loved going to the dances in the village hall every weekend and it was on one of these nights that she was introduced to Harry Issac. He was a cousin of a former classmate who had come through from

Inverness that weekend and from that night on he became a regular at the dances.

Jean was really keen on Harry but did her best not to show it, however as time passed they grew very close, both living for the following weekend and over the space of a year they fell in love. Harry was a couple of years older than Jean and was working for a bakery in Inverness after serving his apprenticeship there. He was having tea with Jean and her mother one Sunday evening when he asked Chrissie if he had her permission to marry her daughter - the answer a resounding yes!

They had been engaged for five months, their wedding only a couple of months away and they had been having long discussions about what they could do to improve the shop. One Sunday afternoon over tea, Jean and Harry had a long talk with Chrissie, telling her their ideas to expand the shop and between them it was decided they would take over from Chrissie, Harry putting his trade to good use by selling fresh baked goods every morning.

Chrissie was now approaching sixty and felt the hours were too much these days, so she was more than happy to retire. She was also delighted to be able to leave the flat and move in with her widowed sister Moira who owned a cottage in the village. Chrissie refused any payment for the shop, insisting it was Jean's inheritance for which she had worked very hard since her father died - she deserved it! Harry managed to get round Chrissie though, eventually persuading her to accept a weekly payment to enable her to live comfortably with her sister.

Jean and Harry had a wonderful wedding and as everyone in the village knew them from the shop, the church was packed as most of them wanted to attend the ceremony.

They held the reception at a hotel in the square having a wedding breakfast for their family and close friends followed by a brilliant ceilidh in the evening, to which the rest of their friends were invited.

They were showered with gifts for their home and Jean reckoned they wouldn't have to buy anything at all! They had decorated the flat before the wedding, moving Chrissie's favourite bits and pieces of furniture to her sisters, keeping some others and selling the remainder. After buying a new bed, a dining table and chairs and a settee they were very pleased with how the flat looked.

They started married life together with a one-day honeymoon as they couldn't go away and leave the shop. They had breakfast in bed, lunch in bed and topped the day off by sitting in front of the open fire wrapped up in a huge blanket eating poached eggs on toast! Honeymoon over, they headed back to bed for an early night as Harry would have to be up at 5am to bake bread and rolls for the shop.

Their first two years as a married couple were spent working hard to improve the shop, Harry expanding the range of baked goods, which sold out every day. They also increased the range of stock and therefore had to replace the shelving and buy new display units. They were very happy and everything was going very well for them until Jean began to suffer from severe abdominal pain. After several visits to the doctor, she was sent to hospital in Inverness where she received the devastating news she would need a hysterectomy, which meant that sadly she would not be able to have children.

As Jean recovered from her surgery, she had long talks with Harry about how their lives would be without children, but neither of them wanted it to be that way as they felt they could provide a caring and loving home for a child. After much discussion, they decided that just because Jean couldn't have a child of her own, it didn't mean they could not give a child a secure and loving home. Harry made some enquiries, they made an application to adopt a child and although it was a long drawn out process, they didn't come up against any problems. Within the year, they were approved by Social Services and began the wait for a child who would become the newest member of their family!

One morning Jean was serving in the shop when Harry came down from the flat with a second basket of fresh bread. He walked over to one of the shelves, picked something up and walked towards her, a wide grin on his face and one hand behind his back. "What are you up to Harry?" she laughed. Harry winked at her and put a tin of baby milk powder on the counter. It took Jean a few seconds to catch on to what Harry meant and suddenly she clasped her hand to her mouth, her eyes filling with tears! Harry gave her a tight bear hug and smiled down at her - they were going to be parents very soon!

CHAPTER 12

Although Abbie knew something happened with Maggie and Simon on the night of her birthday party, no amount of coaxing had persuaded her to 'kiss and tell'. Whatever it was, she knew Maggie was different somehow and when she wasn't aware she was being watched, Maggie sometimes looked very sad. Maybe Simon hadn't been so keen on her, or they argued about something, but whatever it was, Maggie didn't even look in his direction now.

When Maggie returned home on the Sunday after the party, she spent the rest of the day in the sanctuary of her room 'studying'. She went over and over the events of the previous night and came to the decision that as there were only two months until she left school, she would hold her head up and count down the days until she could walk away from all of this and start a new life at university.

Around six weeks after the party, Maggie's father was passing the bathroom when he heard her vomiting and insisted on checking her over, coming to the conclusion she had probably eaten something that disagreed with her. However, over the next few days, Maggie continued to vomit every so often. All the family were having breakfast one morning when a pale Maggie raced off to the bathroom to be sick again and her mother, worried it could be something more serious than a virus, insisted on making an appointment with their doctor for after school the following day.

The following afternoon Maggie was called into see Dr Mackay, who welcomed her into the surgery with a shake of the hand and a friendly smile. "Now, what is troubling you today?"

"I think I may have a virus as I've been vomiting on and off for near enough a week but I'm afraid my mother seems to think it may be more serious," Maggie said apologetically as she felt her mother was being over-anxious as usual.

"Okay. Have you had a temperature at all?"

"No, most of the time I feel fine, but every now and then I suddenly feel ill and have to run to the bathroom."

"Right, if you just pop onto the couch I need to feel your tummy," she smiled at Maggie and followed her over to the couch where she gave her a thorough examination. She then asked Maggie to go to the toilet and provide a urine sample, which she tested.

"Okay, let's sit back down. Now then Maggie, do you know when your last period was?" She watched as Maggie thought back and suddenly her face turned pale. Maggie looked at her and started to shake her head.

"No! You're not suggesting I'm pregnant?"

"I take it from your reaction that you have been sexually active Maggie?"

"Oh god! It was only once! A stupid situation at a party with a boy I thought liked me," she bowed her head and shut her eyes for a moment. "My parents will kill me!"

"I'm sure when they get over the shock everything will be alright Maggie. I'm guessing you are only a few weeks, can you tell me the date of this party?"

Tears were running down Maggie's face as she answered the doctor. "It will be seven weeks tomorrow," she said quietly whilst wiping away tears.

Dr Mackay chatted with her for a few minutes, concerned about how Maggie was going to tell her parents. She told her if she wanted to get her mum to come back in with her she would be happy to tell her. Maggie shook her head, "It's okay, I will tell them once I've had time to think and work out what I'm going to do, thank you." She calmly walked out of the surgery wishing she could turn the clock back seven weeks.

As Dr Mackay wrote up Maggie's notes, she felt both frustrated and sad to record yet another unplanned teenage pregnancy.

That evening, when Maggie's parent's asked what the doctor had said, she told them it was just some virus she had picked up and it should gradually improve. Luckily Maggie only needed to get through the next two weeks and her days at high school would be over. Until then she would try and spend as little time as possible around her parents, which wouldn't be difficult as she only ever saw them at mealtimes and even then her father didn't always make it home from the hospital in time to have dinner. Meanwhile she had a lot of thinking to do...

CHAPTER 13

Peter had been waiting for what felt like hours when finally one of the nurses came into the room pushing a cot. "I've brought your son to meet you," she smiled, "I'm Marie and I will be looking after your son today. Now if you sit down you can hold him and let him get to know his daddy!"

Peter stared at his tiny son. He was a miniature version of Laura with his big eyes and dainty wee nose, just perfect with long fingers and toes! He was so small he almost fitted into Peter's hands! "Do you know how much he weighs?"

"He is 6lbs 2 ounces Mr Cameron, he's just a wee tot!" she smiled down at his baby son.

"What about Laura, when can I see her?"

"When they finish the operation she will be kept in recovery until she has come round and the doctors are happy with everything. I think the wee chap might be hungry so I will take him along to the nursery and give him a bottle."

"Can I not do that? I've been practising so I know what I'm doing," he cocked his head to the side and gave Marie his best smile.

Marie smiled, "Of course you can, I'll pop along and get a bottle and once he's fed and happy we can give him a wash and put him down for a sleep, he's had a bit of a journey into the world!"

Peter fed his son, never once taking his eyes off his tiny face. He was so much like Laura and his heart was just bursting with love for this tiny bundle. They had decided on names not long after Laura found out she was pregnant. A girl was to be named Charlotte after Laura's mother and a boy was to be Joseph, Peter's middle name and a family name going back generations. "Welcome to the world young Joseph Peter Cameron."

"That's a beautiful name," Marie said as she entered the room with a basin and towels. "Now let's get this young chap cleaned up, he must be tired!" Peter looked on as Marie washed his son, put on a little gown, wrapped him up snuggly and put him down for a sleep in his cot.

"Right, I shall just tidy up here, go and find out how your wife is and come back to give you an update." Peter smiled and when she left the room he stood over his son watching him as he drifted off to sleep. Wait until Laura saw him, she would fall in love the instant she set eyes on him. They were so very lucky!

Nearly an hour passed and Peter was becoming anxious. Surely it didn't take as long as this to bring Laura round and take her back to her room. He thought Marie would have been back by now and he was starting to feel uneasy. What if there had been a problem during the surgery?

Another twenty minutes passed before Marie came back into the room, this time followed by a doctor. The look on their faces started alarm bells ringing in Peter's head straight away.

"What's happened? Is Laura okay?" The doctor came forward and shook Peter's hand introducing himself as Dr Alex Ross.

"I'm afraid the news is not good Mr Cameron." Peter closed his eyes as he could feel his chest tighten and as he couldn't find his voice he nodded at the doctor. "When your wife was in labour she complained of a headache and her blood pressure became dangerously high as you know. When we got her into theatre we just managed to deliver your baby as your wife went into heart failure." Peter closed his eyes as his world started to crumble. Marie had crossed the room and was crouched down holding and patting Peter's hand as he allowed the tears to fall unchecked.

"We did manage to restart Laura's heart and we have been carrying out tests but we think your wife suffered a massive stroke and she remains unresponsive. We are helping her with her breathing and will continue to monitor her for any sign of improvement, but I'm afraid I must warn you we don't think it likely she will recover. We will do everything we can for your wife and will repeat the tests in the morning, but if there is any change meantime, we will call you. I know this is very hard on you and if you have any questions I will do my best to answer them."

Peter felt dead inside and prayed this was a horrible nightmare and any second now he would wake up but he knew that his perfect world had crashed spectacularly. "Can I see Laura?"

"Of course, Marie can stay with your son and I will take you along now."

"No, I want to take him with me, Laura needs to meet her son." The doctor looked at Marie who was barely holding back the tears herself and she nodded.

"Okay we will all go along."

Peter stood up, his legs so weak he felt as though they would buckle underneath him but he managed to make it to Laura's bedside. She was deathly pale, there were wires attached to her chest, drips in both arms and the machines surrounding her bed constantly bleeped. Her beautiful face was hidden by a mask attached to a tube, which was attached to one of the machines. Peter felt numb and sick, how could it have all gone so wrong?

Peter was aware of someone leaning over him patting his hand and when he managed to open his eyes and focus, Marie was smiling at him.

"There now, that's better, when you feel ready we will get you up." A few minutes later Peter was sitting on a chair and had been given a cup of tea by another nurse. "Now then," said Marie, "you need to drink that tea, it's hot and sweet and it will make you feel better." Peter did as he was told and slowly he began to feel a bit more human.

"What happened?"

Marie smiled down at him, "You just fainted, but don't you worry about it, it's quite a shock when you see your loved one surrounded by wires and monitors. Most people don't cope very well at first and you are by no means the first to faint. You've had a devastating shock today and it's only to be expected that you're not quite yourself. Now, once you have finished your tea we can think about trying again, but only if you are sure you feel okay."

After a few minutes Marie moved the chair closer to Laura's bedside and made Peter sit down again, just to be on the safe side. He stroked her hand and told her how beautiful and perfect Joseph was, how she was strong and would show the doctors she could pull through and come home to be with her family. Marie left him sitting for five minutes until she felt he was looking a bit stronger and then she wheeled Joseph's cot over to the bed.

"I thought it might be time to introduce your son to your wife?" Peter stood up, lifted Joseph out of the cot and held him close to Laura's neck and cheek.

"Meet our son Laura, he's beautiful and he needs his mum so if you can hear me at all then fight sweetheart, fight with everything you have!" Marie dug her nails into the palm of her hand as hard as she could. She could hardly bear the sadness any longer and was desperately trying to hold back her tears.

After Marie reassured Peter that Joseph would be well looked after in the hospital nursery he agreed to go home and try to get some sleep. Marie walked him along the corridor to the hospital entrance to make sure he got into a taxi and then headed back to the nursery to check on Joseph as promised. As she looked down at the tiny sleeping face she finally allowed herself a few tears. Today had been her worst day as a nurse and she hoped she never had to witness anything like it again.

Peter lay on his bed fully dressed, eyes wide open. He was completely numb and stared at the ceiling for hours unable to comprehend what happened.

As he walked into the hospital the next morning, Peter felt as though the world was resting on his shoulders. He hadn't managed to sleep at all as he replayed the events of yesterday over and over in his mind. He was hoping, that by some miracle, he would walk in to her room today and Laura would be sitting up in bed cuddling their son, but he knew deep down that wasn't going to be the case. He walked along to the room where Laura had been last night and hoped he wouldn't see her lying there, machines keeping her alive, but as he approached the open door he could see nothing had changed.

He walked over to Laura's beside and gently stroked her face, desperately searching for any sign of improvement, but he could see for himself Laura was just as he had left her the previous night.

After a few minutes Dr Ross came in to talk to Peter and explained all the tests had been repeated earlier that morning, but unfortunately Laura was showing no signs of attempting to breathe on her own. He said he would repeat the tests for the final time in a few hours but he did not expect there to be any change. Peter asked what would happen if there was no improvement and the doctor told him they would have to discuss withdrawing the breathing support.

"You mean allow her to die?" Peter asked in disbelief.

"Yes, I'm so sorry but if we don't see any sign of activity in the brain at this stage, there will be no recovery. At the moment the machine is breathing for your wife, but if we remove all the support Laura will not breathe on her own and will not survive more than a few minutes. We do tests to check if Laura's brain responds to stimulation but unfortunately so far there has been no response. I will be back to see your wife in a few hours to repeat the tests and once we have the results we can have a talk and make some decisions." He shook Peter's hand, gave his shoulder a firm squeeze and headed out of the room.

Peter couldn't make sense of it all. The doctor was saying Laura was technically gone, the machine breathing for her. Why Laura?

Marie appeared a few minutes later with Joseph in his cot. "I thought you might want Joseph to snuggle into his mum again today?" Peter nodded and she passed Joseph over to him. He laid his son alongside his wife, placing her arm round him for a cuddle and he stroked Laura's forehead for more than half an hour, until Joseph started to cry. "I think this little fellow might need fed," said Marie. "Would you like to come along to the nursery and feed him?"

"No I'll let you see to him, I need to stay with Laura."

"I understand, I will come back to see how you are getting on after I've got him settled." As she pushed the cot back to the nursery, she had an uneasy feeling. She noticed that compared to yesterday, Peter barely looked at his son and, apart from placing him beside his wife, he didn't hold him either. It was understandable as the poor man was distraught, but he would need his son more than ever now, just as Joseph needed his daddy. She decided to take baby Joseph back after his feed and see if she could get things back on track.

When Marie returned with Joseph, Peter was still standing in the same spot stroking Laura's hair. "We thought we would pop back and see mum and dad as little Joseph here is wide awake. She picked Joseph up and handed him to Peter, "There you go dad, it's your turn for a cuddle this time." He took his son but again placed him on the bed against Laura. Marie looked at Joseph and his mum snuggled up together, "My your son really does look like you Laura, he has all your features except for dad's slight dimple on his chin," she smiled at Peter.

"She was always joking the first thing she would be checking was his ears," he gave a little smile and Marie kept him talking by asking questions about Laura.

"Does your wife work?"

"Yes she teaches primary school and she adores every one of her children."

"How long have you been married?"

"Only ten years," he said and Marie could see he was welling up again, so she smartly changed the subject by asking Peter about his profession and kept the conversation on a safer subject until he regained his composure.

Peter stayed with Laura all day, only taking a couple of breaks to get a coffee but he couldn't face eating anything as his stomach was constantly churning. The doctor came back, as promised, to repeat the tests and Peter went outside for a walk to get some fresh air. In a matter of hours he would probably have to say goodbye to his wife and he just couldn't bear it.

As arranged, Dr Ross came to see Peter to discuss the results of the tests, which were as expected. There was no improvement and the test results confirmed Laura would not sustain life if they withdrew medical support.

Peter sat with his head in his hands but managed to hold onto his composure, he needed to be strong for Laura because if the roles were reversed he knew she would be strong for him.

At ten o'clock he left the hospital after the worst night of his life. At eight o'clock Dr Ross switched off the machines keeping Laura alive and then removed her breathing tube. Marie insisted on staying after her shift to be with Peter and both herself and Dr Ross discreetly moved to the back of the room as Peter climbed onto the bed beside Laura, gathered her to his chest and held her while she passed away. He sobbed into her hair, telling her he would never forget a minute of their time together and promised to love her for eternity.

Eventually he laid her back on the pillow, stroked her hair and kissed her forehead, the tears running down his face as he turned away and walked out into the corridor. Dr Ross took him into a side room to have a brief conversation about what would happen next and then he managed to make it to the front door of the hospital before completely falling apart. Luckily it was so late there were very few people about to hear his tortured sobs. He found a quiet bench where he sat and cried until he was too exhausted to cry anymore. How could life change so drastically in the space of two days?

It started to rain and he somehow managed to get in the car and drive home, dazed, exhausted and running on autopilot... When he got home, he wandered around looking at photos and keepsakes they bought on weekends away, the carved elephant he bought for Laura for her thirtieth birthday and the glass chess set they played with on rainy days. He crossed to the patio door and looked out at the garden. Laura loved to sit at the table and prepare her lessons for the following week - she called it her haven.

He poured a large brandy, made his way through to the bedroom, lay on top of the bed and cried himself to sleep. It was 5.30am when he woke and his first reaction was to roll over to cuddle his wife, but of course the bed was empty and always would be from this moment on. He rolled onto his back and stared up at the ceiling. Why did Laura have to fall pregnant? They would have been happy just the two of them, they had said it often enough. They could have carried on living happily together, been one of those old couples who sat on benches in the park holding hands. They had been so looking forward to having a baby and now he had a baby but no Laura. He had a baby - a baby who killed his mother! Joseph was the double of Laura and he would never be able to look at him without seeing her and he couldn't bear that....

After a shower, Peter got dressed and made some coffee, still unable to face anything to eat. He phoned their friends and families, having to endure repeatedly telling them the tragic news that Laura had died during childbirth. When questioned about the baby, he told them he was okay and was in the nursery at the hospital. When asked when he would be taking Joseph home, Peter lied and said they wanted to keep an eye on him for a few days. Some relatives he spoke to, were so distraught, they had to hang up and call back when they felt able to speak again. It was the worst thing he ever had to do.

Thankfully 'the gang' appeared one by one and while the guys helped organise the funeral, as Peter hadn't a clue where to begin, the girls shopped, cleaned and cooked. They persuaded Peter to try and eat and all sat at the table with him, trying to eat for his sake even though it was the last thing they wanted to do either.

He telephoned the hospital and arranged for Laura's body to be collected by the undertaker and for his son to stay in the nursery until he "got things organised". They assured him that under the circumstances a few days more would be absolutely fine.

The girls in the gang offered to take turns staying over to help look after Joseph once Peter brought him home and he thanked them saying he had to get through the funeral first and then he would make arrangements.

On the day of the funeral, Peter was in pieces but the gang were fantastic and were by his side the whole day. The guys all took a chord to carry Laura's coffin into the church and following the very sad service they stood either side of Peter at the graveside, keeping him upright when his legs threatened to buckle under him.

They made sure everything went to plan and at the wake there was always one of them to take over when Peter was faced with a relative or friend who started to cry and hug him, telling him life wouldn't be the same without Laura. He was well aware of that and knew they were hurting too, but right now he just couldn't deal with other people's grief. One of the gang would gently lead them away offering a brandy or cup of tea and Peter was extremely grateful to have such good friends.

Eventually, just Peter and the gang remained. Bob, who helped arrange the funeral, handed him a large brandy, "For medicinal purposes, get it down you." He did as he was told and looked around at his friends.

"I can't thank you enough for everything you have done. I simply could not have made it through this alone and I will be eternally grateful to each of you."

Bob raised his glass to Peter, "We are your friends Peter and you and Laura are like family to us, we all loved her." They all nodded in agreement and one by one they told of their favourite memory of Laura, each time raising their glasses to toast her. Eventually they headed home, except Bob, who insisted in staying over with Peter. When they reached the apartment Bob poured them both another large brandy before they headed to bed.

Peter lay in bed remembering some of the comments people made throughout the day. Just about everyone asked where Joseph was as if they expected him to be there. Did they not realise Laura would still be here if they hadn't had a baby? One comment he heard repeatedly was "At least you will have your son as a reminder of Laura," a well meaning solitude, but each time he felt as though someone was sticking a knife into his gut.

Firstly, he didn't need a baby to remind him of Laura, he would never forget her! Secondly, did they not understand he didn't want to be reminded of the way Laura died and that's what would happen every time he looked at Joseph?

He knew he wouldn't be able to cope with his feelings and it wouldn't be fair on his child to carry the blame for his mother's death. There and then he made the decision to speak to someone as soon as possible about finding another home for Joseph. He fell asleep dreaming of the picnic he and Laura shared just after they met.

As soon as Bob left the apartment the next morning, Peter phoned Social Services and had a long conversation with a social worker, who seemed very understanding and sympathetic about the situation Peter found himself in. She suggested he might want to take some time to think about his decision as grief often clouded choices, maybe a family member or close friend could help look after his son until he was absolutely sure? He told her he didn't have anyone who would be able to look after such a young baby and assured her he had not made the decision lightly - this was the best option for the child. She arranged to visit him at home the next morning, suggesting he might think about the possibility of having someone to live in and look after the baby if that was possible?

It was not a meeting Peter would ever forget. Although Mary Campbell was very pleasant, she was very thorough and asked a great deal of questions about Peter and Laura's life before she died. He found it all very painful and when she suggested they go to the hospital together to see Joseph, he flatly refused. "I can't do it. I know it sounds harsh but I have lost my wife because of my son and will blame him all his life for her death. I know it sounds cruel but I just can't do it without Laura, please can you just find a home for him with someone who can love him as he is. Can you imagine how it would be for him as he grew older to realise he was to blame for his mother's death?"

Mary had done her best to try and persuade Peter Cameron to keep his son, but it was clear he blamed the baby for his wife's death and it would be better for the child to be raised in a home where he was wanted and loved. She filled in the consent forms and Peter signed away his son for adoption. She told him his son would be moved to a children's home until they could find suitable adoptive parents and he simply nodded and shook her hand as she left.

Mary left the apartment feeling so sad for Peter. It was thankfully an unusual situation, but she only hoped his poor wife was not looking down on him as her heart would be breaking as she watched him give away her child. It was quite possible that a couple of years down the line Peter would regret his decision but by then it would be too late. When she got back to the office she would go through her files and find this poor wee soul loving parents who would cherish him and make up for his tragic start in life....

CHAPTER 14

Marlene arrived at her aunt's house around lunchtime on Saturday and was given a huge welcoming hug! She was very touched at the lengths to which Christine had gone to make her feel at home. Her room had a double bed with a pretty quilted cover, a comfy armchair and pretty chintz curtains. There was a large wardrobe, chest of drawers and a bedside table complete with lamp. Once she added her own bits and pieces, Marlene had a lovely room in which she would be very comfortable.

Over the next few months Marlene and her aunt talked about the baby and what would happen when he or she arrived. After hours of talking they agreed Marlene would look after her baby for the first couple of weeks but would then have to look into adoption as she needed to work and, unfortunately, Christine's health prevented her from looking after a baby. Although initially Marlene wanted to avoid adoption, in time she realised she had no option due to her circumstances and was grateful to her aunt for helping her until she could fend for herself again.

Staying with her aunt allowed Marlene to see out her pregnancy in a stress free environment, in fact in a loving and caring environment. She did the majority of the housework leaving her aunt to do the cooking and baking. They worked really well together and were great companions, sitting in the evenings sewing and knitting baby garments, as even although her baby would be given up for adoption, Marlene wanted to at least provide his or her first clothes.

However as her due date approached, Marlene became increasingly upset at the thought of giving her baby away. Her cousin Jamie and his wife Julie initially stepped in saying they would bring up the baby as their own but, as fate would have it, Jamie's wife fell pregnant and they felt it would be an impossible task to have a five month old baby when the next was born.

The day Christine asked Jamie to go into the loft and bring down a crib, a trunk of baby clothes and a box of blankets was almost too much for Marlene. Herself and Christine sorted through the contents of the trunk and picked out anything suitable, washing and pressing it ready for the new baby. Marlene cleaned the crib and made it up with newly washed bedding. She could already imagine her baby sleeping there and realised she would have to cherish every minute, as the memories of the first two weeks of her baby's life would have to last her a lifetime.

With only just over a couple of weeks until the birth, Marlene became very distressed at times, knowing she was growing closer to doing something that would break her heart. However, nature decided Marlene wouldn't have those two weeks as she went into labour and after a long nineteen hours, she gave birth to a beautiful 6lb 5oz baby girl with whom she instantly fell in love!

Christine also fell deeply in love with her new great niece and it was her suggestion to extend their time with the baby to a month instead of the initial plan of two weeks. Marlene was grateful to her aunt but realised it would result in her becoming even more attached to her baby before having to give her up. Marlene thought very hard about what name to give her child and decided her baby should be named after someone who was good and kind and therefore named her daughter Christina, after her aunt. Aunt Christine was honoured and delighted and as her great niece approached a month old she made a decision, one that would change all their lives.

As they ate dinner one evening, Christine told Marlene she had been thinking about the adoption again. Marlene's heart started to race as she loved her baby more than she could ever have imagined and it was going to destroy her to be parted from her. Noticing the colour draining from Marlene's face, Christine leant over and patted her niece's hand. "It's alright love, it's not what you think, in fact, I may have found a way to allow you to keep Christina."

Marlene shook her head in disbelief, "How?"

"Well, when uncle James died he left me quite comfortable financially and I invested some of the money. I have never touched it, but now I would like to use it to see us through for as long as possible. I've been doing some sums and I think, if we are careful, there is enough to get us through until Christina starts school, then you can work again."

"Oh aunt Chris, I can't let you do that, the money is for you, not me!"

"If your uncle James was here, he would be the first person to give you the money. In fact, he would be disappointed in me if I didn't help you!"

Marlene got up and hugged her aunt, tears of relief and joy spilling down her cheeks - she could keep her precious baby girl!

CHAPTER 15

After the call from their social worker, Miss Harvey, Jean and Harry spent a hectic couple of weeks getting ready for the arrival of their fourteen week old baby girl who they were going to name Olivia. Harry spent the weekend decorating the small attic room next to their bedroom and it looked just perfect! Chrissie's sister Moira was a seamstress and could run up anything on her sewing machine. Chrissie bought a couple of rolls of material and between them they made a pair of curtains, a matching quilted cot cover and cushions for the rocking chair.

Within days they had also made vests, nightdresses, dresses and a hooded jacket. The two sisters stayed up late every night, Moira on the sewing machine and Chrissie sitting by the fire putting the finishing touches to all the garments. Jean had gone into Inverness and arrived home with bags full of baby shopping and Harry's sister had given them her cot as she had recently put her little boy into a bed.

Two days before Olivia was due to arrive the room was finished, they had bought the basic essentials and had enough baby clothes to keep them going for the first few weeks. Harry suggested they keep her arrival a secret, choosing not to tell anyone except Chrissie and Moira, as they wanted to have Olivia to themselves for at least the first night! It was purely by luck the social worker phoned asking if Wednesday lunchtime would be suitable to deliver their baby daughter, which was perfect, as the shop was closed half day and therefore shutting the shop would not arouse any suspicion among the locals!

Neither Harry nor Jean slept a wink on the Tuesday night, in fact Harry gave up trying at 2am, getting up to start making the bread and scones for the shop. He also made some scones and cakes for themselves as they were sure to have visitors when the news of Olivia's arrival spread round the village. Jean stayed in bed longer than usual to get some rest, as Olivia might be unsettled on her first night in her new surroundings.

Harry brought her some tea and toast at 6am and as Jean watched him pour the tea she was overwhelmed with love for him. He was such a kind, caring, loving man and he was going to be a brilliant father to Olivia. "This will be our last morning alone," she smiled as Harry handed her a cup of tea.

"I can hardly take it in! This time tomorrow there will be three of us! I feel as if I'm dreaming!" Harry grinned back at her and leant down to give her a long kiss.

"Enjoy your cup of tea my love and savour every minute of today as this is going to be our best day ever – WE are going to become a mummy and daddy in a few hours and our lives are going to change in the best way I can ever imagine!"

Harry shut the shop at 1pm, turning over the closed sign on the shop door. Tomorrow, when he turned the sign back to open he would be a daddy to a darling, fourteen week old baby girl! Jean had gone up to the flat just after midday to make them some lunch and make sure everything was ready for the social worker's arrival. She wasn't quite sure exactly what would happen? Surely the social worker wouldn't just hand the baby over and then leave? How long would she stay?

Harry came into the kitchen at that moment and Jean was glad to busy herself and make the tea. As they ate their lunch, she told Harry what she had been thinking and he said he had been thinking exactly the same. They both found it surreal to think a woman was going to turn up at their home, hand them a baby and then leave! Jean washed up their cups and plates and Harry was heading through to the bedroom to change his clothes, when the doorbell rang. He stopped dead, turned and grinned at Jean, then ran down the stairs to answer the door and meet his daughter!

As Miss Harvey drove away after delivering the baby to Mr & Mrs Issac, she felt pleased they had found such a nice couple to adopt the little girl. She had read the file and although her birth father had done his best to look after his daughter, he couldn't manage alone and asked them to find her parents who would love her and take care of her. She had no doubt this little girl would have a very loving home with the Issacs.

That evening Harry and Jean sat in front of the fire, Harry holding a sleeping Olivia, both already deeply in love with their baby daughter. Six hours ago, they had never met this darling little girl and now they were her mummy and daddy – she was here at last, she was here to stay....

CHAPTER 16

Lesley's recovery from surgery wasn't straight forward as she developed a bad infection which resulted in her having a second operation, a hysterectomy. She was upset, not about the surgery but at not being able to visit her son for a couple of days until she was able to get in a wheelchair and be taken to the nursery to see him.

He was a real little fighter and the doctors were amazed at how he struggled on, proving them wrong. He needed surgery but it was very complex and had not yet been carried out on such a young baby, a baby they had not expected to live beyond his first week.

Steve and Lesley had already been told on four occasions that it was unlikely their son would make it through another night. However, he was now three weeks old and they both spent every moment possible sitting by his cot in the nursery, taking every chance to hold their little boy.

Steve asked Reverend Peters, who married them, if he could come and baptise Steven, explaining the fears for his life. He gave a short but lovely service in the nursery, Lesley proudly holding her baby with Steve by her side, a protective arm around them both. They christened their baby boy Steven Louis Thomas.

When Steve arrived to visit Lesley the night before she was due to be discharged, he found her upset and anxious about leaving her baby in the hospital. They were walking slowly towards the nursery as Lesley was still recovering from her surgeries. Steve was doing his best to reassure her about leaving Steven in hospital, telling her they would drive over to visit their son every day, when they saw one of the nurses running towards them. At first they didn't think too much of it but then realised she was looking at them. Lesley's heart missed a beat and deep down inside she knew, she knew it was Steven.

Two hours later, a sad and drained Steve had to persuade Lesley to hand him their baby and he kissed his tiny hand and forehead, laid him in his cot and tucked his blanket around him saying "Sleep tight little chap." He turned away, tears running down his cheeks, helped his wife to her feet, placed a firm arm around her and they left their baby son in the nursery for the last time…

A week later the last of the mourners left the graveside leaving Steve and Lesley standing in the churchyard saying their goodbyes to their baby boy. Reverend Peters held a short but lovely service fitting for a baby, such a sad occasion that not one person who attended was able to hold back their tears. Most of the villagers attended but Lesley asked that none of the children attend, as she did not want them to witness grief at such a young age. She would visit them all one afternoon when she felt able and explain her baby had gone to be with baby Jesus.

Over the next six weeks Lesley slowly regained her strength. At first there was so much she couldn't do such as change the bed, hang out the washing and absolutely no lifting or stretching. Mrs Campbell, who cleaned the police house before they got married, proved to be an absolute angel. She bustled in the day after the funeral with a large pan of stew and vegetables for their supper and got stuck in to the housework without being asked, chatting all the time about this and that. Secretly she was there at Steve's request to keep an eye on Lesley and make sure she didn't do anything she wasn't meant to and also to keep her company as he knew it would take her a long time to come to terms with losing Steven.

Mrs Campbell arrived every morning after that, the house was spotless and there was a nice meal warming in the oven ready for when Steve came in for dinner in the evenings. Mrs C, as Steve and Lesley nicknamed her, would be cooking or ironing and telling Lesley about when she came to live in the village, about her family, stories about other families and when she thought Lesley was ready she told her that she too had lost a wee one.

Lesley was drinking a coffee at the time and watched as Mrs C cleaned the cooker and although she never looked up, there was a change in her voice and Lesley felt the emotion, still, after all these years. From that point on there was an unspoken bond between them, although neither of them talked about it again.

Gradually, Lesley began to feel better and felt able to do more around the house, but Mrs C still did all the heavy work. Steve and Lesley didn't shy away from what happened to their baby, nor from the fact they would be unable to have another. Accepting they had a beautiful wee boy but sadly lost him as his heart wasn't strong enough, made them even stronger than before and together they made the decision to look into adoption, but they would give themselves at least a year or two to come to terms with losing their son…

CHAPTER 17

The light was just starting to fade as James and Sara walked home hand in hand after visiting Grace's grave. Today would have been her first birthday and it had been a peaceful but sad day. They placed a teddy bear at the base of the little heart headstone and planted a miniature pink rose in her memory. The past year had been tough but their love for each other carried them through. They cried when they needed to and gradually stopped feeling guilty whenever they laughed. Everyone had been brilliant, saying the right things and giving them time to grieve in their own way.

When Sara eventually returned to work it was exactly what she needed to help her regain some normality and although she had days when she found life hard, gradually it became easier. Visiting Grace today was about accepting the past but also moving on with the future. They would always carry Grace with them in their hearts and she would never be forgotten.

Another six months passed and Sara was on night duty with her friend Sue. It was 3am and all was quiet so they made some tea and something to eat. They were talking about a young baby on the ward who's teenage mum had walked away from her and a social worker was coming to pick her up the following day. "Stop me if I'm talking out of turn, but you have said you're not going to try for a baby again yourself because you couldn't cope with the worry of another stillbirth," Sue glanced at Sara who nodded. "It's just I was wondering if you and James have considered adopting?" Sara had the same thought when the baby was brought into the ward but she hadn't yet broached the subject with James. She was looking for the right time but there would never be a right time, she would talk to James this weekend.

"Yes Sue, it did cross my mind but I need to sit down and discuss it with James and he might not like the idea of adopting," she gave Sue a grateful smile thinking what a good friend she had been to her since she lost Grace.

The following Sunday James was making a raised bed for Sara under the kitchen window. She made them both a coffee, cut a slice of James's favourite cake and headed out to the garden bench. "Come and have a break, I've got a slice of cake for you as a reward for your hard work," she grinned at him.

"A slice of cake! I was hoping for better payment than that!" he laughed and bent to kiss her nose before sitting down beside her. "Don't tell me! You are up to something?" he cocked his head to the side and gave her a long look.

He knew her so well and she liked that about him. Oh well, it was now or never! "Well I don't want you to get upset and I will completely understand if you don't feel the same way but lately I've been thinking about looking into adoption…" her voice trailed off as she watched his reaction. At first his expression didn't change and then he looked straight into her eyes.

"I thought the idea might upset you, but one of the boys at work had a chat with me about it a while back. His sister couldn't have children and she has adopted twice now. I couldn't put us through having another baby. The stress of watching you all those months and worrying if the baby would survive would kill me. If you are sure this is what you want to do then yes, let's look at adopting a wee soul who needs a loving mum and dad." Sara could not believe how much she loved this man and she flung her arms around his neck, kissing him until, laughing, he said he hoped he deserved another slice of cake!

The application process to adopt was long and slow. There was a great deal of form filling; they had to provide financial details; give permission to view their health records; disclose information about their families; ask people to give character references and have both friendly chats and formal interviews with social services. All the information gathered by social services was then used to assess their suitability to adopt.

It was nearly seven months before Sara received a call from their appointed social worker, Mary Campbell, giving her the happy news that their application had been approved and they would receive a letter confirming this. "Hopefully the next time I call I will have good news for you." Sara was very excited and couldn't wait to tell James.

Six weeks later, Mary Campbell arrived back at the office after visiting Peter Cameron - it was a heart-breaking situation! The baby was just over a week old and because of the tragic death of his mum after giving birth to him, his father blamed the wee soul for his wife's death and left him in the hospital nursery to be looked after by the nurses. If she could, she would like to place this baby straight away and avoid placing him in the care system.

Sara arrived home after an early shift at work, kicked off her shoes and headed upstairs to change into her old jeans as it was a lovely day and she wanted to get out in the garden to get some weeding done. Pottering about in her garden was her way of unwinding and relaxing and she always felt much better after a weeding session! She was just heading out the door when the phone rang and for a split second she almost kept going but worried that it might be work, she ran back into the room and grabbed the phone. "Hello?"

"Hello, am I speaking to Sara Andrews?"

"Yes you are, can I help you?"

"Ah I'm glad I've caught you! Sara this is Mary Campbell from the adoption service. I spoke to you on the telephone a few weeks back and as I haven't met you yet, I was wondering if it would be possible for me to pop along and have a chat with you and your husband?"

"Well yes, certainly, when would you like to visit?"

"Would you both be around about four this afternoon? I know it's short notice but I have another call to make not too far from yourselves and I could pop along then if it's convenient for you?" Sara knew James was doing paperwork at the office all afternoon so he could easily come home early. She told Mary that four would be fine and she looked forward to seeing her then. She gave James a quick call telling him there was another routine visit from the adoption service that afternoon and he said it wasn't a problem for him to finish early.

James and Mary walked through the door together and Sara popped the kettle on to make a pot of tea and organised as ever, she had prepared the tea tray earlier along with a selection of home baked cakes. They went out into the sunshine to sit at the table on the decking which overlooked the garden. Sara poured the tea and offered Mary a cake. "I really shouldn't," Mary frowned, then smiled, "but one piece won't do any harm! Now then, how have things been since hearing you have been accepted to adopt?"

"Well initially we were really excited and could barely sleep! I jumped out of my skin every time the phone rang, but we have settled down now and are prepared for the wait, however long it might be," Sara smiled at James and then at Mary.

"How is everything with your business James, plenty work?"

"More than I can handle at the moment Mary, I'm looking at adding another member to my workforce so I won't need to turn down any work!"

"That's good news, it's always good to hear someone's making money!" They all laughed and Mary tucked into her cake and complimented Sara saying it was as light as a feather! Mary instantly liked this couple, they were relaxed, down to earth and friendly – and it was obvious they adored each other. She finished her slice of cake and sipped her tea as they discussed some of Sara's plants in the raised bed.

"Well, I think it's time to confess and tell you I am not just here for a chat, but to tell you about a child who has been placed with us for adoption." Sara and James glanced quickly at each other. "He is just under two weeks old and is still in the hospital nursery but is ready to be released into our care. I can tell you his mother has tragically passed away due to complications arising from the birth and the father is unable to cope with looking after a child on his own. You are aware it can take up to a year to legalise the adoption through the courts and the child's father still has parental rights until that point?" Sara and James both nodded. "It is a sad, sad situation but nonetheless we have to find a loving home for this wee chap and after reading through your file

I wondered would you be happy to come and see him and we can take it from there?"

Sara looked at James and they both broke into wide smiles. "Just try to stop us!" said James. "Where and when can we visit the wee fellow?"

Mary smiled. "Tomorrow at the hospital? You would have to travel through to Edinburgh though."

"That's not a problem," said James. "How long would we have to wait before he came home with us?"

"If you decide to go ahead and adopt him, there will be some paperwork to complete which we could also take care of tomorrow and then I will bring him through to you once that's all in order. He could be here with you as early as the weekend." Sara couldn't believe it, her mind racing at how quickly this was all happening. She thought she was going to burst with happiness!

They chatted for a bit longer about the paperwork they would need to sign and the arrangements for meeting the following day and then Mary said her goodbyes, but not before Sara handed her a small box with a further slice of cake for her tea. Mary was delighted and waved her hand out of the car window as she drove away!

Sara and James just couldn't take it in and went over and over their discussion with Mary. They knew, without seeing the baby, they would take him into their home and give him a mum and dad who would nurture and love him. They decided not to tell anyone just yet, not until they had him home with them…

As expected, the visit went very well. Mary showed them into a private room and then returned a few minutes later wheeling a cot. She picked up the bundle in the cot and handed him to Sara. One look at the adorable wee face and they were instantly head over heels in love with him! James also held him and felt very emotional, as the last baby he held was Grace. Mary left them alone for a few minutes and James turned to Sara, "Well Mrs Andrews, what do you think? Will we take this little boy into our home and give him the best life possible?" Sara was too emotional to answer and simply nodded.

A week later Sara and James were sitting together by the open fire looking at the darling little boy who was now their son. Two days ago Mary walked through their front door with a carrycot and changed their lives.

That first night they laid their baby on the bed between them and studied his dainty little features. He had a very pale complexion; tiny button nose; cute mouth; blue eyes and light brown hair. They hadn't even thought about a name until this point but James had a brother who died young and he asked Sara if they could call him after Jack. Sara thought it was a lovely idea and so little Jack Andrews became part of a new family that evening...

CHAPTER 18

Patrick and Lucy loved family life and were looking forward to having at least four children! Patrick had a brother and sister, Lucy had four sisters, and between them they had twelve children with another on the way as Patrick's sister Becky was expecting an imminent arrival!

However, sadly things did not go to plan as after two years Lucy fell pregnant only to miscarry very early into the pregnancy. They remained positive and put the loss down to nature's intervention but when Lucy miscarried again only six months later, they took a bit longer to bounce back. A further two years passed and Lucy went to the doctor to see if there was a reason why she hadn't fallen pregnant again. After some investigations she was told they found an abnormality and if she did fall pregnant again, she would be unlikely to carry a baby to full term.

At first, after hours of talking, Lucy and Patrick decided there was nothing to be done but to accept they would not be blessed with any children and must be content as a couple. Although they loved each other deeply and put everything they had into having a happy marriage, a tinge of sadness hung over them as they tried to come to terms with not having a family.

A few months later they were attending a friend's wedding breakfast and Lucy began talking to a woman who was sitting opposite her at their table. They chatted about all sorts of things, including families, children and home life. It turned out she worked for social services and after hearing about Lucy's miscarriages, she explained about adoption and gave her a phone number should she wish to find out more. Patrick and Lucy took a couple of months to think about it, eventually making the decision to go ahead. They would love an adopted child just the same as one of their own – in their eyes all children were precious!

They didn't waste any more time in contacting social services to begin the process of being vetted to adopt…

CHAPTER 19

Baby Olivia settled in very quickly in the Issac household, only having a couple of unsettled nights where she woke a few times, however within a week she was sleeping right through the night. She was a happy baby, only crying if she was really hungry or if she hurt herself. Harry and Jean coped very well with the shop and employed a young girl named Zoe, who just finished school, which made their lives easier. Having Zoe working in the shop meant Harry could go up to the flat to have lunch with his wife and have a cuddle with his daughter. When Jean needed to work either her mother or aunt Moira were more than delighted to babysit, taking every opportunity to proudly walk through the village pushing the pram!

Once Olivia started school, Jean only worked in the shop during school hours, meeting her daughter every day as she ran happily through the playground waving her latest painted masterpiece! At least twice a week they would walk along to see granny Chrissie for tea and cake before going home, where Olivia would sit on Harry's knee and tell him every detail of her day at school.

From an early age Olivia loved animals and they walked along to the Wilsons' farm to see the animals at least every other day. Ruth and Robbie Wilson had a huge soft spot for Olivia, quite often taking her with them to the farm for a couple of hours if she was around when they came into the shop. As she grew older, she would cycle along herself to help Robbie in the milking shed or at lambing time she would be found sat cross-legged on the floor in front of the Aga feeding the lambs who had lost or been rejected by their mums. By twelve years old, Olivia had already decided she was going to be a vet and, over the next few years, poor Ruth and Robbie always had an orphaned or injured animal in their kitchen courtesy of Olivia.

Jean and Harry knew their daughter well and took her ambition seriously, starting a college fund not long after she made her announcement and if she didn't go to Veterinary College, the money would be there for whatever she chose to do.

The years passed, Olivia excelling at high school and again at college. Joe Briers, the local vet, encouraged her love of animals by allowing Olivia to spend weekends and school holidays helping out at the surgery.

One of the best days in Olivia's life was when she walked through the doors of Veterinary College in Edinburgh. She loved every minute of her time there and all her placements were brilliant! To her it wasn't work but a dream come true! She passed all her assessments and exams with flying colours and when she was on her final placement she met Matt, who qualified five years previously and was working for a small practice in Livingston. Matt and Olivia became close friends and when she qualified, Olivia was lucky enough to be offered a permanent position at the same practice as Matt, as one of the vets had bought into a partnership in West Yorkshire.

It took them a couple of years to get together as a couple, but when they did they fell deeply in love very quickly.

Two years later they were married in Beauly village church, the service very emotional with hardly a dry eye among the congregation! Jean and Harry were so pleased for their daughter and bounced from smiling to weeping as 'their baby' took her final step and left the nest! It was the happiest day of Olivia's life and she felt blessed to have everything in life that she could ask for!

CHAPTER 20

Maggie walked out of high school for the last time and instead of feeling elated and looking forward to going to university, she was dreading going home to break the news to her parents that she was pregnant. She had gone over and over in her head what she would say to them, trying to think of the best way to tell them and make it easier, but no matter how she told them, it was going to be anything but easy!

Whatever reaction Maggie expected from her parents, she couldn't have imagined the scene that unfolded that evening.

Her brothers had finished their meal and were allowed to leave the table to play for half an hour before bathtime, leaving herself and her parents sitting drinking their coffees. Her father pushed back his chair after a couple of minutes, saying he had some work to do in his study, but before he could stand Maggie blurted out she had something very important to tell them. Her father relaxed back in his chair expecting a discussion about Maggie's move to university but he couldn't have been more wrong.

Maggie took a deep breath and stared into her coffee cup. "A few weeks ago I spent some time with a boy that I've liked for quite a long time…"

"You are not going let some teenage fancy interfere with your education, so if you…"

"STOP DAD!" Maggie raised her voice and her father stopped, shocked at being spoken to that way. "I'm trying to tell you something really stupid happened and I'm pregnant! There I've told you now." For a couple of seconds there was a shocked silence until her parents processed her news and then in a very angry, but controlled voice her father told her to get out of his sight, go to her room and stay there.

Maggie lay on her bed and waited. She had expected her father to explode with rage when she told him her news, but maybe it was the calm before the storm and she had yet to face his wrath. About an hour later Maggie's stony-faced mother opened her bedroom door, "Downstairs now!" Maggie did as she was told, returning to her seat at the dining table without looking at her father. Her mother sat down and leant back in her chair, stony faced and arms folded.

"Right," her father began, "be under no illusion we are taking your news well because that is not the case and we feel deeply betrayed by your actions - you were raised to know better! We are NOT going to sit back and let you trash our good name because of your stupidity and lack of morals. I take it you have told no-one?" Maggie shook her head. "Well at least you still have some sense! I have telephoned your grandmother and next weekend I will drive you up to Ullapool, where you will remain until that child is born when it will be immediately handed over to social services for adoption. Your time there will not be wasted as I will organise a private tutor who will come to your grandmother's house. You do not leave the house at any time without your grandmother. Clear enough?" Maggie nodded. "Now get upstairs out of my sight, you don't leave this house again until we leave next week. You can spend the time packing up your things."

"What will I tell my friends?"

"You will tell them you are going to stay with relatives for the summer. Use what's left of your brain!" he replied sarcastically.

Maggie closed the bedroom door behind her and slumped to the floor – what a mess! Her father was cold and unfeeling and yes she had messed up big time, but neither him nor her mother had given any thought to how she was feeling, as usual it was all about them. They were so shallow and only cared about their reputations, not their teenage daughter's physical or mental well being!

In that split second, Maggie decided she would never come back to this house. She grabbed her notebook and wrote a list of everything she wanted to take away with her. She would wait until she was at her grandmothers before she wrote to Allie explaining why she was never coming back!

CHAPTER 21

The Andrews family's first year together was amazing! Jack was a very content baby, adorable and loving. He was now managing to pull himself to his feet using the furniture and could toddle across the room until he lost his balance. Sara and James had just been notified Jack's adoption had been granted in court and he was now legally their son! They had a joint adoption/birthday party, inviting their family and friends, to announce Jack was officially their little boy and they could now relax and look to the future!

As Jack grew older they told him the bedtime story of the little boy who was loved very much by his mummy and daddy, but because they couldn't look after him, they chose a new mummy and daddy for him. When he was old enough they explained he was the little boy in the story and as a result Jack was a very happy, secure and settled child. He sailed through his teen years, was very popular with all his fellow pupils and proved to be highly academic.

Jack met his long-term girlfriend Mollie during his first year at college and when they both applied and were accepted to the same university to study accountancy, they were ecstatic! They were inseparable and on the day they graduated, Jack proposed to Mollie and she happily accepted! They both found good jobs and, with the help of both sets of parents, were able to put down a deposit on a little cottage. They were very much in love and very excited about their autumn wedding! Their families met up to discuss all the arrangements and everyone was really looking forward to their special day. For them, life just couldn't get any better!

Three weeks before the wedding Jack received a call from the police asking him to come to Perth Royal Infirmary as his parents had been involved in a road accident. He phoned Mollie and asked her to meet him at the hospital and headed off straight away. As he drove along the country roads, he hoped neither of them had broken any bones as it would spoil the wedding for them and they deserved to enjoy the day as much as he would. They were the best parents anyone could ask for and he adored and loved them unconditionally, as they loved him.

He reached the A&E department, gave his name to the receptionist and explained his parents had been brought in after a car accident. She asked him to take a seat and within minutes a doctor appeared and took him to a private waiting room. Jack listened silently as the doctor explained both his parents had been seriously injured when an artic lorry jack-knifed and crushed their car.

"They were cut out of their vehicle by the fire brigade and neither were conscious on arrival at the hospital. Your dad was rushed straight to theatre as he had been pinned down by his pelvis and has internal bleeding. Your mother has injuries to her spine and chest and was in a serious but stable condition as she went into surgery. I'm afraid I can't tell you anymore at the moment as they are now both still in theatre having surgery but as soon as I know anything I will come and tell you."

The doctor asked if he had any questions and a very shocked Jack asked how long they could be in theatre. "I'm afraid I can't say, it all depends on the severity of the injuries and whether or not there are any complications."

"Are you telling me their injuries are life-threatening?" asked a very pale, shocked Jack.

"I'm afraid their injuries are very serious, but the surgeons will do everything they can to stabilise your parents. You can stay here and when either of them comes out of theatre I will immediately come and let you know. There is a coffee machine just across the hall and a small café down the corridor to your left. Is there anybody you need to call?"

"Thank you, my fiancé Mollie, Mollie Jones, is on her way, can someone tell her where I am?"

"Yes I'll get someone to bring her along when she arrives, sure you okay? Would you like me to get you a tea or a coffee?"

Jack shook his head, "No thanks, I'll wait until Mollie arrives. I'm okay, just shocked - I thought we were talking a few cuts and bruises, the police didn't say..."

The doctor nodded and left the room. Jack sat with his head in his hands unable to take in the news that his poor mum and dad were so badly injured. He couldn't bear to think of them hurt, in such pain and prayed the ambulance crew got to them quickly. The door opened and Mollie came into the room, knelt down and gave him a tight hug. "What's happened? Are they alright?"

"You better sit down." Jack waited until Mollie sat down on the sofa and he sat beside her, taking her hand and holding it tightly. Mollie was very fond of his parents and she was going to be very upset when he explained about the accident. "I thought they'd had a small bump in the car and were maybe shaken up a bit, but a lorry crushed their car and they had to be cut out. They are both in a serious condition and are in theatre having surgery already." Mollie hugged Jack tightly and fought hard not to burst into tears.

"So have they said if they will be okay?" she asked in a wobbly voice.

"They don't know yet. The doctor said he doesn't know how long they will be in theatre, it all depends on the extent of their injuries and whether there are any complications. Dad's smashed his pelvis and is bleeding internally and mum has damage to her spine and chest. This is a nightmare Moll, I'm hoping I'm going to wake up any minute now and it's all been a bad dream."

Mollie couldn't hold it together any longer and burst into tears, shocked at how serious the injuries were. Jack held her until she gathered herself together. "There's a coffee machine across the hall, I'll go and get us a couple, I think we could both do with one." Jack arrived back with the coffees a couple of minutes later and could see Mollie's eyes were red from crying and his heart went out to her. She was such a lovely girl and his mum and dad adored her.

About an hour later, the doctor came back to speak to them and this time he had another doctor with him who was dressed in scrubs. "Jack, this is Mr Reynolds, the surgeon who operated on your father." The surgeon shook hands with both Jack and Mollie, then sat on the coffee table to face Jack on the same level.

"Your father sustained a crushed pelvis, severing the femoral artery and he lost a great deal of blood. I'm afraid, as hard as we tried, we just couldn't get the bleeding under control in time to save him and he died during the surgery." Mollie started crying uncontrollably and Jack held her tight and tried to soothe her. He wanted to scream, shout and punch the walls but he nodded and thanked the surgeon for everything he had done.

"What about my mother, is there any word on her yet? Nobody is to tell her about my father, it needs to be me, and only when I think she is strong enough," he looked up at the surgeon, "they were inseparable." The surgeon nodded and said he would go and check on his mother and let him know as soon as he could.

Jack and Mollie sat on the sofa shocked and upset, both trying to be strong for the other. They talked about how they would have to support his mum, as she would be distraught when she found out his dad had died. They immediately decided to postpone the wedding indefinitely to allow his mum to recover fully from her injuries and allow them all time to come to terms with losing his dad.

They briefly talked about phoning their relatives to let them know about the accident, his dad's death and to cancel their wedding. When Mollie said Sara would probably not be able to attend his dad's funeral, Jack couldn't hold back the tears any longer and Mollie held him tightly as he sobbed uncontrollably.

It was over an hour since they had been told of his dad's death but as yet they had no news about his mum. Jack hoped this was a good sign as surely it meant they were managing to repair the damage? He was pacing around the room, unable to sit and wait any longer and he needed to know his mum was okay - he desperately wanted to see her!

He was just going to get more coffees, for something to do, when the door opened and a different surgeon came into the room, introducing himself as Nick Mason. "Your mother made it through the surgery and is in intensive care. I'm afraid she has a serious injury to her spine and although we were able to get her stable, she will need to undergo more surgery. We also had to remove her spleen and some of her ribs were broken in several places so we removed as many fragments as we could. She also has a punctured lung and her liver has been damaged."

"Oh dear god!" Jack shook his head in disbelief, "You said she has to have more surgery, what has to be done and when?"

"Your mother is still in a critical condition and as I said we managed to stabilise her and we are doing everything we can to keep her that way, but she is very weak and we need to get her through the next twenty-four hours and hope her condition improves. We need her to be stronger before we can take her back into theatre. I'm sorry, I wish I could give you better news."

Jack nodded. "Can I see her?"

"You can have a couple of minutes, but I must warn you she also sustained some lacerations to her face. We removed several glass fragments and stitched up the cuts but her face is also swollen and bruised." Jack felt sick, his poor mum, she was such a lovely person and this just wasn't fair. He put his arm around a very pale and tearful Mollie as they followed the surgeon along the corridors to intensive care.

Looking back, Jack wasn't sure what he expected but his legs almost gave way under him at the sight of his mum. He barely recognised her! Her faced was stitched in several places and she was badly bruised and swollen as the surgeon had said, but he was horrified! She had a tube in her mouth, wires, drips and other tubes engulfed her and she was on a heart monitor. Mollie couldn't bear to see Sara like that and had to leave. She slumped to the floor in the corridor outside the room and cried like a baby.

Jack stroked his mum's hair and told her she needed to get better quickly because they had to reorganise his wedding as he wasn't getting married without her there. He told her he loved her to the moon and back, just as she used to say to him every night when he was little. He was only allowed a couple of minutes and a nurse came over and smiled reassuringly. "I'm afraid I can't let you stay much longer, your mum needs to get as much rest as possible. You can come and see her again tomorrow and you can give us a ring at anytime and we will tell you how she is."

Jack kissed the top of his mum's head, left the Intensive Care Unit and found Mollie sitting on the corridor floor. He knelt down, gathered her up and they held each other as they sobbed. In an instant their world had changed, Jack had lost his dad and his mum was fighting for her life...

Jack glanced over at Mollie to see she had finally fallen asleep, exhausted and drained. It had been the worst day of his life and he was thankful she loved him so much, as he wasn't sure he could get through this ordeal without her. He had been lying staring at the ceiling wishing he could fall into the oblivion of sleep and escape from this living hell, but every time he closed his eyes he could see his mum's bruised and battered body lying in the hospital bed.

He must have eventually drifted off to sleep and jumped when the phone rang. Barely able to open his eyes, he reached out to answer his phone.

Jack's perfect world was no longer. The doctor looking after his mum had called to say he was so very sorry, they did everything possible, but due to the severity of her injuries, his mother died a few minutes ago...

CHAPTER 22

Marlene and baby Christina loved living with aunty Christine and true to her word she used her savings, very cleverly, to allow them to live a careful but comfortable life. Marlene took on the role of housekeeper, cooking and cleaning, helping her aunt when she was not keeping too well and raising young Christina. Her aunt's health had deteriorated quite a bit over the past two years and only two days after Christina's third birthday, Christine suffered a stroke, which shocked all the family as she had been really well for a few weeks. At first she seemed to make good progress in hospital and just when the doctors were thinking of discharging her, a second stroke caused her death.

Marlene was absolutely distraught! She became very close to Christine since coming to live with her and she was very shocked and sad. The day of the funeral was really hard for her and even more so for Jamie as his brother Douglas didn't even bother to turn up, which upset him even more.

Jamie came to see Marlene a couple of days after the funeral, telling her just to sit tight in the house, as he had no intentions of selling. Marlene was very grateful to Jamie for his kindness to her and Christina. He was so like his mother in nature, a truly lovely person and Christine was very proud of her son. Luckily for Marlene, her aunt did not put her money into a bank account but hid it in the house and she told Marlene that if anything should happen to her, she must take the remaining money and use it to look after herself and the baby. As long as she stayed in the house with no rent to pay, she might just manage, but if she had to move out and pay rent then she wasn't sure how much longer she could carry on.

Her worst fears were realised when a few weeks later Jamie came to see her to let her know Douglas had been to a solicitor and was demanding the house be sold as soon as possible. The house had been left to both sons in Christine's will and Douglas was demanding his half of everything. In all the time Marlene lived with her aunt, three and a half years, Douglas only phoned his mother twice, to 'borrow' money on both occasions. Jamie was the complete opposite to his brother, visiting his mum at least twice a week without fail and phoned her most days.

Jamie was very concerned about Marlene's situation and knew his mother would have wanted her to stay in the house until she got back on her feet again, but unfortunately the decision was no longer his. The best he could do was to let Marlene stay in the house until the last minute possible and he advised her to try to put off potential buyers, with his full backing, to buy her more time. Marlene was extremely grateful to Jamie, she only wished her own family had a fraction of his kindness!

The first two people to view the house found it unsuitable for different reasons and shortly after the second viewing, Douglas came to the house and accused Marlene of doing something to upset potential buyers. Marlene assured him that was not the case and the last people had said it was too small for their family. Douglas refused to listen and threatened her saying if she continued to put buyers off the house he would personally throw her and her brat out onto the street!

Marlene was extremely upset at Douglas's behaviour and she felt quite scared at the thought of what he might be capable of if she annoyed him.

However, the next couple to view the house the following week were delighted and bought the property for the asking price. Of course that meant Marlene found herself in a situation where she had to get out within six weeks and she started looking for somewhere affordable to rent.

After looking at several unsuitable rooms, she managed to find a large bedsit in a boarding house for a reasonable rent. It consisted of one very large room with a bed, sofa, small table and chairs, a few kitchen units, sink, cooker and a fridge. Jamie insisted she take whatever furniture she needed to make it homely and comfortable and he came to help her pack up and move into the bedsit. He was upset she had to share a bathroom with two other occupants on the same floor but although she hated the idea, she had no option, it was all she could afford.

Together they hung the chintz curtains from her bedroom at the house and Jamie helped to make up the bed with her bedding. Jamie insisted in packing quilts, towels, kitchen crockery, pans, kettle plus anything else she needed to make life more comfortable. When they finished unpacking they stood back and were pleased they had managed to make the room look comfortable and homely.

Little Christina was very unsettled to begin with, as not only was she confused about where aunty Chris had gone, but couldn't understand where they were. However, after a couple of weeks she began to settle and adapted well to her new surroundings.

They had been living at the bedsit for nearly four weeks when Marlene heard raised voices out in the hallway followed by someone knocking on her door. When she opened it, her landlady was standing there with an angry looking Douglas behind her. He was insisting that he needed to speak with her in private but Marlene refused to let him in and stepped out into the hallway instead. "My baby is asleep Douglas, please keep your voice down. What is it you want?"

"I said private!" Douglas growled, scowling at the landlady who moved away back down the hallway saying there was to be no trouble or she would call the police.

"I said what do you want?" Marlene was feeling very scared, she didn't like or trust Douglas and couldn't understand how he knew where she lived or why he was here.

"Where is my mother's money? Dad left her pretty well off and now most of it has gone!" Douglas was furious and moved threateningly close to her, fists clenched tightly.

Marlene hoped he couldn't see she was trembling, "I have no idea what you are talking about, I don't have any money, I never had access to your mother's bank account, never!"

"So where the hell has it all gone then? You must know, you have been living off her for the past few years!" he stepped even closer to her and Marlene stepped back and held onto the bannister.

"You need to leave NOW Douglas," Marlene glanced over her shoulder and looking down could see the landlady hovering at the bottom of the stair.

Douglas grabbed Marlene by the hair pulling her head to the side causing her to cry out in pain. "Take your hands off me and get out or I will call the police!"

What followed happened so fast and was so unexpected, Marlene still couldn't recall exactly what happened years later. Fortunately, the landlady witnessed the assault and gave a statement to the police saying Douglas hit her with such force that Marlene crashed against and went over the bannister, bouncing off the steps at the bottom of the stair and landing in a broken heap at her feet in the entrance hall...

CHAPTER 23

The first three months of married life were simply perfect for Matt and Olivia. When talking to her parents on the telephone, Olivia told them they were living in a blissful bubble and never wanted it to burst! It had been a very busy three months as, after coming home from their week on honeymoon walking in the Lake District, they decided there just wasn't enough room in the tiny cottage Matt rented.

On a call out to an injured bull, Matt was talking to the farmer about how much he enjoyed the Lake District but was back to reality and now house hunting. He offered Matt one of the farm cottages and after a look round he took Olivia to see it, three weeks later they moved in.

It was a quaint cottage, lovely big open fire, bay windows with window seats, rustic kitchen with an Aga and a couple of bedrooms with slanted ceilings which Matt took a bit of getting used to! Olivia enjoyed having her own home and threw herself into making it homely and cosy for her and Matt, however with work, moving and doing so much at home, she was now feeling washed out!

Matt noticed she was falling asleep on the couch nearly every evening and had a talk with her about slowing down a bit. "You have done a brilliant job of turning the cottage into a lovely home but I think you are doing far too much

Ollie. I think you have to slow down, concentrate on work and when we are at home you need to take time to yourself and relax a bit more. From now on our Sundays are going to be relaxing days. When the weather is bad, we can cook a nice roast and sit in front of the fire and on good days we can get out walking, we haven't a moment since coming home from our honeymoon!" Matt gave her a bear hug and went to make a couple of mugs of hot chocolate before they headed off to bed.

Initially Olivia did start to feel slightly better and everything was going well, but six weeks later, after staying up all night to deliver a calf, she began to suffer from back pain. Thinking she had hurt herself pulling the calf out of her mother, she carried on knowing it could take some time for an injury to heal.

A few weeks later, Matt and Olivia travelled home to Beauly to spend Christmas with Harry and Jean. They were so excited at both being able to get the time off work as Jeff, the other practice vet, agreed to cover for Matt at Christmas if he came back to cover New Year. Matt had been worried about Olivia for months now as she was still experiencing severe tiredness, even now she was sound asleep as he drove north. She had also hurt herself delivering the calf and always seemed to be tired, cold and pale. He wasn't so sure anymore that it was all down to the pain in her back, as she admitted, just a couple of days before, she also had pain in her leg and now and again felt dizzy.

At first he wondered if she was pregnant, which might have explained her fatigue but that was three months ago and they had ruled that out. He made her promise to see the doctor as soon as they got back home after Christmas. Ollie loved going home to the Highlands, especially at Christmas and Matt hoped the trip would do her good.

A huge fuss was made of them on arrival at the village shop! Chrissie and Moira were there and Harry had been busy baking cakes and scones for a lovely late afternoon tea. Ruth and Ronnie popped in just to say welcome home, telling them not to leave without coming up to the farm to tell them all their news. There were hugs all round as they left to get back to the animals and as Ruth hugged Olivia she whispered in her ear "Are you alright pet, you are looking very pale?"

"I've been working more hours than usual to get time off to come home, that's all," she smiled reassuringly at Ruth.

There were lots of questions about their honeymoon, the cottage, work and it was almost seven o'clock before Harry drove Chrissie and Moira back along the road to their cottage. "Olivia doesn't look well Harry," Chrissie said as soon as they were in the car. "She is white as a sheet, has lost weight and isn't her usual bright and bubbly self."

"I noticed it too Chris, maybe she's overdoing things at work and she's had problems with her back for some time now, it might be taking its toll. Don't worry I'll get a chat with her or maybe I'll have a word with Matt and see if there's anything else going on."

When Harry left with her gran and aunt, Olivia felt exhausted. "Right love," Jean put her arm around her daughter's shoulders, "you look shattered, the long journey and all those visitors have worn you out. Now I've put a bottle in your bed, I want you to get yourself comfortable and I'll bring your supper through on a tray, bit of pampering is just what you need, that and a good night's sleep!" Olivia didn't have the energy to protest and did as she was told.

It was Harry who took in her supper tray, making sure she was propped up enough and comfortable before setting the tray across her knees. "Thanks dad, this looks lovely," she smiled up at him.

"My pleasure sweetheart, no point in having a daughter if you don't get to spoil her now and again!" he grinned, noticing the black shadows under her eyes. "Now you just shout if you need anything else and I'll be back to get your tray once I've finished my supper," he patted her hand and headed back through to have a talk with Matt.

As it turned out, he didn't even get a chance to say anything about Olivia as the minute they sat down at the table Matt broached the subject of her health.

"I know you have all noticed how tired and pale Ollie is, at first I thought she was doing too much with work and moving into the cottage. Then she seemed to be looking slightly better when this pain in her back started and now it's in her leg too. At first we put it down to a difficult delivery of a calf, but I'm not so sure anymore. She's not as sharp as usual, no spark in her and she just told me a couple of days ago that she gets a bit dizzy now and then. I made her promise to go to the doctor as soon as we get back, in fact, I will be going with her to make sure she tells him the whole story."

Harry and Jean had been watching him as he spoke and it was very clear to them that Matt loved their daughter and was taking charge of looking after her. Because of this, they agreed he was doing the right thing and they wouldn't say anything to Olivia about her health, instead they would make sure she enjoyed a restful but enjoyable Christmas.

True to their word, that is exactly what they did, going out of their way to make the holidays as special and fun as possible, only venturing out shopping or visiting when Olivia looked well enough.

Christmas day had been very enjoyable, with Chrissie and Moira over for an excellent lunch plus sherry trifle and later turkey sandwiches and of course Harry's special mince pies! They were all so full, they could hardly move by eight o'clock and it was Matt who volunteered to walk Chrissie and Moira home, singing carols all the way!

All too soon the holidays were over and there were hugs and tears as Matt and Olivia set off on their journey home. There was also a secret promise from Matt to Harry and Jean that he would phone and tell them about their visit to the doctor.

Harry stood with his arm round Jean and waved as the car pulled away. He had a horrible feeling the news from the doctor was not going to be something they wanted to hear....

CHAPTER 24

Lesley's first day back at school was a bit tearful for her and some of the children, but together they got through it and by the end of the day all the children went home, happily looking forward to the following day as they were going to spend the whole afternoon making paper lanterns. Tomorrow would be easier thought Lesley as she cleared up the classroom and got ready to head home.

She was relieved Mrs C would have taken care of dinner. She was tired, but not as bad as she thought she would be, however she was secretly pleased Steve had suggested they ask Mrs C to stay on for another few weeks until Lesley was fighting fit again. Of course Mrs C was delighted but would only accept half the money they wanted to pay her. Steve had a dreadful time trying to get her to accept a wage when he asked her to look after the house after Lesley came home from hospital. She had flatly refused to take one penny more than the shopping cost, telling him it was her pleasure to be helping and she would be deeply offended if he mentioned money again!

As she turned to put some books back on the shelves, Lesley saw something move out of the corner of her eye and turned to see Johnny had come back into the classroom.

"Hello Johnny," she smiled at him, "have you forgotten something?"

"Can you not have a baby of your own now Miss?" he was looking at her very seriously, and frowning.

Taking a deep breath Laura smiled at him. "That's correct Johnny, I had an operation which means I can't have another baby." She gave him another smile to reassure him she was okay.

He looked thoughtful and then carried on. "Well Miss, my ma says to my da that you can still have a baby if you adopt one like my aunty did, so you see Miss you can do the same as her and get another baby," he was nodding as he spoke as though he was trying to reassure her.

She looked at the innocent child in front of her, so touched he cared enough to tell her all was not lost and he had found a way for her to have another baby.

She gave him a huge smile. "You know I think that is an amazing idea Johnny and it deserves a big reward. In fact," she said opening the drawer of her desk, "it deserves a gold star." She leant forward and stuck the star to his shirt and he beamed from ear to ear.

"Wait till my ma sees this Miss, she will be dead pleased with me tonight!"

"You tell your mother you were my best pupil today and a great help to me. Now you take this as an extra thank you from me for being so kind and I will see you tomorrow." She handed him a bar of chocolate and was rewarded with another huge smile!

"Gee, thanks Miss! See you tomorrow." Johnny ran all the way through the village holding the chocolate in one hand and keeping his Gold star flat against his shirt with the other to make sure he didn't lose it on the way home.

Over dinner that evening, Lesley told Steve the touching story about Johnny and, although there were tears in her eyes, she was smiling. Steve reached across the table, took her hand, raised it to his lips and kissed it. "You are an amazing person and I am very proud of you. I could not love you anymore if I tried."

On the second anniversary of baby Steven's death they visited his grave and over dinner that evening agreed they now felt strong enough to look into adoption. The following day Steve set the ball rolling by making a call to social services, a call he hoped would be the start of a new and happier chapter in their lives...

CHAPTER 25

Jack was absolutely distraught at losing his parents and on the day of their joint funeral he felt like he was having a nightmare but couldn't wake up. By the time all the mourners left he was completely numb, unable to process the finality of it all. He knew it was irrational but at times during the day he had almost felt disloyal to be carrying on without his mum and dad. He knew his life would never be the same and time and time again over the past few days he would have given everything he had just to be able to talk to them one last time.

Over the coming weeks, with help and understanding from Mollie, he gradually began to work his way through the fog of grief. He managed to get the important things sorted and had been to the solicitors where James lodged all the documents regarding the house; some to do with the business; life insurance policies and a joint will which left everything to Jack.

He had long conversations with Mollie about what he should do with his dad's company and they came to the decision that the best thing to do would be to sell it.

James had always said his employee and friend George was the best electrician he ever met and always referred to him as his right hand man. If they came up against a tricky job, James would send George, as he was the man to solve any unusual problems. He was always happy to leave the business in his capable hands when he and Sara were away on holiday and Jack knew his dad would want him to take over the firm.

He arranged to meet George in the local pub as he couldn't face going into the workshop and seeing his dad's office which evoked so many childhood memories. He told George he knew his dad would have wanted him to take over the business and although at first he offered to take on the role of manager and run it for Jack, he eventually agreed to buy it but on the proviso it was valued independently and he paid that figure as he wouldn't pay a penny less. It was a great weight off Jack's mind and he thanked George for everything he had done for James over the years and hoped his dad would have approved of his decision.

It had been six weeks since the funeral and Jack still hadn't been to his parents' house. Mollie was worried about him as she had tried to get him to go over a number of times, saying they needed to collect the mail or water the garden, but every time he came up with an excuse and got her to go alone.

The solicitor had phoned regarding a missing insurance document and asked if Jack could have a look for it. This time he would have to go, as Mollie did not feel it was her place to look through Sara and James's personal things.

Over dinner that evening, Mollie talked to Jack about the call and as expected he said he didn't have time and started to tell her where to look for the document. "No Jack," she put her hand over his, "this time, my love, you have to do this. It's not my place to be searching through your parents' belongings when you are not there with me, it makes me feel uncomfortable. I know how hard this is for you," she stroked his cheek, "but you need to do this, I think it's time," she gave him a reassuring smile and he managed a faint smile in return.

Jack felt physically sick as he opened the front door and stepped into his parents' front porch. He was met with the sight of their jackets hanging on the pegs, walking boots and wellies neatly lined up underneath. A pair of his mum's wellies with a pink flower design brought tears to his eyes. He bought them for her last year on Mother's Day as a bit of a joke as she couldn't pass a pink flower and frequently arrived home with yet another plant for her 'pink' border! The border had to be extended several times and now ran the full length of the garden, he was sure she succeeded in finding a flower in every possible shade of pink!

Mollie gave him a quick hug and they carried on into the large kitchen/dining-room. His dad loved this room, they all had, it was the heart of the house with double patio doors leading into the garden, his mum always said she felt as though she was outside, not inside. Her garden was her haven and she loved nothing more than to potter about out there for hours.

Jack thought he would hate being at the house but it was quite the opposite, he could still 'feel' his mum and dad's presence around him and unexpectedly found it comforting. They spent a couple of hours sorting out the mail, watering the plants, checking that everything was okay around the house. He managed to find a folder, in the small study, full of neatly filed paperwork, which included the insurance document they needed and he silently thanked his mum and dad for being so organised.

As they drove home, Jack told Mollie he wanted to spend the weekend at the farmhouse sorting through his parents' belongings and she nodded in agreement, relieved he had finally managed to move forward.

They were surprised at how much they managed to do that weekend. Jack sorted through all the paperwork in the study, keeping anything important and burning the rest. He asked Mollie if she would sort through the bedroom wardrobes and drawers as he wasn't comfortable going through his parents' clothes, especially his mum's things. Mollie made three piles, one for charity, a charity or keep and a definitely keep. She put all Sara's jewellery, some photos, letters and other keepsakes into a box for Jack to go through when he was ready.

She had almost finished clearing a large chest, which sat at the base of the bed, when she came across a beautifully carved wooden box and inside was an envelope with the name Grace written on it. In the envelope was a small silver locket with a tiny lock of hair inside. There was also a leather bound journal and on the inside page was written *'Jack'*. A quick glance through the pages revealed the story of Jack's adoption from the first phone call enquiring about adopting and detailing every step throughout the process, including the day Jack had been delivered by Mary Campbell. There were entries logging every new step Jack took, right up until he left school. Mollie was overwhelmed at the love poured into every page and she held the book close to her chest and cried for Sara who was such a beautiful person and didn't deserve to be taken from them so early. Mollie could just imagine the love she would have shown her grandchildren. She placed the envelope and journal in the box knowing this was not the right time for Jack to read it. One step at a time...

They headed home on Sunday evening having made a huge dent in clearing the farmhouse. Mollie glanced at Jack trying to gauge how he was coping and was surprised to see him looking more relaxed than he had since the accident. He turned to look at her and caught her staring at him intently. "I can feel you staring at me you know," he said smiling and raising one eyebrow. "Let's have it then, what are you thinking?"

Mollie laughed! "I swear you have eyes in the back of your head! I was just admiring my handsome fiancé and thinking how proud of you I am! You did amazingly well this weekend and I know it must have been one of the hardest things you've ever had to do," she leaned over, stroked the back of his neck and kissed him on the cheek.

"It was hard, but not as bad as I thought it would be, although I had my moments," he frowned. "You did well too Moll, none of this is easy for either of us and I couldn't have got through this without you. There is something bothering me though and I need you to think about an idea I have. It's the farmhouse, it's my home, all my memories are there and somehow mum and dad are still there. They poured so much work and love into making it the perfect home and I can't sell it Moll, I just can't. What do you think about selling our cottage and moving into the farmhouse?" Jack glanced at Mollie to see what her reaction was but couldn't tell one way or the other.

Mollie looked out at the passing fields and thought about what Jack had just suggested. She had wondered what he would do with the farmhouse but didn't want to broach the subject until he was ready to deal with it. She did love the house and knew that Sara and James would have wanted them to carry on living in the family home they had worked so hard to create. She looked back at the man she loved so dearly. She knew the best place for Jack was at the farmhouse, where he could live among the memories and where he could still feel his parents' love. Jack gave her a quick look and she smiled, nodding. In that instant, she knew it was the right thing to do as she watched the tension ease from Jack's shoulders.

CHAPTER 26

Marlene woke up in intensive care, immediately becoming very distressed about Christina's whereabouts. The nurses tried to reassure her and said she was being very well looked after by social services, but that only upset her more. Her little girl would be wondering where she was; nobody would know her favourite foods; her routine; her favourite teddy or bedtime story – the list was endless and in the end Marlene had to be sedated again. It took several days before she managed to remain calm but even then she was so agitated about Christina she still required mild sedation.

Eventually she was able to accept she could not do anything about the situation and held onto the promise that once she looked a bit better and some of the bruising faded, arrangements would be made to bring Christina to the hospital to see her. Marlene understood it would only frighten her if she saw Marlene hooked up to machines, all battered and bruised, but the thought of her little girl in some strange place broke her heart.

When she was much calmer the police were able to talk with Marlene and formally take her statement. She told them what she could remember and the officer then told her Douglas had been charged with attempted murder, although there was a possibility the charge could be reduced to grievous bodily harm. Douglas had already been in front of the magistrate and she remanded him in custody until his trial. No matter what the outcome, Douglas would be imprisoned and she would be awarded damages, however, how quickly she received those would depend on Douglas's finances.

Jamie was allowed in to see her for a few minutes but he was very upset and had to keep wiping away tears. He repeatedly apologised for allowing Marlene to live alone before his mother's estate had been settled, saying how ashamed he was that his brother was capable of assaulting her. He felt so guilty and heartbroken at how distraught Marlene was about little Christina and told her his mother would be turning in her grave with the shame of giving birth to a son who could do such a thing!

Jamie had been in contact with social services to get visiting rights to see Christina on a regular basis to make sure she was happy and well. He told Marlene someone from social services would be coming to obtain permission from her to allow him access and she thanked Jamie saying it would stop her worrying so much if she knew he was keeping an eye on Christina.

Marlene asked Jamie if he could go the bedsit to get some of Christina's favourite toys and books for her to play with when she came to visit, along with some things for herself, and he was only too pleased to help out in any way he could.

Jamie stayed as long as he was allowed and promised he would return with the things she asked for within the next couple of days. He was true to his word bringing in everything she asked for plus some magazines, grapes and a selection of paperbacks for her to read when she felt better. He was brilliant and visited her every couple of days, sometimes bringing along his wife when she could get a babysitter. On her bad days, Jamie would read quietly to her from newspapers and magazines, but on days when she felt well enough they would talk about practical things, which needed taking care of, and Jamie quite often left with a list of things Marlene needed him to sort out for her. One of those was to speak to her landlady about the rent for the bedsit, which he did. Marlene was relieved to hear, at least for the next couple of months, her landlady would let her keep her room with no charge, which was such a kind thing for her to do as she was losing rent money. When the police came to take her statement, they said her landlady did not want to claim against her for damages and had insisted on paying to have the bannister repaired.

On one of his visits, Marlene asked Jamie to write down a list of questions she had for her doctors and social worker as she needed to find out how long they expected her to be in hospital and what would happen to Christina meantime.

Once the doctors began to wean Marlene off heavy medication they explained that apart from her obvious broken legs and arm, she had sustained bruising and trauma to her spine and would have to be kept on total bed rest. This would mean lying flat for weeks to allow for the swelling and bruising to dissipate before they could tell just how much damage had been done, how it could affect her mobility and whether there would be lasting damage.

Finally, after four weeks in hospital a social worker arranged to take Christina into see Marlene and although she was desperate to see her little girl, Marlene found the visit very distressing. To her surprise, Christina seemed quite happy and showed no outward signs that she had been through such an ordeal.

Over the next few weeks Marlene had a visit from Christina once a week for about an hour, but each time she became very distressed as she lay watching her little girl play on the floor with her toys. She couldn't hold her or do much with her, although one of the nurses would lift Christina onto her bed and hold her along side Marlene as she read a storybook to her. However, Christina's attention span didn't last long and it wouldn't be long before she wanted to be back down on the floor to play again.

When the visits ended, the social worker would lift Christina up to give Marlene a kiss and cuddle before they left. Christina would then wave goodbye to her mum when prompted by the social worker, happily leaving without a backward glance.

Part of Marlene wanted her little girl to be upset because she was missing her mummy but deep down she was of course relieved that Christina seemed so happy and content. It didn't stop Marlene crying for hours after each visit and it would take her a couple of days to recover and become more positive again.

Jamie continued to visit as much as possible and happened to be there on the day the doctors discussed the results of the latest scans. Marlene had unfortunately suffered permanent damage to her spine and although there was no certainty at this stage, they felt optimistic she would eventually be able to walk again but probably not unaided. She would require months of treatment, physiotherapy, then rehabilitation and they stressed at this point they could not say how much mobility she would regain and could only guess at the outcome.

When she asked how long they thought it would be before she could leave hospital and go home, wherever that would be, she was shocked when the doctor said it would be a long process, but they were hoping around six to eight months if things went well. She could then continue her physio as an outpatient.

Jamie stayed with Marlene for a few hours and, in between breaking down in tears, she talked to him about what would be best for Christina. She was going to be in foster care for close to a year in total and even when she did get out of hospital, where would they live and how was she going to look after a small child? Jamie told her he would be there for her and help in anyway he could and she thanked him again for all his support, but pointed out he had a job to hold down plus a family of his own.

Marlene needed to come up with a solution, one that didn't involve relying on Jamie or anyone else, but most importantly it had to be in Christina's best interests. It was late afternoon and although Marlene was much calmer, she looked exhausted. Jamie put on his coat, kissed Marlene on the cheek and told her she needed to rest, he would come back again tomorrow when they would come up with all the answers.

As he left, a nurse arrived with an injection to help Marlene relax and get some sleep. As Jamie walked through the corridors of the hospital he was riddled with guilt, as it was his brother who caused Marlene and her little girl all this pain. It was pretty clear Marlene was not going to be able to look after Christina and he knew she already realised this. He walked away from the hospital with a heavy heart and dreaded the next few days when life-changing decisions were going to be made by Marlene, which would affect her future with Christina.

Jamie arrived as promised the next morning, but he didn't come alone as, after talking to his wife Julie, she felt three heads would be better than two when it came to decision-making. A young mother like Marlene, Julie could understand how she must be feeling faced with such an awful situation. When they arrived, Miss Duncan, Marlene's social worker, was already sitting by her bedside and Marlene asked them to come in and join the discussion.

Marlene explained to Jamie and Julie that she was trying to find out what options and help were available now, whilst she spent months in hospital, and later, when she was eventually discharged.

"Do you have any idea from your doctors how long they think it might take before they can discharge you Marlene?" asked Miss Duncan.

"My doctors told me yesterday I am looking at a minimum of six to eight months, maybe longer depending on my progress."

They all saw the frown cross Miss Duncan's face and Marlene immediately asked if that would be a problem.

The next half an hour was very stressful as Miss Duncan explained they would have to place Christina with long-term foster parents for the duration of Marlene's stay in hospital. As Christina was now under their care, they would also have to assess Marlene's ability to look after her, once discharged. Jamie looked at his wife and shook his head on hearing the last comment. Miss Duncan then asked Marlene about her accommodation.

"Well we are staying in an bedsit at the moment, but that won't be suitable anymore as it's on the first floor and stairs are not going to be an option for quite some time, if at all."

"I see," Miss Duncan frowned again. "Well before we could think of returning Christina, you would have to be living in suitable accommodation and…"

"Hang on a second, she's my daughter and she will be coming back home to me as soon as I get out of here!"

Marlene looked at Jamie, then Julie who was shaking her head in disbelief! "Surely those rules don't apply in this situation?" intervened Jamie. "It isn't as though Christina was taken into care because Marlene couldn't look after her or was maltreating her, she was attacked – she is a brilliant mother!"

"I understand what you are saying, but regardless of why a child is placed in our care, our criteria for returning that child is the same in every case. Do you have a husband or partner Marlene? If there was such a person living with you, it would change things."

Marlene shook her head. "No it's just the two of us."

"I'm sorry Marlene, Christina has been placed in the care of the department and we are now responsible for her welfare. We must be absolutely sure she is living in a suitable home and that you are able to look after all her needs."

"I need to be absolutely clear on this," Marlene glared at Miss Duncan, "you are saying that even if I get home, you will not automatically return my daughter to me?"

"Yes, I'm afraid those are the rules."

"So what happens if I have a walking frame or sticks or something?"

"We would arrange for an assessment at your home to make sure you can cook a meal, do all the tasks involved in looking after a child and most importantly, be able to ensure the child will be living in a safe environment."

"And if you don't consider me fit and my condition doesn't improve, what then?"

"Why don't we just take a step at a time, that's a long way down the line and there's no need to look that far ahead?"

"I need you to answer my question Miss Duncan."

"Well, if that was the case and there was not a capable adult living permanently in the home, then I'm afraid we would not be able to let Christina return home."

Seeing that Marlene was becoming increasingly upset, Jamie stepped in and asked Miss Duncan if she could leave them alone for a few minutes to allow them to have a discussion.

As the door closed behind Miss Duncan, Marlene let out a tortured sob and Julie rushed to comfort her. After a couple of minutes Marlene's sobs subsided and Jamie came over and held her hand. "I know it all sounds impossible at the moment, but if everything goes well, you *will* get Christina back."

Marlene shook her head, "I might not! What sort of childhood is she going to have if she's a year in a foster home waiting for me to get out of here, only to spend another year or however long it takes for social services to deem me fit to look after her. And, more worrying than that, what if there is too much damage for me to ever be considered fit to have her home with me? How many years is she going to be in foster homes?

I want my little girl to be settled in a permanent home with parents who would love and care for her and give her a happy and fun childhood, one where her parents can afford to buy her everything she needs! How am I ever going to provide for her if I'm not able to work? How am I going to pay for all the things a growing child needs?"

As Jamie drove home that afternoon he thought about the events of the morning and was full of admiration at how

Marlene handled the discussion with Miss Duncan on her return. She must have been screaming inside but calmly discussed her decision with the social worker.

"Miss Duncan as I have no idea how, or even if, I will be able to look after my daughter again, I have decided it would be in her best interest to be adopted at this age. In time she will forget her past and only remember her new life with new parents."

Miss Duncan looked shocked and asked whether it was the right time to make such a decision, suggesting Marlene should take a few more days or even weeks to think about it.

Marlene shook her head. "I have done nothing but think about this since my accident. You told me earlier I may not get my own daughter back if I am not deemed fit enough to look after her and that statement confirmed I have to do what is best for my daughter and not put her through any further distress. She needs a stable and normal childhood, which she will not get with me now because of my injuries. When my doctor told me how long my recovery could take and was not able to say how well I will be able to walk, or even if I will walk again, I knew it was the right thing to do for Christina. Please do as I ask and don't make it any more difficult for me by questioning my decision." Miss Duncan nodded her agreement and Marlene continued.

"There are things I need you to give to her new parents, can you do that?" Miss Duncan simply nodded, in awe of the selfless decision Marlene was making. "I will make a list of Christina's likes and dislikes, give you her favourite toys and books etcetera, which I would like her to take with her to her new home. I would also like the adoptive parents to be told the reason for her adoption as we don't know if she will experience any problems resulting from the traumatic way she was separated from me."

Although unusual, it was agreed the adoptive parents would be informed Christina's mother was injured in an accident and was now physically unable to care for her. Marlene didn't want Christina's new parents to think she had just abandoned her baby.

Miss Duncan asked Marlene one last time if she was absolutely sure this was what she wanted and Marlene nodded her agreement.

"Okay Marlene, I will prepare the paperwork and come back in a couple of days to get your signature, meanwhile I will start the process and we will do our best to find Christina a new home as soon as possible. Would you like me to bring her in for one last visit? I can let you see her before you sign the adoption papers?"

That would have been too much for Marlene to bear and she shook her head as the tears coursed down her cheeks, but she did ask Miss Duncan if she could arrange for a photograph to be taken of Christina for her to keep and she agreed saying she would do that personally.

Two days later Marlene signed away her baby girl, and in return she was handed the photograph she asked for. Miss Duncan said she would visit again to let her know Christina was settled with her adoptive parents for which Marlene was very grateful.

As she lay in her hospital bed that night, her heart broken, she wished she had died at the hands of Douglas rather than suffer life without her baby...

CHAPTER 27

As soon as they arrived home after their Christmas holiday with Olivia's mum and dad, Matt phoned the doctor's surgery and made an urgent appointment for his wife the following day. He then escorted Olivia to bed, insisting he would see to the unpacking, tucked her in and watched as she fell into a deep sleep just a couple of minutes later. Matt looked down at his precious wife who was very pale with dark circles under her eyes. She looked extremely fragile and Matt felt terrified that she might be seriously ill.

Olivia described her symptoms to the doctor, had blood taken, did a urine test and was given antibiotics to treat a suspected kidney infection. The doctor said he would send the samples to the laboratory and once he had the results he would call them. Meanwhile, if Olivia's condition suddenly worsened, she was to call him straight away and not leave it, as a kidney infection could turn very nasty, very quickly.

Olivia spent the next couple of days at home in bed, at both Matt and the doctor's insistence, most of which she spent sleeping. Her hands and feet were swollen and she had a hot water bottle tucked in to her back to try and help ease the pain. The following day she received a phone call from the doctor who said an appointment had been made for her at the hospital the next morning as they needed more bloods and wanted to do a scan as a precautionary measure.

Olivia and Matt saw a very kind specialist at the hospital who carried out several tests and did an ultrasound scan. They were asked to wait at the hospital until all the test results came back from the lab and go back to see the doctor again at 2pm. They went for a coffee and a sandwich and then sat in the waiting area where Olivia leant against Matt and promptly fell asleep. Matt had a feeling the doctors already had an idea what was wrong with Olivia and were repeating the tests for confirmation. Whatever it was, she was very ill and Matt feared the doctor was going to give them bad news.

They sat in the doctor's office and listened carefully as he explained they now knew for definite what was wrong with Olivia.

"All the tests we ran today confirm Olivia's kidneys are not functioning as they should and we need to arrange for you to have dialysis to give your kidneys a bit of a rest and at the same time make you feel much better. You will also have to take several medications, which will help with the symptoms you have."

Matt's fears were confirmed, Olivia was very ill. He asked her if she was okay and she nodded saying she was glad they had found out what was making her so ill.

"Can you do the dialysis here?" asked Matt.

"I'm afraid not. We are going to send you to the University Hospital at Middlesbrough for the dialysis Olivia. Initially, because of the distance involved you will be admitted to the renal ward, have dialysis three times over the space of a week and will be monitored throughout. The medical team will then decide on a plan of action to prevent you from becoming so ill again."

"Do I have another problem which is causing the strain on my kidneys or is this permanent?"

"No, there isn't another problem. At the moment your kidneys are struggling, failing to do their job, but we can help by taking the strain off them and that's what the dialysis will do. Most people feel better than they have done in months and that's because the artificial kidney removes the bulk of the toxins and waste products that have built up in your body and are making you feel so ill. Your kidneys are in effect already failing but we will be able to find out to what extent once we get you into hospital. Now Matt, will you be able to drive Olivia over to the hospital?"

"Yes and I will stay up there with her for as long as it takes." Matt gave Olivia a reassuring smile and her grip tightened on his hand, grateful that she was lucky enough to have someone who cared about her as much as Matt did.

The doctor smiled at them as he stood up, "Right then, I'm just going to pop out for a minute and make the arrangements."

Matt held Olivia's hand tightly, "Don't get upset love, from what the doctor says, they will soon have you feeling much better."

"I'm not upset but I am anxious about having dialysis. I just want to feel better and hopefully, if it all goes okay, I'll be my old self again!"

The doctor came back a few minutes later to tell them there was a bed available for Olivia the next day, stressing the sooner she had the dialysis, the sooner she would start to feel better. He gave Matt an envelope to give to the doctors at the renal unit, explaining it was the results of the tests they had done along with a covering letter detailing Olivia's symptoms. "It might be worth mentioning the doctors on the renal ward will do a very detailed medical history on you, so it would be helpful if you made notes on when this illness started, how you felt and if possible a timeline of it's progression."

Matt and Olivia thanked the doctor and made their way back to the car. Olivia was exhausted and as soon as they arrived home she had to go straight to bed and sleep. As promised, Matt took the chance to phone Harry and Jean to tell them what happened at the hospital. As he expected, they were both desperately worried about their daughter and listened very carefully to what Matt had to tell them. As their call ended, he promised to ring them the following day once he got Olivia settled in at the hospital and they made him promise to tell them absolutely everything, good and bad.

That evening after packing a bag for himself, he helped Olivia pack and told her about his conversation with her mum and dad who were obviously very worried about her and sent their love. He told her he had promised to phone them and let them know how she got on at the hospital and she just nodded, whereas a few weeks back she would have been annoyed he was worrying them needlessly.

Once they finished packing, Matt made them both a hot chocolate, taking the mugs through to bed where they talked briefly about the plan for the morning before Olivia fell asleep. Matt lay in the dark, cuddling his sleeping wife, so worried about her, he couldn't sleep. All he wanted was for Ollie to get better, but he knew deep down they had a long and probably rocky road ahead of them...

CHAPTER 28

Maggie felt relieved and yet very sad on the day she left her home to live with her grandmother, relieved to be escaping from her over-bearing parents but sad to be leaving her brothers as she wasn't sure when she would see them again. She was also sad because she was saying goodbye to her childhood and her childhood home as although her parents and brothers were expecting her to return in a few months, Maggie had other plans.

She sat in the back seat of the car, watching the scenery flicker past like an old movie, as they travelled north to the fishing village where her grandmother lived. The house wasn't in Ullapool itself, but quite remote on the outskirts, far enough that you needed transport. That was of course the reason why she had been banished to the back of beyond, she would have very little contact with the outside world. The tutor her father employed was female, which only highlighted his lack of trust, as no men would come within a mile of her as long as he had anything to do with it!

Her grandmother, Jess, was the complete opposite of her father and Maggie often wondered if she was really his mother as there was nothing of her in him. She was always smiling; kind; caring and most of all she believed in encouraging everyone to do what their heart desired.

Jess gave Maggie a welcoming hug and ushered her into the kitchen where they sat at the table and had sandwiches, fresh home-baked scones and tea. Maggie let her father and grandmother catch up and only spoke when Jess asked her a question. She avoided mentioning the reason why Maggie had come to stay with her and kept the conversation with her son about her brothers, her mother and work. She was telling him some news about some of their relations as he finished his tea when he suddenly stood up and announced he was heading away to get home in time for dinner.

At the door, her father gave Jess a quick peck on the cheek, barked an order at Maggie to do as her grandmother asked, got into his car and drove away without a backward glance.

Over the following months, Maggie studied hard and tried not to think about the baby growing inside her as her father had already made arrangements with social services for her baby to be adopted. Jess talked to Maggie several times about how the birth would be as she felt it would be better for her granddaughter to know what lay ahead. Arrangements were in place for the baby to be born in the cottage hospital where he or she would immediately be taken away to the nursery, spending no time at all with Maggie. Jess thought it would be better for Maggie if she had no memories of the baby being at the house and no contact at all with her child after the birth.

Maggie wrote to her brothers and surprisingly received long letters from them telling her all the news at home. She thought her parents wouldn't allow the boys to write to her, but as they didn't know she had been sent away, only that she had gone to stay with their grandmother for the summer holidays, her parents had to keep up the charade. When

Maggie did not return home at the end of the summer, the boys were told she was waiting for a place at University and had chosen to stay and help their grandmother until the spring.

In January, Jess and Maggie were completely cut off from civilization due to a blizzard and there was a deep snowdrift across the track leading to the house. They couldn't even get out of the house, as the snow was a good five to six feet deep. At the height of the blizzard, two weeks before her due date, Maggie's labour began.

At first things progressed slowly and Maggie carried on helping her grandmother take in plenty of logs from the utility room which was used as a wood store during the winter months in case of bad weather. In the early hours of the following day her labour stepped up to the next stage and considering she had no pain relief, Maggie coped extremely well and Jess was very proud of her.

At 5.15am on 15th January, Jess delivered her great grandson! She wrapped the tiny boy in a towel and handed him to Maggie who wept as she examined her beautiful little boy with his copper red hair, Simon's hair. Her grandmother smiled down at her, knowing how Maggie's heart must be breaking at the thought of giving the wee soul away, but it was the wrong time for her. She would now be able to go to university, have the career she wanted in medicine and eventually have another baby when she was in a settled marriage.

Due to the snow, the original plan to take her baby away immediately could not be carried out and Maggie was able to spend a few unexpected days with her son. She cherished every second of their time together, holding him as much as possible through the day and taking him into her bed at night. She spent hours just studying his tiny face in the hope she would always be able to close her eyes and picture him after they took him away from her.

As the snow began to clear, Jess told Maggie her son's birth would have to be registered and she should think about choosing a name for her baby. "I have already chosen a name - Gran, meet little George Roberts." She looked up at Jess and smiled through her tears, "After granddad."

On the day the social worker came to collect little George, Maggie said her goodbyes on her own, handed her baby to Jess; went upstairs; lay on her bed; covered her face with a pillow and sobbed her heart out. When the social worker had gone, Jess wiped her own tears away before going upstairs to Maggie's room. She lay on the bed next to her sobbing granddaughter and held her tightly in her arms, tears running down her own cheeks at Maggie's pain. She sobbed uncontrollably until she eventually fell asleep, totally exhausted, in her grandmother's arms.

With Jess's love and understanding, a devastated Maggie slowly came to terms with losing George and a few months later, in late summer, Maggie left Ullapool to start university in Glasgow...

CHAPTER 29

It was the first anniversary of his parents' death and Jack had just finished planting a rose at their grave, pink of course as there could be no other colour for his mum. They had been buried next to their baby girl Grace and Jack also planted a new miniature pink rose below her headstone. Mollie was down on her hands and knees, weeding round the headstones and giving them a scrub with a hard brush. She hadn't been herself at all today and Jack had a feeling there was more to it than the memories from this time last year. He sat back on his knees and watched as Mollie tidied up and knew from her face there was definitely something worrying her.

"You made a good job of that Moll, come and sit by me for a minute before we head off home." Mollie did as requested and as she went to sit down Jack pulled her onto his lap. "Now, we are not moving from here until you tell me what's bothering you." Mollie looked down at her feet and knew she was going to have to tell Jack and he was going to be so upset with her!

"Well first I have to say I didn't do it on purpose, I didn't tell you at the time because you were so upset and I thought it was too soon after the accident. Then with selling the cottage and moving into the farmhouse and redecorating, we were so busy and I honestly forgot all about it," she had been desperately trying to hold back the tears but a few escaped and trickled down her face.

"Okay, I believe you and I promise, whatever it is, I accept you did what you thought was the right thing, but maybe you should explain what it is you didn't tell me."

Mollie took a deep breath, "When I was clearing out the chest at the bottom of your mum and dad's bed, I found an envelope with Grace's name on it and inside there was a little silver locket with a small wisp of her hair. I put it in the box with all your mum's jewellery, the one that's on the shelf in the study."

Jack nodded, "That's okay Moll, I can remember mum showing me the locket once but I had forgotten all about it until now."

"It's not just the locket though Jack, I also found a book, well more of a journal with your name on it and written by your mum. It has the story of your adoption, phone calls, dates, meetings with social workers and it goes right up to when you left school. I'm so sorry, I meant to give it to you when you were over the shock and upset, but I put it in with the jewellery and forgot about it. I remembered this morning when I was watching you plant the rose on Grace's grave."

Jack gave her a tight hug and kissed her forehead. "It's okay Moll, you know mum and dad told me all about it as I was growing up, mum liked to write everything down, you know how many diaries we found in boxes."

"I'm sorry, I completely forgot about it."

"I tell you what, we can have a look at it tonight. Now, it's getting quite warm, so how about we pick up these bits and pieces and head home for a coffee break in the garden?"

That evening Jack read through Sara's journal and was amazed at the amount of detail it contained. She made a note of every phone call and meeting. The letter from the court granting his adoption was pinned to one of the pages. His first birthday card was there, a card from all Sara's colleagues at the hospital and so many other keepsakes.

It was such a lovely record of his mum's thoughts, all his 'firsts' as he grew up and he was glad his mum had gone to so much trouble to save the memories, especially now when she wouldn't be here to tell him herself. He flicked through a few blank pages at the end of the journal and was just about to close it when he noticed writing on the last page. It was a message to Jack from his mum.

> My Darling Jack
>
> I hope I am the one to hand you this journal one day when the time is right, but if not I want you to know that every second dad and I spent with you, brought us only joy we could never have imagined. The first night you came into our lives we didn't close our eyes for one second. We studied your tiny features, stroked your tiny hands, hardly daring to breathe in case we disturbed you. We have always loved and adored you with all our hearts and I pray that your life will be as rewarding and fulfilling as ours have been, although without you that would not have been the case.
>
> I know we never hid the fact that although you were our son we adopted you from your biological parents, as, for reasons of their own, they

were unable to keep you. All the details of your adoption are logged in this journal and should you ever wish to find out the circumstances surrounding your adoption, or seek out your birth parents, we give you our blessing my darling. Don't ever think for one minute we would be offended or hurt, because we have had the gift of having you all these years and are secure in your timeless love for us.

I fully intend giving you this journal once you are happily married and thinking of having a family of your own but as I said if I'm not here, know that you have my blessing. If dad is still with you, please look after him for me because I think he might be lonely on his own, although he would never admit that to you.

Love you to the moon and back my darling

Mum xxx

Tears poured down Jack's face and Mollie came over and hugged him. "I'm sorry if it's upset you, I was worried this would happen."

"It's not the adoption bit, it's a letter to me from mum, here read it."

Mollie was sobbing by the time she finished reading the letter. It was so touching and her love for Jack was almost tangible. She snuggled into Jack and he held her until she was able to speak. "You are so lucky to have been showered with such love and affection Jack. Having you as their son made your mum and dad so happy and content, they loved their lives."

They didn't really talk much about the journal again, bar an occasional comment, until months later at the beginning of spring when Jack told Mollie he had been reading through his mum's journal again and his curiosity was getting the better of him!

However, he felt if he did look into his adoption, he would betray the memory of his mum and dad. Mollie got him to read the letter Sara had written again, pointing out the line saying he had their full blessing. They discussed it over the next few days, the main questions being, if he did trace his birth parents, would he contact them? What if they didn't want to meet him? Did he want a relationship with them? In the end they decided it would do no harm to contact social services and take it from there.

A fortnight later, Jack had a meeting at the social work department. He explained why he was there and asked if it would be possible to see any files they held regarding his adoption. He provided as much information as he could, even down to the name of the social worker responsible for handling his case at the time. The woman who was interviewing him was surprised at how much information he had and he explained about the journal, which she thought was a lovely idea, apart from being very helpful!

She advised him to apply for a copy of his original birth certificate which would give him his birth mother's name, maiden name if applicable and his father's details, if he was named on the certificate. Their address at the time of registering the birth would also be on the certificate, plus their dates of birth and the date they married, if that was the case. She said it could take up to six weeks for them to trace his file and he would receive a letter, hopefully telling him the search was successful.

"If we do trace your file, you will be asked to make an appointment to come in and discuss it's content."

"Hopefully successful?" he queried.

"I'm afraid we have been unable to trace some adoption files from the 1950's/early 60's as it seems some were only kept for a certain time after the adoption was finalised through the courts, and then unfortunately destroyed."

Jack hoped his file was not one of those destroyed and he did as advised and applied for his original birth certificate. He was surprised at how apprehensive he felt when he received the envelope from the registrar and waited until he was cuddled up on the sofa with Mollie to open it.

It was not what they expected. His father, Peter Joseph Cameron, registered the birth, his occupation an Accountant. They both smiled at the coincidence but seconds later were shocked to read the words, in brackets after his mother's name, Laura Jayne Cameron (died in childbirth). He was named Joseph, presumably after his father and there was an address in Edinburgh. Jack handed Mollie the certificate and came back with a bottle of wine and two glasses. "I know we don't usually have a drink during the week but I think we can make an exception tonight," he said pouring them both a large glass. "I wasn't expecting that, it certainly alters the assumptions I made as to why I was put up for adoption."

Mollie sipped her wine and read through the certificate for a fourth time. "Well we know from the journal the social worker told your mum your parents did not keep you due to complications. Personally, I thought they had split up before you were born or you may not have been your father's child or something along those lines, but it never crossed my mind that your mum could have died. It must have been awful for your father!"

"I can't imagine what it would be like to go through that. Imagine looking forward to having a baby and your wife dies leaving you all alone to look after him. I wonder if she was ill before she had me? Maybe my father blamed me for her death and simply didn't want me because I lived and she died?"

"Surely not, how could he blame you? Things sometimes go wrong in childbirth, but it's not something you can blame on the baby! I would have thought he would want to keep you more than ever because you were a part of his wife, a reminder of their love?"

"I don't know Moll, maybe we have got it wrong. What if he didn't want children, his wife got pregnant so he had no option but to go along with it, but when she died he got rid of me?"

"Oh don't say that Jack, surely he wouldn't have done that? Maybe he simply couldn't cope, he might never have held a baby, he had to work and might not have had anyone to help him, we don't know. Let's wait and see what it says in your file, hopefully you will find out what happened when you get to read it."

CHAPTER 30

Lucy and Patrick finally received the news they had been desperately waiting for, they had been approved to adopt and now they had to be patient again until social services found them a baby or child of their own. They did not dare tempt fate and decorate their little bedroom until they were approved, but now it was painted lemon and Patrick had put stickers of teddy bears on the walls. There was a cot which they would change to a bed if they needed to, a chest of drawers, a little wicker chair and several teddies and soft toys, mostly donated from their families.

At first they received daily phone calls from their siblings asking if there was any news, but after a couple of weeks they realised they were only adding to what was already an anxious time and now they were all very good at not mentioning the wait for a baby. Lucy and Patrick had been the same at first but managed to settle back down, concentrate on work and carry on as normal, but it was difficult and every morning Lucy woke up wondering if today was the day she would get a call from their social worker.

Lucy was busy making up a spray of flowers for a funeral, absently thinking about what she would make for dinner that evening, when Rhona called her to the phone and, at last, she realised it was the phone call she had been waiting for!

Alice, their social worker, asked Lucy if she could call at the house at six o'clock that evening as she would like to talk to them about a child who had been placed with them for adoption. Lucy did not hesitate to tell Alice both she and Patrick would finish work early and six o'clock would be perfect. Rhona looked at Lucy and thought it was bad news as Lucy was very pale and looked as though she was going to burst into tears. She walked over and gave Lucy a hug, "It's alright Lucy, just take a minute and then you can tell me what has happened."

Lucy whispered, "I think they might have a baby for us Rhona, well Alice said a child."

"Oh my god Lucy, that's wonderful! I thought from the look on your face something had gone wrong but that is fantastic! You and Patrick deserve it, you will be wonderful parents!" She gave Lucy another tight hug and then looked at her, "How are you going to let Patrick know?"

"He's working in town today, they are refurbishing the old bank in the square."

"Well get yourself across and tell him the good news and I will get the kettle on and have a nice cup of tea waiting for you when you get back," Lucy who was slowly regaining a bit of colour as the shock wore off, smiled and hurried out of the shop.

Lucy ran over to the square, questions racing through her head. Why was the baby/child up for adoption? Was it a boy or a girl? When would they get to see him or her? How long did it take before they let the child come to live with you? Rhona always knew she would be giving up work if they were lucky enough to adopt, but now she would have to talk to her when she got back to the shop.

Just as she arrived at the square, she saw Patrick getting wood out of the back of the van and shouted his name at the top of her voice. Patrick looked round and saw Lucy grinning at him - he knew there was only one thing that would light up her face like that! Lucy excitedly told him word for word what Alice told her and they arranged to meet at the square at five o'clock to give them enough time to get home and make sure everything was spotless at the house. Patrick kept telling her Alice knew the house was clean and to stop worrying, but Lucy wasn't going to let a speck of dust affect their chances when it came to having their own child!

Lucy and Rhona talked about what news Alice would have and went through all sorts of scenarios. Lucy also voiced her worries about how much notice they would get if they were given a child but Rhona told her not to worry, as soon as she needed to, she could stop work as her other employee Val, who worked part time, had recently asked if there was any chance of working more hours, so she would be able to take over from Lucy. It was like a dream and Lucy could not wait to sit down with Alice and Patrick to hear about the child who could be theirs. Every minute felt like an hour and she had never been so glad to walk out of the shop to meet Patrick and get home.

Lucy had a tray with tea and biscuits ready when Alice knocked at the door and once they sat down, Alice began to tell them about Christina. She explained that although they would not be told her surname, as she was three years old, it would be too confusing if they were to change her first name and Lucy and Patrick were in complete agreement. Alice also told them as much as she could about the circumstances surrounding Christina's adoption and Lucy became quite upset as she thought of the poor mother who was having to give up her baby girl because she had an accident, she must be heartbroken! Once Alice told them everything she could about Christina, she asked if they were happy to meet her and if all went well, go ahead with the adoption. After a quick glance at Lucy, Patrick smiled and said they could not wait to meet her!

Alice suggested they visit Scotscraig Children's Home and spend Saturday afternoon with Christina, and if everything went well, they could visit again on Sunday and let her get to know them a little before she came to live with them.

The visits went brilliantly! Lucy and Patrick simply fell in love with her on sight and were desperate to see her again on the Sunday. Christina seemed to take to them straight away and quite happily sat on Patrick's knee as her showed her a picture book and they made animal noises together. Alice said Patrick was a natural and Lucy smiled at the little girl who was laughing at her husband's impression of a goat!

Just over a week later, after two further visits to the home, Lucy and Patrick waited anxiously for Alice to arrive with Christina. Just after 11am the doorbell rang and Lucy, who had been on tenterhooks all morning, nearly jumped out of her skin. Her pulse was racing as she opened the door to Alice holding Christina's hand and on the doorstep sat a small suitcase and a box of toys and books. Alice explained about Christina's mother asking if these things could go with her to her new home and Lucy agreed it was only right she should have her own things, which would be of comfort to her.

"Christina's mother also asked if this list could be given to you and although we don't normally allow contact of any sort from the birth parents, due to the tragic circumstances and to help make life easier for this little girl to settle, we have allowed her to provide a 'favourites' list," as she spoke Alice handed the sheet of paper to Lucy who smiled and nodded.

"If you can, then please tell Christina's mother thank you for the list and reassure her we will take the best care of her little girl and give her all the love we have," Lucy broke off as emotion overwhelmed her.

Alice nodded, smiled at Lucy and stood up to leave. "I will visit on Tuesday morning to see how she is settling in, but meanwhile if you have any questions or are worried about anything, I am at the end of the phone to help you in any way I can," and with that she waved to Christina, who looked up, smiled and went straight back to playing with her teddies.

That first evening Patrick and Lucy didn't take their eyes off their beautiful little girl. They put her to bed together and as she hugged her teddy Patrick read her the story of Goldilocks and the three bears, but before he even got half way through the book Christina was sound asleep. They stood looking down at her, neither able to believe how quickly they were falling in love with this precious little girl...

CHAPTER 31

Olivia's first week in hospital consisted of tests, rest, sleep and most importantly, three sessions of dialysis, which resulted in her feeling much better and more like herself again. Matt was so relieved to see the 'old' Ollie back and delighted to report some good news to Harry and Jean for a change.

Olivia found her first dialysis session very stressful and was freaked out about her blood leaving her body, to go through a machine and back into her body. The process took just over three hours and she constantly asked her nurse questions, needing reassurance throughout. Matt held her hand, talked to her and tried to help her relax but she was almost rigid with fear.

She was the same during her second session until a young boy came in with his nurse and jumped onto one of the beds. As the nurse was setting up the machine the boy and her were chatting and laughing. Once his dialysis began, he opened his bag and took out his schoolwork. It was just what Olivia needed to see and Matt knew it was a good opportunity to show her just how safe it was. He started chatting to the boy, who told them his name was Calum, he was ten years old, had three younger brothers and was on his own as his dad couldn't take any more time off work and his mum had to look after his brothers. His gran would be in later though and would take him home as she quite often stepped in to help on his dialysis days. Olivia felt so sorry for the poor little lad and forgot to worry about her own situation, for her it was a turning point.

During her third session, Olivia actually fell asleep and couldn't believe it was nearly over when she woke up again.

Her test results were much better after that session and when the doctor did his ward round later that afternoon, he told her he was pleased as she was now more stable and looking much better. As her results had shown a marked improvement, she could be discharged and continue her treatment as an outpatient every Monday, Wednesday and Friday and he would see her every Friday after her dialysis.

On the drive home Matt and Olivia discussed how they would manage the trip to the hospital three times a week, as Matt would have to return to work. It was Matt who suggested her parents came down to stay with them for the first few weeks. "Your dad could drive you to and from Middlesbrough for your dialysis and your mum could take over running the house and looking after you." Olivia agreed with his plan, telling him her parents had already hinted at the idea, saying they would rather be with her than at home worrying about her.

When they reached home Matt dialled Jean and Harry's number and handed the phone to Olivia.

"Hello."

"Hi dad, it's me."

"You sound much brighter sweetheart, how did you find the dialysis?"

"I was terrified to start with, if you think about what's really happening, it freaks you out! Then this young boy, Calum, came in on my second session and once he was all set up, he got all his books out and started doing his schoolwork! I thought if he can do this so can I!"

"That's my girl, you stay strong and let the dialysis do the job of keeping you well. Your mum and I are very worried about you sweetheart."

"I know dad, please don't worry, I have to go for dialysis three times a week and that will help keep me stable."

"How are you going to manage with Matt working, you surely can't be driving?"

"Well I was wondering how you and mum might feel about coming down and staying with us for awhile, just until I am a bit better. Maybe you could take me over to the hospital and mum could help me in the house and make sure Matt has a decent meal on the table each night?"

"You don't have to ask twice my darling, mum and me will get packed up tonight and set off early in the morning."

"You don't need to do that dad, give yourselves some time, I don't have my next dialysis till Monday so you have all weekend to travel down!"

"No my love, we are desperate to see you and if we come down tomorrow we will have Sunday to get ourselves organised for next week."

"Okay dad," Olivia was getting upset just hearing her dad's voice and was desperate to see both him and her mum, "just come whenever you want, Matt will be pleased to have some help."

"Okay love, I will see you tomorrow evening. Your mum is here so I'll put her on and get cracking with the packing!"

Olivia spoke to her mum who was as keen as her dad to get down to look after her. They talked for a few minutes more and then her mum said she was off to supervise dad's packing. Just before hanging up, she told Olivia they both loved the bones of her and couldn't wait to spoil and look after her!

Matt came over to the sofa and took the phone off his wife, knelt down and gave her a gentle hug. Olivia looked worn out, so Matt rearranged her pillows, tucked her up in the patchwork quilt her mum made for her and sat next to her on the edge of the sofa.

"Your mum and dad are coming down?"

"Yes, they are running around packing now and are leaving early tomorrow morning. They will look after us and take the pressure off you," she stroked Matt's face, noticing how tired he looked, "I love you so much!"

Harry and Jean arrived just after 4.30pm the following day and there were hugs, kisses and a few tears. They had packed every inch of their car with gifts and cards from relatives, friends and well-wishers back at home; some of Olivia's favourite things from her room; a box from the bakery full of cakes, rolls, bread and two boxes of groceries.

They all settled into a workable routine very quickly. Harry took Olivia to hospital three times a week, Jean usually tagging along on the Wednesday. Hospital days were long and tiring for both Harry and Olivia but Harry never complained once. He usually waited until Olivia was settled on dialysis and went to the café for coffees and a couple of sandwiches. Harry would read the newspapers and do his best to complete the crosswords. Olivia always took along her book but she found it hard to concentrate, so Harry would read to her. On the drive back Olivia always fell asleep quite quickly and Harry would listen to his favourite radio station. When they arrived home, Jean would have a meal ready and some home-baked cakes or an apple tart.

Olivia saw her doctor on Friday afternoons after her dialysis and they would have a discussion about how she felt in herself, her latest test results and whether or not they needed to tweak her medication.

Everything was going well and the doctors were pleased until the ninth week, when unfortunately Olivia began to deteriorate again and her doctor upped her dialysis and also added a new medication. Although everyone was disappointed, the doctor was reassuring, explaining it could just be a blip and he was hopeful she would improve again.

Initially, she responded well to the new regime, had much more energy and didn't need to sleep quite so much. Matt and her parents were very pleased and relieved to see a marked change, although they were all aware she needed to remain stable this time.

Luckily, Olivia's condition did stabilise and she continued to feel better. After a family discussion round the dinner table one Sunday, they agreed Harry and Jean should go home, but only on the understanding they would be asked back straight away if Olivia's condition changed again.

Olivia was transported back and forth to the hospital, along with two other patients, by a volunteer car agency the hospital used and she continued to remain stable for a couple of months. The following month Matt was on holiday and took over the hospital run. Over the past couple of weeks he suspected she was deteriorating again, her appetite was poor and she was back to sleeping nearly all day when she wasn't at the hospital.

At the doctor's appointment after the dialysis on the Friday, both Matt and Olivia were stunned when her doctor explained Olivia was no longer responding to the dialysis and medication and her condition was now considered 'critical'. He suggested she stay overnight and have a blood transfusion for her anaemia, which could be repeated as necessary along side the dialysis.

Matt could feel his heart racing, "I have to ask, does Ollie need a transplant? She is on the transplant list?"

"Yes Matt, Olivia was placed on the list as soon as we began dialysis but the chance of a suitable match is down to luck I'm afraid."

Matt glanced at Ollie, but she looked as if it was all going over her head. "So how long a wait could we be talking?"

"As I said, each donation is matched to the best recipient, however, the best option would be to have family members tested as live donor transplants have a higher success rate. Ask everyone in Olivia's family to get tested, it would be the best outcome if one of them was both a good match and of course a healthy donor."

"Olivia is adopted!" Matt felt as though he wanted to curl up and cry one second and punch something the next. He felt so helpless!

"Aah, not the reply I was hoping for, however I had a patient in the same position once before. He traced his birth parents and is now back playing football after his father agreed to be his donor. It's worth a try Matt, Olivia isn't doing well on dialysis," he looked at Matt's face. He had seen that look of hopelessness and devastation before many times and really hoped it would work out for Olivia.....

CHAPTER 32

Lesley and Steve's application to adopt was a long but relatively smooth process, as taking into account their professions; the references provided by their employers, family and friends and the backing of both their doctor and the reverend, it was no surprise they were eventually approved by social services. Eleven weeks had passed since they were placed on the waiting list and now they had to be patient and wait until they were contacted with news of a baby or child who needed a loving home.

They had a second good-sized bedroom and when Lesley was expecting their baby, they turned it into a nursery. After baby Steven died and Lesley felt well enough, she packed everything into cases and boxes but couldn't bring herself to give anything away or do anything with the room. So, it was with a mixture of joy and sadness she cleaned the room, unpacked everything, washed and ironed all the clothing and blankets and got the nursery ready again for the new baby who would be coming into their lives. Of course they had no idea how old the baby or child would be so they might need to buy a whole wardrobe of new clothes.

Lesley stood at the door looking at the cot and the row of teddies waiting for their new owner to arrive. Somewhere out there was a child who was destined to change her life and she hoped it would be soon, but for now she would just have to wait patiently.

However the wait proved not to be as long as expected as, only three weeks later, Lesley was sitting at her desk having a cup of tea and a sandwich while the children were having a singing lesson in the church when Steve appeared at the classroom door.

"Hello Mrs Thomas, are you enjoying your sandwich?" he winked at her. Lesley laughed at him! She loved it when he turned up unexpectedly just to say hello.

"Well hello to you too Sergeant Thomas, to what do I owe the pleasure or are you checking up on me again?"

"Well I came to tell you something but for the life of me I can't remember what it was – now, what was it? If you were to offer me a bite of the cake Mrs C gave you for lunch, it might jog my memory!" His eyes twinkled as he teased her!

"You may as well have a cup of tea with the cake and keep me company for a while!" Steve winked at her, pulled up a chair and poured himself a cup of tea. He took a large bite of the cake, all the time smiling at Lesley!

"Okay Steve Thomas, you are up to something!"

"That's Sergeant Thomas to you," he winked at her again and she burst out laughing, she knew he was up to something! "Oh I've just remembered what I had to tell you and if you were to let me finish that slice of cake……"

"Oh go on then – but if you haven't got anything to tell me, you are in a lot of trouble mister!"

His eyes crinkled up with wickedness and he finished the cake, then patted his stomach, "Mrs C is a very good baker, I am going to have to watch my figure!"

"Stop stalling and tell me!"

Steve smiled, leant across the table and kissed his wife. "I came to tell you it's time to arrange for your replacement to get here pretty quickly Mrs Thomas, as you are soon going to be a mum again!"

Lesley looked at him wide-eyed. "Honestly? When? Did someone call?"

"Yes honestly! I'm not sure when and yes a social worker called and is coming to see us this afternoon after school and will tell us all we need to know then!" he got up and walked round her desk to give her a long, firm kiss. "It's finally going to happen sweetheart, WE are going to have an addition to the family!"

That afternoon they sat intently listening to Miss Sutherland's every word. She told them she had two children to find adoptive parents for, a baby boy who was just three weeks old and a little girl who was four months old. They could come and see both the children who were, for the moment, in a children's home. However if they had a preference the papers could be signed today and she would personally bring the baby to them in around a week's time. Lesley looked at Steve and he knew what she was thinking. "As our little boy died from a heart condition, we would very much like the chance to have another." Miss Sutherland smiled at Steve and took a file out of her briefcase.

"I took the necessary paperwork with me today in case you made a decision without going to see the children, so if you are both happy to go ahead with the adoption we can get these forms completed now. I will get this processed and if everything is in order, I will be in touch next week and we can arrange a day for me to come back down with your new son!" she looked from one to the other and they both nodded. "Don't look so worried!" she smiled at them, "the hard bit is over and now you are rewarded with your baby boy - it's all good from now on!"

Once all the paperwork was completed and signed, Miss Sutherland left saying she would be in touch within the week, and suggested they make the most of their last few nights of unbroken sleep!

The following day Lesley contacted her replacement teacher, a local woman, who taught before having her own family. Now they were all in school she was eager to return to her profession. Esme Woods, who had already been approved by the school board, had been happy to wait until Lesley received news of a baby. She was delighted to hear Lesley and Steve were going to have another little boy and agreed to take up her post the following Monday. Lesley hoped to shadow Esme for a few days to allow the children to get to know her and also give Lesley time to give her both a background and progress report for each child. When Miss Sutherland phoned the following Friday to say she was delighted to be able to deliver their baby on Wednesday morning, Lesley was happy to hand over the reigns to Esme.

Her last day was emotional for both her and the children with each child bringing a small gift for the new baby, mostly clothes knitted by their mums. There were also gifts of soft toys, a rattle, some bibs and Lesley was very touched by the cards some of the children made and the kindness of the parents. She in turn, had bought each child a book and wrote a personal message to each one on the inside cover. There were lots of tears as they all left for home but Lesley had promised she would bring the baby in to meet them. After all the children had gone, she handed over her keys to Esme, thanked her, wished her good luck in her new job and headed home to prepare for the new arrival.

On the day their tiny son arrived, Lesley and Steve were overwhelmed with love and although they found themselves transported back to the day their Steven was born, they made no comparisons as both their sons were equally precious to them. It took a few days to choose a name for the new member of the Thomas family and finally they decided on Michael as both their grandfathers shared the name...

CHAPTER 33

Five weeks after the first meeting with social services, Jack received the letter he had been waiting for. They had successfully located his file and could he phone and make an appointment to discuss the contents.

The following week Mollie and a curious, but slightly anxious Jack, sat opposite Lauren Oliver, a social worker who specialised in fostering and adoption. She began by explaining most people who came to them for details of their adoption coped well when they discovered the reason their birth parents approached social services. However, some found it upsetting, others were angry and if the adoptive parents were not aware of the search, it had in some cases caused problems.

"Now Jack, you have had some time to think about finding out the details of your adoption, if you are still sure we can carry on?" Jack simply nodded and took a deep breath.

"Okay, now just before I go through your file with you can I ask if you have a copy of your original birth certificate?"

"Yes, I have the names of both my parents and it also states my mother died in childbirth."

"Yes it seems your mother suffered serious complications during her labour and they resulted in her death. I have here a report from the social worker who supported your father with regard to placing you with us for adoption. You were just a week old and still being looked after by the hospital where you were born. Your father was very distraught because of your mother's death and adamant he would not be able to care for you on his own. He told us he had no relatives who could help and felt it would be better for you to have both a mother and father who could give you a stable, happy home. He signed the necessary papers straight away and the social worker was able to place you with your adoptive parents very quickly." She looked up at Jack, "Are you okay?"

"Yes, I'm fine. It's more or less what we imagined from the information on my birth certificate."

"I do have a bit more to tell you, it's rare but not unusual for a parent to write a letter to be placed in a file when they give up a child, however, in your case I was surprised to see your file had been accessed long after your adoption. It seems your father contacted our department almost five years ago and asked for a letter to be placed in your file and given to you if you ever came forward for information regarding your adoption." Jack looked at Mollie and she squeezed his hand, "It's your choice Jack, you don't have to take it, but if you do, you can open it now, in ten years or never, it's up to you."

Lauren Oliver smiled at Mollie who looked fit to burst! "I'm just going to pop out for a few minutes and leave you to read through your file. I can't let you take any of the papers but here's a pen and notepad and you can make notes to take away with you. We can decide about the letter when I come back," and with that she left them alone to look at the file.

As Jack wrote down some of the details, he discussed the letter with Mollie. It was something he had not expected, in fact, he didn't think it would be allowed. He decided he couldn't come this far and not read something written by his father, which could provide him with more information about who he was. As they drove home they decided to make their favourite supper, open a bottle of wine and then open the letter...

CHAPTER 34

Marlene's recovery was a slow and painful process. After giving up Christina for adoption she went into deep depression, wishing she could die, as she had nothing to live for anymore.

After a couple of months the plaster casts came off her arm and her legs, the right leg healing very well, but the left required further surgery and was set in another cast. At this point Marlene was introduced to her physiotherapist Connor, who was from County Tyrone in Northern Ireland. Although he was unable to treat her body as a whole, he concentrated on getting full movement and muscle strength back into Marlene's injured arm and her right leg. As he worked, he chatted away about growing up back in Ireland with his seven siblings, relating stories of the antics they got up to and how his poor mother coped with them all!

Marlene never talked much, just a nod here and there, but Connor knew, behind the blank expression, she was listening and hoped by telling her personal stories about his family life she would grow to know and trust him, which would aid her recovery. However, he needed to understand Marlene and voiced his concern to her doctors regarding her lack of interest in getting mobile again. Although normally a patients' private life stayed that way, they felt in Marlene's case it would be helpful if Connor knew the circumstances surrounding her accident and her decision to give her daughter up for adoption. Connor now understood why Marlene was so withdrawn, but also felt more determined than ever to help her in any way he could.

Five weeks had passed since Connor started working with Marlene and he had been limited to treating her arm and right leg, both of which were much improved, especially her arm.

At this point the second plaster came off her left leg and the doctors carried out more tests. When they had all the results, they told Marlene the swelling and bruising at the base of her spine had reduced significantly and they felt it was time to start therapy and see if she could regain some feeling and movement in her legs. "Hopefully in time we will get you up on your feet again Marlene," her doctor smiled encouragingly.

"But I can't feel my legs! How am I going to stand up?" Marlene shook her head at the doctor, "I may as well accept I'm never going to get out of this bed on my own!"

"We cannot promise anything Marlene, we don't know to what extent the damage has affected your ability to walk, but let's see if intensive physiotherapy can get some feeling back in your legs and take it from there. Connor is very experienced and if you trust in him and do as he asks I am confident you should see some improvement."

"He is wasting his time, you are all wasting your time, I can feel nothing and I'm never going to walk again," Marlene whispered, tears running down her cheeks onto her pillow.

"Let's just give it a try, work hard, do as Connor asks and prove yourself wrong," he patted Marlene's hand, smiled and left sighing to himself as he doubted she would walk again.

Early the next morning Connor came into the room, his usual bright, breezy, chatty self. "Morning Marlene! Now then, today we are going to begin with some strengthening exercises to wake up those lazy muscles in your legs and remind them they are there for a reason!"

Marlene couldn't feel anything as Connor bent and straightened her legs. All the time he kept up his usual constant chatter and Marlene closed her eyes wishing he would finish up and leave her in peace. Eventually, Connor announced she had worked hard enough this morning and deserved a lunch break but he would be back again in the afternoon. Marlene simply nodded and closed her eyes praying for sleep to escape reality.

Connor walked down the corridor and decided he was getting nowhere with the friendly, softly, softly approach. This afternoon he would try a different tack and hopefully get some reaction out of Marlene. At the moment she was totally disinterested in trying to get better and was void of any emotion, but this afternoon he was going to initiate the 'cruel to be kind' approach.

That afternoon, after discussing his plan with Marlene's doctor, Connor strode into her room with a different mind-set. He picked up a pillow and walked round to the left side of Marlene's bed. "Right Marlene, your first exercise this afternoon is to punch this pillow as hard as you can."

The punches were feather-light, no more than taps. "Come on Marlene, a child could do better than that!" She continued to put no effort into the exercise. "You need to get angry Marlene, picture someone you're angry with, what about the man who did this to you? Surely you would put more effort into punching him!" Marlene glared at Connor, she hadn't realised he knew how she had been injured. "Hit him Marlene, come on, hit him hard! Get your own back, come on!" Marlene was getting angry at Connor and started to hit slightly harder. He raised his voice slightly, "Is that all you've got? He put you in this bed Marlene, he caused horrific damage to your body, he robbed you of your life with your daughter!" That was the trigger, suddenly something in Marlene snapped and she started lashing out, hitting as hard as she could and crying until she was too exhausted to lift her arm anymore. Connor quickly went round the bed to the other side and started winding her up again. "You have another arm Marlene, you're not finished yet surely? Picture his face Marlene, make him pay for what he has done to you, come on!" His raised voice did the trick again and this time Connor could feel her punching for all she was worth, all the pent up emotion and anger was being channelled into her fists. She was sobbing and totally exhausted when Connor stopped her. He fetched a wet facecloth and pulled up a chair at her bedside.

"I'm sorry Marlene, but you needed to get rid of some of that anger, the tension in your body is doing you no good at all and I need to get you to focus on working your muscles and regaining your strength." Marlene nodded as she patted her face with the cloth. "From now on I want you to put all your frustration and anger into your exercises to build up your strength and get you moving about again. No going back, okay?"

"Okay," Marlene whispered.

That was the day Marlene turned the corner. Punching the pillow became a daily work out which served as a release from the frustration and also gradually built up her upper body strength. Connor did an intense workout twice a day to get the muscles in her legs strong again. Marlene would watch him and listen to another of his childhood stories. Eventually, as she grew to trust him, she started chatting back and talked about her own past, however she never mentioned Christina.

It was during one of these sessions, as Connor bent Marlene's leg back towards her waist, she flinched. Marlene was telling Connor about how nosey the locals were in the village where she came from and didn't seem aware of what happened. Connor eased off and did some other exercises before repeating the knee bend to her waist and this time she stopped mid sentence. "Oh my god, I can feel that! Do it again, I can feel something at the bottom of my back!" Connor gave her a wide grin and winked.

"I told you I would get you moving again, now you have to start helping me, try with all your might to move your toes for me."

Marlene tried and tried but nothing happened. "It's okay," Connor reassured her, "you have done more than enough today and we must not wear you out! I will be back tomorrow so be prepared for the same hard work we did today. Tonight I want you to rest but as you are going to sleep I have some homework for you. I want you to close your eyes, picture your toes in your mind and imagine you are wiggling them. Well done Marlene, you made huge progress today and I promise it will get easier as time passes. I'll see you tomorrow morning!" he grinned and whistled all the way down the corridor - although very risky, his plan had worked!

As Marlene drifted off to sleep that night she realised she did in fact want to try and get better and although her health would rule how she lived her life from now on, she couldn't give up and would try to make the best of it. She remembered she had 'homework' and fell asleep imagining her toes were wiggling to music.

The next morning she could hear Connor whistling as he approached her room. He opened her door and in a broad Irish accent, with a salute, he said "Top of the morning to ye!" Laughing, she realised she had been relying heavily on this man, not as her therapist, but as a friend.

They repeated the exercises from the previous day and Marlene continued to feel movement in her lower back when Connor raised her legs. At the end of the session he asked her to close her eyes and concentrate on wiggling her toes but still nothing happened.

"Don't be despondent, your body needs to learn to respond to the brain signals again and you just have to concentrate on sending messages from your brain to your toes." They continued the same regime for the next couple of weeks but still Marlene did not recover any movement in her legs.

One afternoon Marlene became upset at the lack of progress so Connor decided one of his stories was needed. "Okay, you have a rest for ten minutes and I'll give your legs a bit of a workout and tell you about the time my brothers and I decided to climb down the well at my Gran's farm, I can still feel my dad's slipper across my rear end even now!"

Marlene laughed as she listened to the antics of the Irish kids and as he described the feel of the slimy, thick mud at the bottom of the well, Marlene cringed at the thought of it and the toes on her right foot twitched. Connor didn't say anything, continued telling his story and it happened again. He took his pen from his pocket and poked her toes and at first she didn't react but then suddenly she realised she could feel something and as he did it again and again she started to cry and smile at the same time. "I can feel it, I can feel it Connor!"

Progress was slow but steady and the results were much better than anticipated. Five months later Marlene was able to walk a few steps with the aid of sticks although she needed to wear both back and leg braces. Unfortunately, she wasn't pain free, both her lower back and left leg gave her varying degrees of constant pain, resulting in good days where she managed well, interspersed with really bad days when she couldn't do much but rest in bed. Despite this, she remained incredibly positive throughout her recovery, delighted to be walking again, albeit very slowly and she still had to use a wheelchair to go any further than a few yards.

When the time came to start talking about Marlene's discharge from hospital, fourteen months after her accident, Jamie stepped in with incredible news. He had been a regular visitor and anything Marlene needed, he provided. What Marlene didn't know and Jamie never talked about just in case her recovery didn't go to plan, was he had taken his brothers half of the sale from their mother's house, the amount the court awarded her as compensation, and invested it in Marlene's name. It would be enough for her to live on for years if she was careful. She was overcome with gratitude but Jamie insisted it was only right after what his brother had done - he only wished it could be more.

It was time for Marlene to start making plans in readiness for leaving hospital, to get back out into the world and begin living again!

CHAPTER 35

As they sat in the surgery waiting room, Olivia was visibly shaking and Matt tried his best to comfort her. Over the past few weeks, they had tried everything possible to trace Olivia's birth parents. Initially they tried to find her father, Bryan Carson, but had no luck at all and so they turned their attention to finding Olivia's birth mother, Angela Johnson. It was helpful her occupation was noted as Trainee Doctor and after a bit of research Matt was both surprised and relieved to find she had not changed her name and he eventually traced her to a practice in Edinburgh.

Matt telephoned the practice to make an appointment but had difficulty, as he was not registered as a patient so he completed the registration form over the telephone and made an appointment to see Dr Angela Johnson. When they arrived the receptionist told them Dr Johnson was running late but would see them as soon as she could, however that was forty-five minutes ago and Matt was getting worried about Olivia.

"Are you feeling alright Ollie?" he gave her hand a reassuring squeeze.

"My legs have turned to jelly and my stomach is in a tight knot, but apart from that I'm fine, maybe a bit tired."

"Mr Ashford, you can go through now," the receptionist smiled at Matt.

Matt helped Olivia to her feet, putting his arm around her waist for support, and they walked slowly towards the consulting room.

Angela Johnson was not as Olivia imagined her to be, looking much younger than she expected. It had not occurred to Olivia there might be a 'family' likeness between them but sitting behind a large mahogany desk was an older version of herself. It was obvious from Matt's face that he was also taken aback by the resemblance. They both stared at Angela sitting at her desk with her head bowed reading Matt's registration form, until with only a brief glance in their direction she asked them to sit down.

"My apologies for running so late Mr Ashford, how can I help today?" she said looking up at Matt.

Matt took a deep breath and squeezed Olivia's hand, "I am not actually here about myself, but needed to see you on behalf of my wife." He paused and took a deep breath, "Can you confirm you are the Angela Johnson who had a baby girl named Anna with Bryan Carson?"

Angela stared at him, visibly shocked and momentarily draining of colour before quickly regaining her composure. It was only then she turned to look at Olivia and it was obvious she also saw the resemblance. She quickly looked down at her desk and took a moment to compose herself, before addressing Olivia.

"And you are Anna?"

"I was, I am Olivia now," she answered in a weak voice. There was another pause and Olivia noticed the slight twitching of Angela's lips, indicating she was not quite as composed as she appeared.

Angela briefly smiled at Olivia and nodded, "Right, well I imagine you are here with a few questions for me but my office is not really the best place for us to talk. I still have a couple of patients to see and should be finished my surgery in about half and hour. Would it be okay with you if I meet you next door in the bistro, we will get peace to talk there?" her face had softened slightly and this time the smile wasn't so forced.

Matt and Olivia nodded in agreement and stood to make their way out of her office.

Angela watched as the young couple walked through reception before closing her door. Olivia looked unwell, appearing weak and fragile and although she could be finding this situation stressful, she had a feeling there was more to it. She leaned against the door and closed her eyes for a brief moment. The thought this day could happen had lurked somewhere in the back of her mind for years, but as time passed she thought it less likely. She had never regretted walking away from Bryan and the baby, if given the chance to turn the clock back she would do the same again. She chose her career, loved every minute and would change nothing, but she had a feeling she may now have to face the backlash of the choice she made.

Sitting back behind her desk ready for her next patient, Angela's mind was working overtime. Why now? She suspected this wasn't just curiosity to meet a birth parent, no, she had a gut feeling they wanted something from her, but what?

As they sat at a window table in the bistro sipping tea, Matt and Olivia were trying to digest the fact they had just met the woman who gave birth to her. Matt was quiet, knowing his wife, who was noticeably tired and pale, needed time to think about the conversation they were about to have with Angela.

By the time she finished her afternoon surgery and changed into more casual clothes, Angela was running late and she hurried out of her office and through reception where she told her secretary she was out of contact for the rest of the day. She was dreading this meeting but at the same time was curious to know why they wanted to find her. She stopped for a few seconds outside the bistro, took a few deep breaths to compose herself and opened the door…

Olivia had just said she didn't think Dr Johnson was going to meet them, when the bistro door opened and she walked in looking very different without her white coat. She approached their table and began with an apology. "I'm sorry if I seemed to rush you out of my surgery earlier, but I thought the quicker I got through my appointments, the sooner we could sit down and talk in a more relaxed environment." She was still professional in manner but her face was softer now. She asked them what they would like to drink, beckoned the waiter and ordered herself a gin and tonic, a beer for Matt and a fresh tea for Olivia.

Just then her phone rang and she apologised again explaining the call was very important and headed out of the bistro to take the call. The waiter was placing their drinks on the table as Angela returned. She held her glass up, gave a wry smile, said "Dutch courage!" drinking half the glass in one go. They all smiled a little at her comment and it helped them to relax, as until that point Matt and Olivia were unsure of the reception they would encounter.

Angela stared at Olivia then commented that she had both a look of herself and her father. "Have you also contacted Bryan?"

"No, we did try to trace him but every time we thought we were on the right track, we drew a blank. Matt then tracked you with ease as it stated you were a trainee doctor on the birth certificate and we guessed, or rather hoped you were still practicing."

"I see. Can I ask why you have searched for us? Curiosity?"

"I'm sick!" Olivia blurted out, tears pricking behind her eyes.

Matt reached out took Olivia's hand, placing it in the middle of both of his. "Ollie has kidney failure and needs a transplant. Everyone we know has been tested but none are a good enough match. You will obviously know a blood relative has the best chance of a being a match."

Angela's sharp physician's eyes scrutinised Olivia and she realised she had mistakenly thought her pallor was due to the stress of the situation. "I see..." nodded Angela, "So you are here to see if I can help you." It was a statement, rather than a question. She took a large mouthful of gin and signalled to the waiter. "I think we all need another drink, Olivia what can I get you? How about a lemonade?"

Olivia nodded, "Thank you," she whispered.

After ordering the drinks, Angela leant back in her chair. "Right, well I think the first thing I need to do is get hold of Bryan and see if we can get him down here and discuss what we do next," she said giving Olivia a much softer smile.

"You know where he is?" Matt looked surprised.

"I don't know exactly where he is, but I do know he is still in Edinburgh. I know of someone who works at the hospital who will get me his number." She took her purse out of her bag and got up from the table, "I'm just going to make a phone call and see if I can get hold of him."

Matt waited until Angela was out of earshot before turning and hugging Olivia. "Baby, it's going to be alright, one of them will be a match, you wait and see! I love you so much and I'm not going to give up until we get you better." Olivia smiled and kissed him, she could not have wished for a better husband. For the first time in months she felt a glimmer of hope, although she voiced her doubts to Matt.

"She is a doctor who walked away from me when I was a tiny baby. If she didn't want anything to do with me back then, why would she bother to help me now?"

"Shh, she's coming back."

Angela sat down at the table and told them she had left a message with a friend of Bryan's who assured her he would phone him immediately. "The friend works at the hospital and a colleague of mine once pointed him out commenting that he was friends with my ex. I haven't spoken to Bryan since you were born, but I know he won't hesitate in coming to meet you."

"Thank you," said Olivia.

Angela asked a few questions about Olivia's illness, when she was diagnosed; her treatment so far; how many times a week did she have dialysis; what medication she was taking – all medical questions, but then it was her profession. Olivia was aware of Angela talking to her as a patient, not as her dying child but oddly that didn't matter to her. She thought she might feel some connection to the woman who gave her life, but there was nothing and it was obviously the same for Angela who seemed to be taking Olivia's bombshell in her stride, again Olivia suspected it was down to professionalism.

"Why did you give me up for adoption?" she blurted out interrupting Angela mid-sentence. Angela slowly took a sip of her drink and looked directly at Olivia.

"I should have offered to explain your adoption and you deserve an explanation." She took another sip from her glass before continuing. "I wanted to be a doctor from a very early age and studied very hard a school. When I met Bryan I was a student doctor, we went out for about a year and a half and then I moved into his flat. About eight or nine months later I discovered I was pregnant with you and I openly admit to being really angry at how a baby was going to affect my career. I was lucky and managed to hide the pregnancy near enough all the way until you were born, but I had to get back to work quickly or the medical board would have made me repeat the year. I wanted to put you up for adoption but Bryan was furious and was adamant he would find a way to take care of you himself until I qualified. At first I wouldn't agree, but he had been abandoned by his mother as a child and desperately wanted to keep you.

I have to give him his due, he took weeks off work when you were born and did everything for you, and I mean everything, you were all that mattered to him and he adored you. I couldn't get enough sleep at the flat and I started staying at the hospital and one day I just moved out without telling Bryan and left him a note. It was despicable and cowardly, I know, and I make no excuses for myself. All I can say is I worked very hard to become a doctor and didn't have the time to look after a baby, I had to give everything to my career.

I know Bryan did his best, but I imagine it was exhausting when he returned to work and had to look after you including getting up to feed you at night. I don't know why he decided on adoption, maybe he just couldn't cope with it all, but I can assure you it broke his heart. The last time I saw him, he came to tell me he had to do what was right for you, to give you the best life possible and would I sign the adoption papers - he looked a broken man. I don't think I have ever seen such hatred in another person's eyes as I did that day and I don't blame him for despising me." She took another sip from her glass before looking up at Olivia, "Bryan had to do what was best for you, although I think it would have destroyed him – all I can do is apologise for what happened which I know isn't worth anything."

Neither Matt, nor Olivia said anything, then after a couple of minutes, Olivia broke the silence. "I'm not here to blame anyone. I do feel sorry that Bryan wasn't able to keep me and I understand it would not have been possible to manage alone. I have the best parents in the world, they love me, care for me, have given me the best of everything and I have a very happy life thanks to them…. and Bryan. Now I have Matt and I couldn't ask for a better husband so I have been very blessed.

I never had any intention of looking for you until I became ill and as I have exhausted all other avenues and am running out of time, this is my last chance, I had no alternative. It's simple, I need a kidney and you or Bryan could save my life if you are a match. The only questions I have for you are, will you have the tests and will you be a donor if you are a suitable match?" Olivia looked at Matt who was feeling immensely proud of his wife at that moment. She was facing death, facing a woman who ignored her existence from birth and she had just laid her cards on the table with as much dignity as she could muster. He was overwhelmed with love and pride for her and prayed this awful woman who abandoned her from birth would step up and finally do something for her daughter.

Angela looked at Olivia, impressed at how composed and polite she was even in the face of death. "Of course I will, it's the least I can do and I know Bryan will not hesitate to help in any way he can," she gave Olivia a genuine tender smile and Olivia turned to Matt who held her as she gave into the emotion and strain of the day.

Olivia walked back towards the table after fixing her face in the ladies toilet and saw a man sitting opposite Matt who quickly got up to help her. "Bryan is here Ollie and Angela has told him why you needed to find him. He said he will do anything he can to help you," he gave her a reassuring hug and led her back to the table.

Bryan was very different from Angela. He was friendly, soft spoken, did not disguise his feelings and there was something instantly likeable about him. It was blatantly obvious from the way he spoke that he never got over 'losing' his daughter and both Matt and Olivia could not help but like this man who, along with the woman who caused him so much heartache, was now going to try and help save her life.......

CHAPTER 36

M aggie loved university life, and although she hated the fact her father paid all her fees and lodged an allowance in her bank account for her living expenses each month, she viewed it as compensation for his treatment of her over the pregnancy.

She breezed through medical school and chose to specialise in paediatrics, helping, and hopefully curing, sick children so they could get back home to their families and get on with enjoying their childhood. Of course, there were some very sad cases where it was not possible to cure a child, but at least she could help to limit their suffering. Although their circumstances were different, she wanted as few parents as possible to have to say goodbye to their children as she had to with George.

After qualifying, Maggie took a position in Aberdeen at a children's hospital and as she was at last able to support herself, she was able to cut all links with her parents. She had always kept in touch with her brothers, Alex and Charlie, and they were loyal to her, never disclosing the contents of her letters to their parents.

A year after moving to Aberdeen, it was Alex who telephoned her to say their grandmother had died and Maggie decided she wanted to say a personal goodbye after

Jess had shown her so much love and kindness throughout her pregnancy and the months following George's adoption. She was also desperate to see her brothers as she hadn't seen them since leaving home.

Maggie waited until everyone was seated in the church and slipped into the empty back pew as the service began. Her grandmother had been a popular, well-liked member of the community and almost every pew was filled with mourners. Maggie raised herself up as much as she dared, fearful of drawing attention to herself, and tried to see her parents and brothers who were sitting at the front. She just managed to see the backs of their heads and it looked odd to see her brothers heads higher than her father's - they had obviously grown to be tall like her mother's side of the family.

The service was very touching, the minister's final comment, "I'm sure George was waiting for Jess with open arms, they are together again at last," caught Maggie off guard at the mention of her grandfather, after whom she named her son. As the coffin was carried out of the church, Maggie got the chance to get a glimpse of her parents using the cover of other mourners who stood as a sign of respect. Her mother and father looked stony-faced and Maggie could not detect even the tiniest flicker of emotion from either of them. Her brothers walked behind and as she suspected they were now both over six feet, towering over her parents who walked past looking straight ahead. As her brothers drew level with her, she quickly reached out and tapped Alex's arm. He turned his head and the look of shock was followed by a huge smile. "Meet me round the back of the church when you get a chance," she winked at him and he nodded.

Maggie waited until everyone had followed the coffin to the graveyard and slipped out unnoticed to make her way behind the church to the opposite side from the graveyard. After the interment Alex told his parents he and Charlie would follow behind to the wake in the village and when the coast was clear they went in search of Maggie.

It was an emotional reunion, as they had not see each other for so many years. Maggie was enveloped in hugs and they all shed tears of joy at finally being together again. She repeatedly told the boys how much she missed them and they told each other all the latest news. Maggie said she was staying at the Quayside Guesthouse in the village overnight and the boys were delighted, as they had also booked in there. Their parents were staying at their grandmothers house, which was a relief as neither wanted to spend the evening listening to discussions about how to share out their grandmother's belongings. Alex suggested they all go to the pub for dinner and told Maggie she would also get to meet his girlfriend Amy.

The boys had grown into really decent young men and she was extremely proud of them. She had waited until they left senior school before writing to tell them the truth about why she had spent so much time with their grandmother in Ullapool and about her baby son George. Maggie didn't want them to think she abandoned them, but Alex said they began to suspect something major had occurred, as their parents never mentioned her again after she left for Ullapool.

The boys headed off to the cemetery and Maggie went back into the church to light a candle for her grandmother and one for her son, praying that Jess was with her husband again and that George was a content and happy little boy. She often wondered if he liked school, if he was clever like his mum and uncles and if he had brothers and sisters to talk to and have fun with. When she had children in her care who were the same age as George, she would have long chats with them about what they were learning in school, their favourite books and toys and wondered if her son had similar likes.

Maggie and her brothers had a brilliant evening and Maggie took to Amy right away, delighted her brother had met such a lovely girl! They were obviously very happy together and as they left the pub, Alex whispered to Maggie that he was going to ask Amy to marry him very soon! Maggie flung her arms around him and wished him all the happiness in the world!

They headed back to the guest house and all gathered in Maggie's room where they chatted into the small hours, bringing each other up to date on so many things they had missed during the last few years. It was nearly 3am when they all hugged each other and said goodnight, arranging to meet downstairs for breakfast at 8am the following morning.

They lingered over breakfast longer than they should have as they all had a long journey ahead of them. They said goodbye in the car park, the boys promising they would visit now Maggie no longer shared a flat and rented her own closer to the hospital and she was looking forward to seeing them regularly again.

During her time in Aberdeen Maggie met and became great friends with a colleague Stuart MacIntyre, also a paediatrician, and gradually they became a couple. It wasn't long before Stuart proposed and Maggie couldn't have been happier! Stuart had restored her faith in men as, after Simon, it had taken a very long time before she even gave a member of the opposite sex the time of day! Stuart was a few years older than her and very easy going; gentle; kind; humorous and brilliant with the children in the ward, often staying after his shift to play games, which helped them relax and trust him. Maggie knew she had fallen head over heels when her heart started racing the second she set eyes on him and when she asked herself why she was fighting the attraction, she couldn't come up with an answer!

They didn't want a long engagement, choosing to marry quickly and move into the one flat so they could see more of each other outside of work. They had a simple but lovely wedding day, married at the church manse and Alex gave Maggie away. Charlie, Amy, Stuart's sister Katie and her husband Fraser were present as witnesses and after the ceremony they all went to a restaurant in the city for a meal and a few drinks. It really was a lovely day! That afternoon Alex and Amy invited everyone to their wedding in four months time, Alex completely understanding Maggie could not be there because of their parents and promised to send her some photographs.

A year after her brother and Amy got married they had a baby girl and named her Rachel. They did not invite Alex's parents to the christening as by that time Alex had also stopped talking to them after his father made an unforgivable, derogatory comment about Amy's family at their wedding. Maggie and Stuart were delighted when asked to be godparents to baby Rachel and they enjoyed a family day together with a small celebration at Alex's home in Aberdeen. Maggie loved being part of her brother's lives again and they regularly got together. She had been so honoured to be Rachel's godparent and at the church service felt very emotional, wishing she had been able to christen her baby son.

It wasn't long after they had a family get together for Rachel's third birthday when Charlie phoned Maggie and told her the devastating news that Alex, Amy and Rachel had been involved in a road accident and both their brother and his wife had been killed outright. By some kind of miracle, Rachel had been rescued from the car without a scratch as she had slipped out of her mother's arms and got wedged behind the passenger seat which saved her from injury. Alex and Amy left instructions that Maggie was to raise any children they might have should such a situation ever arise, so Maggie and Stuart suddenly found themselves parents to a three year old...

CHAPTER 37

Lucy and Patrick could not have loved Christina more! All the family adored her and she had the best childhood they could possibly give her. She was a very loving little girl, full of fun and very popular at school. She had two very special friends and the little trio were always together, very rarely did you see one out and about without the other two!

As she grew older she proved to be very clever at school and, at the age of twelve, set her mind on becoming a nurse. Lucy thought she would change her mind as she grew older, but she did indeed choose a career in nursing.

Both Lucy and Patrick were very proud of her, she had brought them immense joy and they never forgot how fortunate their were to become Christina's parents at the cost of her birth mother's misfortune.

They decided very soon after she came to live with them that one of her bedtime stories would be about a little girl who's mummy became too sick to look after her and so she asked a new mummy and daddy to take care of her. So Christina grew up knowing what happened to her when she was young and accepted it without question, as she was very happy and content.

When Christina was in her first year of nursing, Patrick and Lucy had a chat with her to explain the details of her adoption. Lucy had written everything in a small notebook at the time, including what the social worker had told them with regard to her mother, and she gave the notebook to Christina. Patrick told her if at anytime she wanted to try and find out what happened to her birth mother, they would support her one hundred per cent and do anything they could to help her.

"Mum, dad, you know I love you both to bits and maybe I will want to find out more at some time in the future but I am very happy with my life and I need to concentrate on my nursing – I have exams coming up soon and that's what I need to focus on. If ever I do decide to look into my adoption, I will come and talk to you first. I am so lucky to have you both!" she said throwing her arms around her dad, kissing him, then doing the same to her mum.

Lucy and Patricks' pride in their daughter grew even more as Christina worked hard throughout her nursing training, passing all her exams with flying colours! However, although they hoped she would find a nursing post close to home, Christina was offered and accepted a nursing post at an Edinburgh hospital, which was over a hundred miles away.

Christina had a hard time deciding what to take with her when the time came to leave home and would have taken everything she possessed had there been enough room in the car! In the end she managed to take enough of her favourite things to help make her new flat feel homely. Lucy baked cakes, made a hearty stew to give Christina something decent to eat for the first couple of days and also made up a box full of essentials for the food cupboard. She bought a beautiful patchwork quilt, for her daughter's bed, and some lovely thick towels as a moving in present.

The car was packed solid as they set off early in the morning and by lunchtime the car was unpacked and Lucy had laid out a tasty lunch of sandwiches, fruit, cheese and biscuits along with a large pot of tea. After they helped clean the flat and made it as comfortable as possible, Lucy and Patrick had to say their goodbyes to their 'little' girl. There were tears all round, but they were all happy she was fulfilling her dream!

Christina settled in quickly at work, got used to her new surroundings very quickly and within a couple of months had made quite a few friends. She was working in the Oncology Unit and at times it could be very busy, but always rewarding and there wasn't a day when she didn't feel she was making a difference to someone's life. Time passed quickly and she loved her job, although when a patient lost their fight against cancer it could be very sad. She felt that in an environment where people with cancer were battling to live, every moment was precious and it was uppermost in her mind at all times when looking after her patients.

Months later Christina was nursing such a patient who was very ill and sadly losing her battle with the disease. On a night shift her patient Maisie was very close to the end of her life and Christina took every chance throughout the night to sit at her bedside. As she held her hand, Maisie woke up and began to talk about things that happened in her life. She told Christina she'd had a good life but did have one regret, she didn't know what happened to her baby boy. Christina asked her was she meant and Maisie explained when she was sixteen, she was made to give her illegitimate baby away. She said it hung over her like a black cloud all her life and she had never been completely happy because of it. Maisie died a few hours later just as the sun began to rise at the start of a new day.

Weeks later, Christina still felt saddened by Maisie's story and found herself frequently thinking about her own adoption, wondering if her birth mother felt the same as Maisie had. Mum and dad told her she was adopted because her birth mother had a very bad accident. Did her mother survive? Was she still alive and living with the same black cloud hanging over her? Christina tried to put herself in her mother's position, how would she feel if she had an accident and had to give up her three year old daughter?

The next time her mum and dad came down to visit, she told them Maisie's story and how it had been praying on her mind for weeks.

"Maisie said there wasn't a day when she didn't think about her son, wondering if he was happy, even wondering if he was still alive? It's made me wonder about my birth mother. What if she has had a black cloud hanging over her every day since she gave me up for adoption? I wouldn't want her to suffer the same sadness, especially as she had no option due to an accident. I am so sorry, I really don't want you both to be hurt, but I have to find out if she is okay and set her mind to rest by explaining about both of you and how much you have loved me and given me the best upbringing. Please don't feel betrayed or think anything has changed, it hasn't and never will as you are my mum and dad, but if my birth mother is still alive, I would just like to reassure her that I'm okay."

Both Lucy and Patrick hugged their daughter, feeling immensely proud at how caring she was and agreed that it was the right thing to do, offering to help in any way they could.

Two weeks later Christina sat in an office at the local social work department talking to a social worker named Ruth, who began with a general chat about why she wanted to begin searching for her mother. Ruth listened as Christina explained what she knew about her adoption and was satisfied that careful thought had gone into the decision to begin a search. Christina provided Ruth with all the paperwork her mum had given her regarding the adoption, her parent's details and when and where the adoption had taken place. Ruth explained she would carry out a record search of the archives with the information Christina provided, but to be aware in some cases records had been misplaced or destroyed in error over a certain period, which unfortunately included the year of her adoption.

Ruth took copies of all the documents Christina provided and gave the originals back to her saying she would write and let her know the outcome as soon as the search was completed.

As she made her way home, Christina's heart was racing – she had actually done it!

After a long five weeks wondering if Ruth would find her adoption file, Christina arrived home one Friday morning after a busy nightshift to find a letter waiting for her. She quickly ripped it open thinking it would inform her that unfortunately nothing could be found, but she was wrong! Ruth confirmed the search had been successful and asked that she telephone the office to make an appointment to come and discuss her file.

Without even taking her wet coat off, Christina immediately called and made an appointment for the following Wednesday morning at 10am. Then she rang her mum to tell her the news and, bless her, she was so pleased for Christina it made her cry – she was an amazing mum!

CHAPTER 38

Dear Joseph

I wrote this letter, as one day you might have reason to contact me.

I felt I should wait until you were twenty-one before making any attempt to get in touch with Social Services and ask if it was possible for them to give you my details, should you ever try to look into your adoption. They suggested I write a letter, which could be put in your file, and so I find myself wanting to say so much but aware it can't all be said in a letter and some things are better explained in person. However, I feel the need to tell you about why you were adopted, which will allow you to know what happened without having to contact me, should you prefer not to do that.

Your mum Laura and I were soul-mates and loved each other deeply.

We couldn't believe our luck when Laura fell pregnant as we had resigned ourselves to not being able to have a child of our own. Laura was a primary school teacher and adored children so she was glowing with happiness throughout her pregnancy, beyond excited about having our baby!

Unfortunately, Laura took ill as she went into labour and had to be taken to theatre to have a caesarean section. Sadly, during the operation, she suffered a massive stroke and her heart stopped. Although the doctors restarted her heart, it was too late for Laura as after several tests it became clear her brain was not functioning and she died the next day.

Although Laura was not aware, you did meet your mum before she died. On the day you were born, I tucked you under her arm so you could cuddle into her until it was time for you to be taken back to the nursery and did the same again the following day.

You were the spitting image of her and she would have loved you with all her heart and soul. The day you were born was the best day of my life, but the worst, all rolled into one and my world crashed around me – I felt like I was drowning. I did not have anyone close enough to help me look after you but I have to be honest and tell you that when I looked at you, it was like looking at Laura and each time it felt as though I was being stabbed through the heart. I was petrified I wouldn't be able to get past the thought that you were the reason Laura died and at the same time I couldn't bear the thought of you being hurt because of my inability to manage my grief.

I was in pieces, struggling with my feelings and could not see how I was going to carry on. I did what I thought was best for you and put you up for adoption in the hope that you would have loving parents and not be subjected to the emotional baggage I inevitably carried with me for several years.

Every year on your birthday I visit Laura's grave, apologise to her for giving away our precious son, hope and pray you have been brought up in a good home, were loved and most of all that you have had a happy life. To find out you have been unhappy would destroy me as I have always believed I made the right decision and did what I thought was right for you at the time.

I hope this letter will give you some understanding as to why I made the choices I did. If you ever need anything or have any questions, please get in touch but if you don't, I will understand. You can always contact me through Lloyd & Young Accountants in Edinburgh and if I am not there for any reason, they will pass a message onto me wherever I am and I will get back to you.

You are always in my thoughts and regardless of what you decide to do with this letter, forever will be.

Peter

"Oh what an awful thing to happen Jack!" Mollie wiped the tears away and Jack put his arm around her, hugging her close to him. "It's just so sad," she sobbed.

"Don't get so upset, Moll. It must have been tough and I don't really know what I would do in that situation, but I'm not so sure he did the right thing. Would it not have helped him to keep me? I was a living memory of my mother and surely it would have been better to keep part of her with him through me?"

"Maybe at the time he was so wrapped up in grief that he wasn't thinking straight and he made the decision to give you up too soon. If he had given it a few weeks he might have acted differently. We can never know how he felt, I know how distraught I would be if anything happened to you Jack."

"I read in mum's journal that he would have had a few months to change his mind, as my adoption wasn't official until it went through a court hearing when I was around a year old. Anyway, it doesn't matter, this is upsetting you too much Moll. You are heading upstairs to run yourself a deep bubble bath while I make us a couple of frothy hot chocolates, now go!" Mollie smiled at him through her tears, blew him a kiss and ran upstairs to do as she was told. Jack was so good, he was always spoiling her and it was all the little things that meant the most to her, especially a hot chocolate in the bath as he sat on the rim and happily chatted away to her while she soaked away the day's stresses.

Neither of them mentioned the letter for a few days, but both thought about nothing else. Almost a week had gone by and Mollie couldn't keep silent any longer. It was Saturday morning, they were having bacon rolls out on the patio and they could feel the heat of the sun beating down on them... Mollie loved weekend breakfasts and she absently wondered if Peter and Laura had enjoyed mornings like these before she died. Jack glanced up and knew from the expression on her face that Mollie was deep in thought. "Okay, spill the beans Moll, I can see that you have something on your mind."

Mollie raised one eyebrow and looked over her sunglasses at Jack. "Clever aren't you! I am thinking about something, but I'm not sure you are ready to hear it yet."

"Well, now I know you have something on your mind, you may as well tell me!" he cocked his head to the side, raised his eyebrows and waited.

"Right okay, but this is just a thought and I'm not saying you should do it but maybe think about it." Jack drummed his fingers on the table and waited. "It's about the letter from your father – Peter, I'm not sure what to call him, but I was wondering what you are going to do. Are you going to get in touch with him?"

"I thought it might have something to do with that," he said, slowly nodding his head, "I have been thinking about it quite a bit myself and I'll admit curiosity is getting the better of me. Should I get in touch with him? Is it the right thing to do? Is it disloyal to mum and dad? I know mum gave me her blessing, but it's still a difficult decision to make. I need more time Moll, I need to be sure…"

CHAPTER 39

A s Christina walked into Ruth's office she felt sick with nerves knowing that when she walked back out she would know her mother's name. She sat down and watched as Ruth placed a file on the desk in front of her and then handed Christina a notepad and pen.

"I can let you see your file but I'm not able to give you copies of anything so it might be helpful if you make notes so you can read them later. Right let's see.... Well, first I feel I should warn you that you might find the information I'm about to tell you upsetting, this is not one of the common reasons we see when children are placed with us for adoption." At this point Ruth moved a box of tissues closer to Christina, which looked ominous.

"Your mother is called Marlene Ross and unfortunately she was the victim of a very bad assault at your home not long after you turned three. Her injuries were severe, your mother was in hospital for a few weeks and you were placed in foster care by social services until your mother recovered. However, the doctors were not sure just how severe the damage was to her spine and couldn't say if she would be able to walk again." Ruth glanced across the table at Christina who was busy writing, "Are you okay Christina? Would you like me to stop for a minute?"

"This is so sad and hard to hear, but I'm alright and I'd rather you kept going."

"Okay, but if you want me to stop, just say. When it became clear it could be a year or more before Marlene would be able to walk again, if at all, she contacted social services and explained the outlook was very poor for her and she didn't want you to miss out on a normal, happy childhood. She was worried about the length of time she would be in hospital and meantime you would be in foster care.

She wanted you to have a stable and loving home, therefore when the doctors confirmed she had permanent spinal damage, saying she might manage to walk with the aid of sticks but certainly walk with some degree of difficulty, she asked social services to arrange for you to be adopted." Ruth looked up at Christina, "Are you sure you are okay - will I stop for a minute?"

Christina helped herself to a couple of tissues, "It's just such a sad thing to happen. I can't imagine being in that position, she must have been heartbroken!"

"Your mother was a very brave woman by the sounds of it. She put your welfare and future first, regardless of how distraught she must have felt."

"Will I carry on?" Ruth asked and Christina nodded.

"Does it say anything about my mother? Do you know what happened to her?"

"There are notes of a follow-up meeting after your adoption had been finalised and there is a comment here saying your mother was still having treatment in hospital a year after the accident. It seems even at that stage her condition had only just started to improve very slightly, although her doctors were still hopeful she would continue to make further progress."

Christina felt relieved as at least she didn't die of her injuries and hopefully continued to get better. However, she doubted Marlene would have recovered fully – she had been unable to walk for a very long time, maybe she never walked again?

Ruth stood up, "I am going to make us some tea and meantime you can catch up on any notes you want to make, you can read through the file until I come back."

Christina wrote down as much as possible, picking out all the important details so she could go over them again later. When Ruth came back she poured their tea and pushed a small plate of biscuits towards Christina. "Have a couple with your tea, helps with the stress!" she said winking at Christina who managed a smile and did as suggested.

"Are there any contact addresses in the file?" asked Christina.

"It does note the address where you were staying when the accident happened, but I very much doubt your mother would have gone back there as it says the flat was on the first floor. The address on the adoption papers is care of the hospital and there is also a contact number for a doctor there. I doubt either of these would help you in any way but you could always try." Ruth wrote down the hospital details and the doctor's number and handed Christina the note. "The number may well not be in use any longer and I doubt the hospital will tell you anything due to patient confidentiality. Have you applied for a copy of your birth certificate yet? I trust it's only an adoption birth certificate that you have?"

"I only have the one from the Adoption Register."

"Well if you supply the registrar office with the certificate number, they match it to your original birth certificate, which will of course contain your mothers address at the time of your birth. Although there's no father mentioned anywhere in your file, your mother may have named him on the birth certificate, it's quite common."

They chatted for a little while longer discussing what Christina should do now and then she thanked Ruth for all her help and made her way out of the building. As she headed home, she tried to imagine what it would feel like to be in her mother's position, seriously injured with nobody to take care of her young child - she must have been so distressed!

When she arrived home, Christina made a coffee and went over the notes she made, rewriting them at the back of her journal. Then she called her mum and spent over half an hour relaying all the information she learned from Ruth.

Lucy sat in her kitchen, listening as her daughter told her the details and although she had always known Christina's mother had a bad accident, she was horrified at what the poor woman had gone through. When Patrick arrived home that evening, Lucy was visibly upset as she repeated everything Christina told her.

"It's just so awful Patrick, the poor woman was attacked so brutally in her own home, the doctors didn't think she would ever walk again. She was still in hospital a year after Christina came to us! God only knows how she coped with it all and bless her for being such a loving mother and giving Christina to us so we could give her a happy and loving home, she is a very brave lady!"

Christina stared at her birth certificate and was surprised to see her father was called Johnathan Mason and he was a solicitor at Mason and Cook, Glasgow. Her mother, she already knew as Marlene Ross, her occupation was a secretary and her home address was in Stirling. Christina looked in the telephone directory and the solicitors were still listed in Glasgow. She spent the evening going over all the information she had, trying to decide what her next step should be. She could try to get information from the hospital but as Ruth said, they probably wouldn't give out any information without Marlene's consent. It would be really difficult to trace her mother after so many years – she wouldn't even know where to begin, although she could try the address in Stirling, but on the adoption records Marlene gave her address as the hospital?

In the end, she decided as the solicitors were still in existence in Glasgow, and her father was a Mason, it should be relatively easy to find out where he was. She looked up the telephone directory again and wrote down the number for Mason and Cook, took a deep breath and rang the number. She told the receptionist a friend had recommended Mr Johnathan Mason to her and could she make an appointment on either Wednesday or Thursday the following week. The receptionist asked her to hold and Christina wondered if Johnathan Mason still worked there.

"My apologies for your wait, Mr Mason's diary was in another office. Now let's see, I have two appointments available on Wednesday, one at 2pm and the other 3pm."

"The 2 o'clock appointment will suit me better."

"Can I take your name please?"

"Christina Edwards."

"That's the appointment booked for you Ms Edwards and we look forward to seeing you on Wednesday at 2pm, Goodbye."

Christina wondered if Johnathan Mason was still in touch with her mother or, if not, did he know her whereabouts. She wondered if he had been around at the time of the accident but she didn't think it likely, as surely he would have taken care of her, or at least paid for someone to look after her – he was a solicitor and therefore she doubted money was an issue. Hopefully, Johnathan Mason would answer her questions, or at least some of them, when she met with him on Wednesday.

As she sat in the waiting room at Mason and Cook, Christina could feel her stomach churning over and over again. She hardly slept a wink the night before as she went through possible scenarios in her head and although she walked into the solicitors' office on a mission, the nerves were now getting the better of her. The receptionist looked up from her typewriter, "Mr Mason will see you now Ms Edwards, it's the second door on the right."

Christina took a deep breath, opened the door and studied the man who was sitting at the desk before he looked up and gestured for her to take a seat opposite him.

"Now Miss....." he checked her surname on his sheet of paper, "Edwards, what can I do for you?"

Christina leant forward and placed a copy of her birth certificate on his desk. He picked it up and when he realised what he was reading his face drained of colour.

"What the hell is this and who are you?" he raged.

"I am Christina Ross and that is my birth certificate you are reading which, as you can see, states I am your daughter!"

At first Johnathan felt like a rabbit caught in headlights, but he quickly regained his composure.

"Marlene Ross sent you here?"

"No, she had to give me up for adoption when I was very young so I don't remember her. I came to you first as you were easier to trace, the name of the solicitors is on the certificate. Do you know where Marlene is?" she watched Johnathan closely and she could see he was very uncomfortable.

"No I don't know where she is," he snapped. "I haven't seen her for twenty years or so."

"How did you know her? Were you a couple?"

"No we were not. She was my secretary and she had a thing for me. Let's just say we got closer than we should have."

Christina could see Johnathan was becoming very agitated, his voice betraying his anger. "Did you know about me? Were you together when I was born?"

"I've told you we were never together! Marlene tried to latch onto me, using all means of emotional blackmail, but I couldn't even be sure it was me who got her pregnant. For all I know, she could have slept with the whole office!"

Christina had a gut feeling he was lying about Marlene and to her surprise she wanted to stand up for her mother.

"I only have your word for that. Maybe it was different, maybe it was you who had a relationship with Marlene and when she got pregnant you decided not to stand by her?"

Johnathan glared at Christina, "Look, I don't know why Marlene decided to put my name of the birth certificate – probably after money and no doubt that's what you're here for! How do I know she hasn't put you up to this, or has she? I'm a happily married man and if you know what's good for you, you will keep your mouth shut and get the hell out of my office!" he leaned towards her menacingly, "I am warning you, I will not allow you to make accusations which you can't prove and if you set foot in this building again, I will make sure you'll wish you had never set eyes on me!" he snarled as he thumped his fist down on his desk.

Christina stood up, picked up her birth certificate and backed away from the desk. "Believe me, I have no wish to set eyes on you ever again and I really hope you are not my father as I would not want to have even one single gene of you in me!" Shaking, Christina turned on her heel, threw open his office door, walked calmly through the reception and out the main door.

Once she was safely out of the office she couldn't hold back the tears any longer and ran down the stairs sobbing uncontrollably. As she reached the entrance hall, she ran full pelt into a man on his way into the building and she hit him with such force, she would have fallen over if he hadn't quickly reached out to steady her.

"Whoa young lady, you're going to do yourself some damage if you can't see where you are going!"

"I'm very sorry," sobbed Christina and tried to move on.

"Just a minute, I can't let you leave here in such a state, lord knows what will happen to you. How about you come back up to the office and we can get you a cup of tea?"

"No! I'm not going anywhere near him again!"

"Him?"

"Johnathan Mason."

"Well, I am in need of a hot drink myself and there's a little café next door. How about you let me buy you a cup of tea and let an old man make sure you are alright before you get on your way?"

Christina only hesitated for a second or two before agreeing to the man's offer. He was clearly a gentleman and had a grandfather-like manner, which instantly made her feel at ease. She nodded and accepted his invitation, she needed to fix her face and calm her nerves after the confrontation with Johnathan Mason.

Alex sat at the window table in the small café and waited for the young girl to return from the ladies room where he guessed she was trying to disguise her tear-stained face.

Christina stared at her reflection after doing her best to hide her red eyes. Accepting the invitation to come to the café and have tea with a complete stranger was totally uncharacteristic and she intended to quickly drink her tea and leave as soon as possible. Today had been a huge mistake and her father's reaction was not one of the scenarios she had anticipated.

Alex stood up and pulled a chair out for Christina to sit down and smiled, "Feeling a bit better now?"

"Yes thank you. I'm very sorry for running into you like that, you really don't need to stay with me, I'm fine now," she smiled.

"Well if it's alright with you, I will join you for tea, it will save my secretary making me one and I will get some brownie points for that!"

Christina smiled at the man who had come to her rescue. He had a very likeable manner and a wicked twinkle in his eye! The waitress approached their table and Alex decided he would have a white coffee, ordered a pot of tea for Christina and a selection of homemade biscuits.

"Well now, I suppose I better introduce myself as I have invited you to afternoon tea," he smiled. "I am Alex," and he held out his hand to shake hers.

Christina shook his hand and smiled, "Christina."

"Now then, would it be too rude or intrusive if I asked what happened to upset you so much?" Alex was not at all happy to see a client leave his office in such a state and he wanted to get to the bottom of why Christina was so upset. He already had several discussions with Johnathan regarding his manner towards clients and by the look of it this would be another to add to the list.

"Oh I don't want to bother you with the details, it's a long story and it wouldn't be of any interest."

"Try me, I am a really good listener, it's my job and you might feel better if you get it off your chest."

CHAPTER 40

Olivia was having dialysis on the day Angela and Bryan arrived to be evaluated as potential kidney donors. They were having blood and urine tests; thorough physical exams; medical history reviews; chest x-rays and an ECG along with anything else the medical team thought necessary. They had both already passed initial compatibility tests in Edinburgh within the last month, but Olivia's condition had been slowly deteriorating and the need for a transplant was now urgent.

The team at the hospital wanted to run more tests and go ahead with the transplant as soon as possible and although initially both Bryan and Angela were acceptable donors, the team wanted the strongest match to give Olivia the best possible chance.

Jean and Harry travelled south to be with Olivia and were staying close by at the same bed and breakfast as Matt. They were trying to be strong for both Matt and Olivia but were extremely worried for their daughter and were anxiously awaiting the donor test results.

Matt was sitting by Olivia's bedside, holding her hand as she slept, when her doctor tapped lightly on the door and came in to her room.

He spoke very quietly so as not to disturb Olivia. "Hello there Matt, I just popped in to let you know we have completed most of the test results on Olivia's donors, all we are waiting for now are the scan results, which we should have later this afternoon. I'm afraid I'm not at all pleased with Olivia's test results today and the team held a meeting this morning to discuss our next move – we have scheduled the transplant surgery for tomorrow morning. We will do last minute blood and urine tests on the donor first thing tomorrow and if everything is still satisfactory we will go ahead as scheduled."

"Who is the donor? Bryan or Dr Johnson?"

"Mr Carson has the best overall results, but to be honest they are both acceptable as donors which is a brilliant result! Mr Carson has been very keen to be the donor all along and Dr Johnson is more than happy not to win on this occasion!" he winked at Matt. "I will let you pass on the good news to your wife - tomorrow will be a big day for you both!" He patted him on the shoulder and quietly left the room letting Olivia sleep.

Matt watched as his darling wife slept and silently prayed tomorrow would go to plan as he knew she couldn't go on for much longer - he just couldn't bear to think of life without her.

Harry and Jean arrived to visit Olivia just as she started to waken and Matt relayed the conversation he had with the doctor. There were tears all round, excited tears, frightened tears and tears of relief! Their precious girl was being given a chance to live! Olivia asked Matt to go and see Bryan to ask if he would come and see her that evening. As Harry and Jean were there, he said he would leave her mum and dad to keep her company, have a chat with Bryan, get the coffees and a nice treat for them all.

Matt made his way down to the cafeteria to get a coffee and went for a wander in the grounds of the hospital to get some fresh air and grab a few minutes on his own before going to see Bryan. He had been praying so hard for a transplant and now it was so close he was terrified! He had to hide his worry, be positive and strong for Ollie as earlier that morning she told him she was petrified something would go wrong during the surgery and she wouldn't wake up again.

As Matt walked back towards the hospital entrance he saw Angela heading out of the building with her overnight bag.

"Angela!" She looked up and walked towards Matt. "Where are you going?"

"Bryan is going to be the donor so I can get back to work now. You will let me know how everything goes tomorrow?"

"Of course, but I thought you might have stayed too."

"I would be hanging about doing nothing when I have so much work to catch up on. You have my number?"

"Yes, I will ring you, hopefully with good news."

"I'm sure everything will go well," and with that she headed off towards the car park.

Matt was dumbfounded! He thought after everything that happened after Olivia's birth, Angela would have at least stayed until after the surgery and show some support, but no! She was a very strange woman and Matt was sure her heart was made of stone!

The next morning Matt was sitting with Olivia, constantly reassuring her and trying to keep her calm. She was very nervous and would shortly be having a pre-med which would make her both relaxed and sleepy. When they heard a tap on the door, they thought it would be the nurse but it was the doctor.

"I'm afraid we have to delay your operation for a few hours Olivia as one of Mr Carson's tests has thrown up a problem. His urine test is showing signs of infection and we cannot transplant a kidney which could be carrying infection."

Olivia burst into tears and Matt was pretty close himself. "You said the operation is only postponed for a few hours?"

The doctor gave Matt's shoulder a reassuring squeeze, "I have to be honest with you, Dr Johnson was very relieved Mr Carson was the stronger donor and told me she had second thoughts about having the surgery, she then left the hospital and headed back home. I haven't been able to speak to her yet but I have left a message at the surgery for her to phone me urgently and they assured me they would also keep trying to get in touch with her, so I'm hoping she will call me back soon.

I'm sure when she hears what's happened with Mr Carson she will not let you down Olivia. I'm also hoping she has not yet had anything to eat so we can still operate today and as soon as I've spoken to Dr Johnson I will let you know," he left the room hoping she wasn't avoiding calling him – she couldn't get out of the hospital quick enough yesterday! Olivia desperately needed the transplant to go ahead today.

After the doctor left, Matt climbed onto the bed and held his wife until she eventually fell asleep exhausted. He had seen a marked deterioration in her over the past few days and she was now very weak and sleeping more than ever. He closed his eyes and he prayed, begged and pleaded for his beautiful, gentle Ollie to be saved. He lay there, tenderly holding Olivia, tears slowly rolling down his cheeks…..

CHAPTER 41

Rachel was coming home from University in the October break to celebrate her twentieth birthday and Maggie was in usual organisational mode. It was the same every time Rachel came home for the holidays and Stuart just nodded and agreed with Maggie, occasionally making the required comment to prove he was listening to her! This time he was actually paying more attention than usual as Maggie was organising a party, which required him to string up lantern lights in the garden, fairy lights in the conservatory and he was in charge of buying and serving drinks.

Of course Maggie would write out a shopping list for the drinks and a 'to do' list for all his other tasks, so he didn't really need to remember anything himself. He loved that she was so organised as it made life so much easier for him. She always knew his work schedule as well as her own and she had been the same when Rachel went to primary school. She must have been the only child who went through the whole of her school life, never forgetting her gym shoes, painting apron or reading book. She was never late for school and if he or Maggie were delayed at the hospital, Mrs Simmons would be there to meet her as she walked through the school gates.

When Rachel first came to live with them she was only three and Maggie managed to take a few months leave of absence from the hospital until the little girl settled in to her new home. Maggie needed her to feel happy and secure before leaving her with a babysitter, and after a great deal of discussion, they decided to employ a live in housekeeper who could also step in when necessary to take care of Rachel. After searching for three months, Maggie finally found Mrs Simmons who was a retired housekeeper. Although she was 'retired' she was only in her mid-fifties and had worked for the same family for twenty years, only retiring once the three children were in their teens and were quite capable of looking after themselves.

She was looking forward to having more time to spend with her husband, but he sadly died only a few months after her retirement, so when she saw Maggie's advert, she knew it was meant for her

.

Stuart had just finished hanging the lanterns in the garden when the phone rang and he hurried inside to answer it. "Hello."

"Hi dad, I was just about to hang up, thought you might have been called into the hospital. Is mum around?"

"No Rach, she popped over to see Mrs Simmons, bit of a problem with her foot, you know what mum's like! Do you need to talk to her or will I do?"

"Of course you will! The thing is if I tell you, mum will make you repeat it word for word so I'll let you decide, I can ring again later and tell her direct?"

"Mmm, you're right, you're best to ring her back and talk to her yourself, cut out the middle man!" he laughed. "Anyway how's things? We are looking forward to seeing you, the house is so quiet - I don't think I'll ever get used to it!"

"Oh dad, don't say that, you'll make me homesick! I miss you too you know and I can't wait to come home. I have loads to tell you and there is someone I want you to meet. Oh I shouldn't have said that! You see that's what I was calling about. You know I've been dating Mike for a few months, well I was wondering if I could take him home to meet you and mum? I know you might feel it's a bit soon, it's just as it's my birthday…"

"Of course you can darling, you know any friend of yours is welcome in our home! There's no way I'm telling mum this though," Stuart said laughing, "I will just say you rang and will call back later, is that okay with you?"

Rachel laughed too, "Yes dad, it will be our little secret! Tell mum I will phone back at four. Do you think she will be okay about me taking Mike home, she hasn't organised anything special has she?"

"No Rach, as far as I know it's just a birthday tea, the usual spread mum lays out on birthdays and of course she'll not mind, although I hope Mike doesn't mind answering questions!" They both laughed, chatted for a few minutes longer about Rachel's latest assignment, then said their goodbyes. Stuart didn't like telling lies to Rachel, but it was only a little white one and if he let the cat out of the bag about the party, Maggie would throttle him! He checked his to do list and headed out to the conservatory to hang the fairy lights before Maggie got home.

Maggie spent longer than planned with Mrs Simmons and had only just come through the door when the phone started ringing. Stuart was on a ladder in the conservatory and tapped on the glass, pointing at the phone and mouthing 'Rachel'. Maggie nodded and answered the phone.

"Hi mum, did dad tell you I called earlier?"

"No love, I've only just walked through the door and dad is out in the conservatory reading the paper," Maggie had almost said hanging up the fairy lights!

"I'm so excited about coming home, I can't wait to see you!"

"Same here darling, we miss you so much, the house is so empty without you!"

"That's what dad said mum, but I'll be home soon and I can tell you all my news then. I was calling to ask you if it was okay for Mike to come home with me for the holidays as he would like to spend time with me on my birthday?"

"Of course it is love, he will be more than welcome!"

"Thanks mum, that's brilliant! I've told him all about you and dad and can't wait to show him where I was brought up. We are going to drive up on Thursday after Mike finishes his lectures so we should be there in plenty time to have dinner at seven if that's okay with you? Oh and can we have macaroni at some point over the weekend mum?"

Maggie laughed! Rachel would have macaroni every night if she could - it had always been her favourite as she grew up. "I'll see what I can do! Now mind and be careful on the road, don't hurry to get here, dinner can always be a bit later. Just you get here safely!"

"Yes mum!" Rachel sighed laughing. "Okay mum I've got to go but I'll see you Thursday night, love you!"

"Okay darling, I'm counting the days, love you too sweetheart, bye!"

Maggie headed towards the conservatory and Stuart busied himself because he knew what was coming. "Hello dear, how did you get on with Mrs Simmons?"

"She's okay, her foot is healing well and she is adamant she will be at Rachel's party next weekend," she smiled.

"Did Rachel say anything to you about Mike coming home with her next weekend?" She raised an eyebrow and looked at him suspiciously.

Stuart gave his full attention to tapping a tack into the door facing to secure the lights cable. "No, first I've heard of it!"

"Well it seems Mike would like to be with Rachel on her birthday, so we have another guest for a few days. You know he is quite a few years older than her, he's a lecturer at a college."

"Yes, you mentioned it to me before. Where did she meet him?"

"At a music concert, seems she was getting squashed and he lifted her up onto his shoulders and walked her out of the crowd."

"Does the age difference bother you? You nabbed yourself a good looking old man yourself you know!" he winked at her and they both laughed.

"No darling, besides you're a young looking sixty!"

"Not for another eight months Mrs M! And while we are on the subject, remember whatever you cook up for my sixtieth will be repeated for your fiftieth!" Maggie just raised her eyebrows and smiled.

"I suppose age is not a problem, at least someone a bit more mature shouldn't muck her about."

Stuart shook his head - the poor man was in for a grilling!

It was just after six the following Thursday when the door burst open, Rachel shouting "I'm home!" at the top of her voice. Stuart welcomed her with a huge bear hug, shook Mike's hand and welcomed him to their home.

"Where's mum?" asked Rachel.

"She's not long in from work so she's just getting changed sweetheart. She'll be down in a minute. Now come on through and let's get some drinks. Now then Mike, what would you like, a beer? lager?"

"A lager would be great thanks. Rachel was right, you have a beautiful home here!"

"It was an old run down farmhouse when we bought it, but it's been an enjoyable labour of love, although the builders helped here and there!" he smiled, "I can't take any credit for that part, although I dabble here and there and am handy with a paintbrush! You'll get a better look at it tomorrow in daylight and when you see the view we have, you will realise why we bought it!"

Stuart's first impressions of Mike were good, he seemed a decent guy and it was clear he and Rachel were besotted with each other! It was hard to say what age he was, maybe late twenties, but the age difference certainly wasn't apparent. He only hoped Maggie would go easy on him over dinner and not bombard him with questions. They were sitting in front of a nice roaring fire, enjoying their drinks', when Maggie came down to join them. Rachel jumped up to hug her and as Mike had his back to her, he got up to introduce himself. When he turned to face her, Maggie gasped, quickly turning it into a cough as a cover!

"Mum this is Mike, Mike this is mum," Rachel grinned at both of them.

Mike held out his hand, "I'm pleased to meet you Mrs MacIntyre."

Maggie looked into the emerald green eyes, shook his hand and smiled, "Pleased to meet you Mike, just call me Maggie."

Stuart handed Maggie a glass of wine and she took two large mouthfuls before putting the glass down on the table. "Had a hard day love?" Stuart laughed, "Want a top up?"

I was just a bit thirsty! Don't be so cheeky," she smiled. "I'm just going to check on dinner, be with you in a couple of minutes." Maggie took refuge in the kitchen and desperately tried to compose herself - she must be wrong but it was one hell of a coincidence if she was right!

Her composure regained, she joined them by the fire and listened as Rachel chatted away, bringing them up to date with the university gossip.

Dinner went well, the conversation covering university life, local gossip and the arrangements for the children's ward Christmas party at the hospital where Stuart was to be Father Christmas again this year. They all got on very well and Mike proved to be very likeable, intelligent and very funny, having them all in fits of laughter at some of the amusing things his students did.

They had their dessert in front of the fire with a coffee, Stuart and Mike chatting away about fishing, Maggie and Rachel discussing what style of dress Maggie was thinking of wearing to the Hospital Christmas Dance.

Everyone helped to clear up the dining room and kitchen and then Maggie said her goodnights as her long day at work had her beaten. Stuart made everyone a hot chocolate before following her. He walked into the bedroom where Maggie was propped up in bed and he handed her the hot drink. "Thanks love," she smiled up at him, but he knew her well and knew something was up.

"Ok Maggs, spit it out love?"

Maggie sipped her hot chocolate. "I'm just tired love."

"Is it Mike? His age? Or don't you like him?"

"None of those, in fact I think he's a really nice man and there's no doubt they are in love."

"So what's bothering you, because I know you well and I know there's something?"

"You are probably going to think I'm losing the plot Stu, but look at this photograph and think about Mike's face, do you see anything?" she took a photograph out of her bedside drawer and handed it to him watching his face closely and she saw it, the flicker of recognition!

"No Maggs, it can't possibly be him although he does have a look of you in this photo. What age were you in this one?"

"It was taken in my twenties, twenty four or five I think?"

"I reckon Mike must be late twenties from picking up on things we talked about tonight. There's no doubt you both have the rare green eyes, I have never met anyone with such vivid green eyes as you......until now!"

"It's also the hair Stu, Simon had Copper coloured hair and Mike's is exactly the same colour. When he turned to face me tonight I could have been looking at Simon!

When they finally got together, Maggie told Stuart about her teenage pregnancy and how she was forced to give her son away. There had been a couple of occasions when Maggie saw someone who had a look of her, but once close up she couldn't be sure. It had been years since it had happened, but this time the likeness was plain to see, regardless of whether he was George or not.

"Okay Maggs, but let's just take it slowly and let Mike tell us about his life in his own time. Even If we do think there is a strong possibility he could be George, you know we can never say anything, don't you?"

"Yes Stu, I know, it's not as bad as it could be, the worst outcome is that Mike and Rach are cousins!"

CHAPTER 42

Peter Cameron stared out the window of his office, trying hard to keep his emotions in check. He looked down at the card in his hand and read it again, for the hundredth time. He had always wondered what this day would feel like, but never in all the years, did he imagine the flood of emotion it would evoke!

When he arrived at the office that morning, his mail was sitting in a neat pile on his desk as usual and when he saw the handwritten envelope he thought it was yet another invitation to some party or other. He picked up the letter opener and sliced open the envelope to find a hand-painted card adorned with bright red poppies. He opened it to find out what occasion he was invited to attend and as he read, he was aware the only thing he could hear was his thumping heartbeat. He couldn't take his eyes off the page, reading the words over and over until finally they began to sink in.

Dear Peter

I have been sitting here, pen in hand, for almost an hour trying to decide how to begin this letter and have come to the conclusion there is no right or wrong way, no guide on what or what not to say!

My name is Jack Andrews but you will know me better by the name you gave me at birth, Joseph and as you will now realise, I have recently been given access to my adoption file and the letter you wrote five years ago.

I must stress, before going any further, although I have known of my adoption since I was a young child, I have never been curious about my birth parents, as I had the best mum and dad anyone could wish for. They were loving; supportive; good; decent people and I could not have been given a home with a more deserving couple.

However, last year I sadly lost both my parents as the result of a car accident. It was only when I was sorting through their possessions that I found a journal my mother kept, detailing my adoption and giving me her blessing to look for my birth parents, should I ever feel the need.

I have been in possession of your letter for a few weeks, unsure whether or not to contact you for reasons I'm sure you can imagine, however the reason for my adoption was not what I had imagined and I'm sure it was a *very distressing and difficult situation to find yourself in.*

I am spending next weekend in Edinburgh with my fiancé Mollie and as you said yourself, there is only so much you can put in a letter, so we thought you might like to join us for dinner. I have made a reservation at Martone, an Italian restaurant, on Saturday at 8pm for four people, as I wasn't sure if you had remarried or have a partner, but should you decide for reasons of your own, that you no longer wish to meet me, I will understand.

Until Saturday, Best wishes
Jack

Peter sat down and stared at the photo of Laura on his desk.

It had taken years to come to terms with losing his wife and son and he tried burying himself in work, but felt tortured by his actions, guilt and regret festering inside him.

He had to face Jack and tell him he had long since realised what he did was wrong and Laura would never have forgiven him. He could never change what happened and had no right to ask for his son's forgiveness, but he could apologise to him in person in the hope Laura would finally rest peacefully...

CHAPTER 43

Christina looked at Alex and decided to confide in this kind man who had come to her rescue. She told him about her childhood including what happened to her mother. She explained how social services had recently given her access to her adoption records and she now knew the circumstances surrounding her adoption. Then last week she received a copy of her original birth certificate, which she hoped would help her find her mother.

"Wow, that's quite a life story and you must only be in your teens!"

Christina had to grin, "I know it sounds like a drama you would see on the television, but it's all true! I've just turned twenty and the drama isn't finished yet as I have to find my mother."

"I'm a bit confused. How does Johnathan Mason fit into your story? Were you hoping he could help in some way to find your mother?"

"I don't know if I should say, I don't even know you and I've just be warned to back off."

"By whom?"

"Johnathan Mason."

Alex sighed and shook his head. "Christina, let me tell you something, Johnathan has been hauled over the coals on several occasions for his attitude to clients. He has been pushing his luck for years now and believe me there is nothing you could say about him that could shock me. I would really appreciate it if you could confide in me because if Johnathan won't help you, I will and I will take care of him in my own good time."

"You work with Johnathan?"

"I am his boss Christina."

"Oh no, I wouldn't have said anything if I had known that!"

"I'm glad you did my dear, I am tired of apologising to clients on his behalf and smoothing things over to keep their business, but that's my problem, let's get back to why you went to see Johnathan?"

Christina kept quiet for a few seconds, at first thinking she should say nothing and leave. However, without help she doubted she would be able to find her mother and maybe Alex could suggest how she should go about tracing her.

"Well I will tell you, but it's only because I don't know what to do next." She reached into her bag and brought out the copy of her birth certificate, looked at it herself, then looked at Alex.

"This is the copy of my birth certificate and once you read it, I think you will know why I went to see Johnathan Mason." She handed over the certificate to Alex and watched as he read it. The look on his face was not what she expected and she wasn't quite sure what to think. If she didn't know better, she would have said Alex was trying hard not to cry.

After a few seconds, Alex looked up at Christina and stared long and hard at her face until she felt so uncomfortable she had to say something.

"Alex, are you okay? I've made a mistake by showing you the certificate, I'm very sorry. I think I should go now."

"No Christina, please stay. I'm sorry, it's just a bit of a shock but it's beginning to make sense now."

"I came looking for my father in the hope he might know my mother's whereabouts or at least give me some idea as to where I might find her."

There were so many things going through Alex's mind, but uppermost was that he was sitting next to his granddaughter. He could not believe it, but when he saw Marlene's name on the certificate and his son's, everything suddenly became clear.

He had always suspected there was something between Johnathan and Marlene and when she left so suddenly, he thought it was because there had been a falling out and Johnathan had made it impossible for her to stay. Little did he know she was pregnant with Christina and his no good, disgrace of a son had abandoned her.

"Christina, your father may not have been prepared to help you but your grandfather is," he leaned across the table and placed his hand on top of hers, "you are my granddaughter - I am Johnathan's father."

Christina put her hand to her mouth in shock! "I'm so sorry, I don't want to cause any trouble, I didn't know you he was related to you or I wouldn't have said anything!"

"Well I'm glad you did Christina because you've just made me a very happy man! I know this is probably all too much for you to take in right now but how would you feel about coming home with me to dinner and we can have a long talk about all of this and make a plan to find Marlene. There is someone I would really like you to meet and believe me she is going to be over the moon! Well, we might need to pick her up off the floor first once we tell her she has a granddaughter!"

Christina couldn't believe she had found her grandparents and Alex was going to help her find her mother, the relief was so overwhelming, she burst into tears again. Alex quickly got up, put his arm around her shoulders and gave her a napkin to mop up her tears. Christina stood up and gave her grandfather a hug. Everything was going to be alright now, this lovely man would find Marlene!

Christina had been back at work for just over two weeks and had a whole weekend off! She was lying on the settee watching a movie on the Friday evening when the phone rang. "Hello!"

"Christina, it's Alex."

"Hello Alex or should I say grandad!" she knew he would be turning pink with pride at the other end of the phone.

"I like the sound of that!" he laughed. "I have some news for you and you might want to get out the tissues…"

"Bad news?"

"Good news!"

"Oh my god, you've found her?"

"Of course I've found her! I'm your grandad, although my private investigator helped a little!" he laughed. "When can you come through to Glasgow so we can go and meet Marlene together?"

"I can't believe you found her! I'm off all weekend, can we go tomorrow?"

"Let me know what train you are on and I will pick you up from the station."

"I must be dreaming! I can get an early train and will call you from the station before I leave."

"Right, I will see you tomorrow, try and get some sleep!"

"See you tomorrow grandad!" Alex could hear the excitement in her voice and smiled to himself. He hoped things would go well tomorrow but he was worried how Marlene might take the shock of them turning up on her doorstep.

Once on the train Christina watched the passing scenery and thought about her last trip to Glasgow. Once Alex found out who she was they had gone to his home to see Betty, his wife, and tell her Christina's story.

When they arrived at the house, Alex could barely contain his excitement and asked Christina to wait in the hall. He turned and gave her a wink before pushing open a door. Alex walked into the kitchen where Betty was busy baking cakes and asked her to sit down as he had something important to tell her.

"I'm busy making cakes for the church fayre Alex, can't it wait?"

"No my love, this definitely cannot wait! I met a young girl today as I walked into work and she was very upset and crying, so I stopped her and took her to the café for a cup of tea. We started talking and I found out that years ago, Johnathan had an affair with Marlene, his secretary."

Betty gasped with shock. "Was that the girl who disappeared without a word?"

"I'm impressed love, that was twenty years ago!"

"I may be getting on a bit, but my memory is still sharp as a tack! So how did you find out about this?"

"Well the young girl, Christina, had gone to see Johnathan to see if he could help find her mother who just happens to be Marlene. She was adopted when she was three years old and has just recently found out who her mother was."

"Oh the poor girl! Why would Marlene have her daughter adopted?"

"Well Christina had been told Marlene had a dreadful accident which left her very badly injured and unable to care for her daughter, so she made a brave and tough decision to have her adopted."

"Oh Alex, the poor girl! The world is so cruel sometimes!"

"There's a bit more love and there's no way to tell you without upsetting you, however, you need to know."

"Tell me Alex!"

"Well as I said our son was having an affair with Marlene when she was his secretary and when she fell pregnant, Johnathan was the father of the baby and I'm not quite sure but I think he fired her, no doubt with a warning not to say anything about the pregnancy!" Alex was shaking his head in disgust, "Our son is a disgrace Betty."

Betty was horrified and she too shook her head in disbelief! "How could he do that? I don't know what happened to that boy Alex but I'm ashamed of him, this is just too much to forgive!"

"I know my dear," he put his arm around her shoulders and kissed her on the forehead. Alex watched Betty's face as the penny dropped and she gasped.

"So Christina is Johnathan's daughter?"

"Yes my love and that makes you a grandmother!" he smiled at the look on Betty's face.

"Why didn't you take her home Alex? We need to talk to her and make sure she is alright. This must be very upsetting for her?"

"Well at first when we realised we were related it was a bit of a shock but it was soon replaced by joy. Christina is a lovely young lady and she would like to meet you too." Alex helped his wife off the chair and led her towards the hall. As the kitchen door opened she saw a beautiful young girl standing in the hall. Betty looked at Alex and he nodded. "Betty my love, meet our granddaughter, Christina!"

Betty almost ran at her, engulfing Christina in a long hug. When she finally let her go, Betty stood back but held onto her granddaughter's hand. "Come and sit down with me love, I need you to tell me all about what happened to you and your mother."

They sat and talked over Christina's story and agreed that Marlene had to be found as soon as possible. Alex said he would get the private detective, who worked for the firm, to start looking. He copied all the information Christina had and hoped it would be enough to trace Marlene.

As she travelled home that evening Christina felt as though she had dreamt the whole day. She had met her horrible father, bumped into her lovely, gentle grandfather, who took her to meet her adorable grandmother and together they were going to help her find her mother!

Now she was heading back to meet her grandfather and together they were actually going to meet her mother – it was like a dream!

Alex met Christina at the station and they had a quick coffee at the café where he brought her up to date with the investigator's findings. "Tom started at the hospital and although he couldn't get anything through the official route, he did speak to one of the physiotherapists who had been there when Marlene was a patient. She had been there for nearly two years so he remembered her easily. He gave Tom the name of the physiotherapist who looked after Marlene along with the name of the hospital he moved on to. Tom was lucky enough to find him and he knew where Marlene went to live after her discharge from hospital, as he did several home visits."

Alex watched Christina's face, "She is staying in a small village about twenty miles outside Edinburgh, she has never moved since leaving hospital."

"That man Tom didn't go to her home did he?"

"No, all he had to do was to say he was visiting the area and relatives of Marlene's asked him to try and find out if she still lived there. The local minister was very helpful," Alex smiled at the look of admiration on Christina's face.

As they drove to the village, Alex and Christina talked about how hard life must have been for Marlene and discussed how they would approach the visit, neither wanting to upset her.

Christina's stomach was doing somersaults as Alex drove through the village but at first they couldn't find the house so Alex pulled over to ask directions from an elderly gentleman who was walking his dog. He very kindly explained where to go and a couple of minutes later, Alex parked outside a small terraced cottage with a small rose garden.

Alex looked at Christina and he could see she was now very nervous. "Are you ready to meet your mother?"

Christina closed her eyes and took a deep breath. "As ready as I'll ever be!"

As Alex knocked on the door, Christina thought her legs were going to give way. This meeting meant so much to her, but what if Marlene didn't want the past dragged up, all the feelings of hurt she may have buried over the years could rise to the surface and she might not want to see her.

The door opened and Alex recognized Marlene straight away. It took her a few seconds longer but after the initial shock at seeing Alex Mason on her doorstep she gave him a warm welcome.

"Mr Mason! You are the last person I expected to see when I opened the door, what a surprise! Come in, please come in off the doorstep!"

"It's good to see you again after all these years Marlene," he took her hand and patted it as he spoke.

"Come through to the warmth and sit down." Marlene walked ahead and Alex watched as she leaned heavily on her walking stick. He stepped forward into the cottage, turned, took Christina's hand and led her forward. "I've brought my granddaughter with me, I hope you don't mind?"

"Of course not! Come in and take a seat, would you like some tea?"

"We don't want to put you to any bother Marlene, however if you are having something yourself, then tea would be lovely."

Alex watched as Marlene walked into the small kitchen and it was plain to see her accident left her with permanent damage.

Christina couldn't take her eyes off Marlene. She was studying her every move, looking for any similarities between them. It was then she noticed a framed photograph of her, which must have been taken shortly before she was adopted as her mum and dad had one taken very soon after she went to live with them and it looked very similar.

Alex caught Christina's eye and mouthed, "Are you okay?"

Christina nodded but signed with her hand that her heart was beating fast and then pointed to the photograph and then at herself. Alex nodded, giving her a reassuring smile and a wink!

Alex could see Marlene was about to lift a tray and he got up and rushed forward saying, "Let me get that for you, we have arrived unannounced and are putting you to a lot of trouble!"

"Not at all Mr Mason, it's such a surprise to see you but I am a bit curious how you know where I live and I imagine there is a reason for your visit?" she said giving him a questioning smile.

Alex put the tray down on the coffee table, offered to be mother and poured the tea, first handing both Marlene and Christina their cups and saucers, then passing round the plate of cake and biscuits. He then sat down and took a deep breath.

"You are right of course Marlene," he said smiling, "and please call me Alex, I am no longer your boss! Well I'm not sure where to start but maybe I should begin by telling you I have just recently been made aware of the reason you left your position in my company." Alex could see Marlene looked both shocked and anxious. "Please don't worry, I am here to apologise for how Johnathan behaved towards you, although I don't actually know the full story but I would be very grateful if you could tell me as, from what I hear, his actions were unforgiveable. Please don't worry about sparing my feelings and you can talk openly in front of Tina, as I said, she is family." Christina nearly choked on her biscuit thinking he gave the game away by using the shortened version of her name, but she realised Alex needed to assure Marlene that she could speak openly about such a personal matter and she obviously hadn't made the connection.

Marlene was very surprised and shocked that, after nearly twenty years, Johnathan's father found out how he treated her and had gone to the bother to find her to apologise.

"So you know I didn't resign and didn't leave willingly?" Alex nodded. "Do you know Johnathan and myself were having a relationship?'

Again Alex nodded, "I would like you to tell me the whole story although I do know that you left because you were expecting a child." Marlene nodded in agreement.

"We had been in a relationship for months and he told me all along he loved me and was just waiting until the right time to break off his engagement with April, then we would be together. I believed him and of course loved him too, but when I told him I was pregnant he said how stupid I was and couldn't I get rid of it somehow? He was hurling abuse at me, accusing me of sleeping with every man in the office, which was not true!

I was five months pregnant and I swear I didn't know, although I was putting on a bit of weight I never thought much of it and was really shocked myself when I found out! I told Johnathan I was having the baby and I would need him to help me financially. He said I could ruin his career if anyone found out and told me to leave before anyone became suspicious.

I accepted he wanted nothing to do with me, but asked him to help support me, I even drew up an agreement promising if Johnathan agreed to pay me an allowance, I wouldn't say anything about him being the father. He was really mad and said he wasn't going to pay a penny and if I said anything to anyone at the office he would tell them I had slept around and chose to try and blackmail him because he had money, that's why he fired me. He also threatened me, saying if I told anyone why I was leaving he would say I was lying and he had caught me stealing from his wallet."

Alex shook his head, "I am so sorry Marlene, believe me if I had known, you would not have been treated like that.

I did wonder if something happened between you at the time but he said you had to leave suddenly as your mother or father was ill, I cant quite remember I'm afraid!"

"Don't worry about it Alex, none of this is your fault. I had no money and was at my wits end with nowhere to live, but an aunt of mine came to the rescue and I went to live with her and was very happy. I had a little girl and my aunt looked after us extremely well and in turn I looked after her as she didn't keep very well, in fact I named my daughter after her."

Christina glanced over at her grandfather, her eyes widening as she learnt something new about herself.

"I am so ashamed of my son, I always knew he was a nasty piece of work but this is beyond belief!" Alex looked over at Christina to make sure she was okay and she appeared to be holding it together. "So how long did you live with your aunt?"

"Just over three years, but then my aunt died. She had two sons, one who was a lovely man and would have let me stay in the house after his mother's death, but the other was out for every penny and forced the sale."

"So what did you do?"

"I had a bit of money that I had saved up and Christine had a nest egg hidden in my room as the horrible son Douglas would sometimes come to the house looking for money but he wouldn't go in my room. She told me that if anything happened to her I was to take the cash to help look after the baby. As it turned out, when I moved to a flat after the house was sold, Douglas somehow found out where I was living. He came round to my flat and started throwing his weight around, asking for his mother's money as he believed Christine had a lot more money than she actually did. I told him I had never had access to my aunt's bank account but he didn't believe me and demanded to know where it had all gone. We were standing on the landing outside the flat, as the baby was asleep, when he grabbed me by the hair and hit me so hard I went over the bannister and landed at the bottom of the stairs." Marlene looked up as Christina let out a gasp and covered her mouth with her hand.

"I'm so sorry, I didn't mean to shock you," Marlene had forgotten the young girl was listening to the story. She must be Johnathan and April's daughter and shouldn't be listening to bad things about her father.

"I am horrified you were attacked like that!" Christina just wanted to rush over and put her arms around her mother but she needed to wait until Alex revealed who she was.

Alex leaned forward with his hands in his head for a few seconds before looking across at Christina. She caught his gaze and he gave a slight nod and she nodded back.

"Marlene, I have something to tell you that might come as a bit of a shock and for that I apologise. A couple of weeks ago a client came to see Johnathan looking for her mother and there is no easy way to say this, it seems she is your daughter and is trying to trace you."

Marlene suddenly looked alert and she studied Alex's face waiting for him to continue. "I asked her to explain what she knew about you and she gave me enough details to piece the picture together. Johnathan was unforgivably nasty, threatened her and sent her away saying he would have nothing to do with her, just the same way he treated you all those years ago. He does not yet know that I met your daughter heading out of the office and she caught my attention because she was very upset. I mistook her for a client and managed to get her to tell me what had just occurred. She explained what happened in Johnathan's office and showed me her birth certificate, it was then I realised she was my granddaughter."

"Is she okay, what does she look like?' Marlene begged, tears streaming down her face.

Christina got up, walked over to Marlene and knelt down beside her chair. Marlene stared at her and her face changed as she realised who she was! "Yes it's me! I am Christina – I'm your daughter!"

After they both stopped crying and hugging, they started to ask each other questions and smiling to himself, Alex picked up the tray and went to make more tea as his granddaughter and her mother tried to fill each other in on the events of all the missed years.

It was hours later when Alex and Christina left the cottage. Alex had even made some sandwiches for them all, insisting Marlene and Christina keep talking.

Before they said goodbye to Marlene, promising they would be in touch very soon, Alex persuaded Marlene to accept a cheque as compensation for the hardship she had suffered, all as a result of his son abandoning her. Although she refused several times, Marlene eventually accepted the money as it was clear Alex was not going to take no for an answer. She felt as though she was dreaming, not in a million years could she have imagined how her life could change in the space of a day! She could not believe her daughter walked into her house today after so many years!

Christina could not believe how well the visit had gone. Her mother was such a lovely person and surprisingly not bitter about how her life turned out. Marlene told her it had taken years to come to terms with knowing she would never see her daughter again. She held Christina's hand tightly for hours as they talked, every now and then stopping to study her daughter's face.

Even in the midst of such an emotional day, recounting the awful events which ultimately her father was responsible for by not looking after Marlene in the first place, she asked Christina to tell her mum and dad how grateful she was to them for being such loving parents, she was a credit to them. She also asked Christina to call her Marlene as she already had a mum who deserved that title - what an amazing woman!

Christina couldn't wait to tell her mum and dad all about the visit as she knew they were concerned for Marlene and would be pleased she had her daughter in her life again.

How lucky she was to have three lovely parents and another set of grandparents!

CHAPTER 44

It was a day none of them thought they would ever see, for all sorts of reasons.

Harry and Jean sat in the front pew remembering the baby girl who was delivered to them all those years ago, how quickly the time had passed. Every day had been worth it, good days; bad days; when she had the measles; the heartbreak when Joanie, Olivia's best pal had to move away from Beauly; the day she broke her arm; when Robert, her ten year old boyfriend chose Marie to dance with at her birthday party; the day she left home to go to Veterinary School; her graduation day; her wedding day; the day they found out she was so ill and then the day of the transplant. They had never, in all those years, experienced the emotions they now felt today...

Behind them, Chrissie and Moira sat with tears in their eyes, the emotion of the day too much for two old women...

Across from Harry and Jean, Bryan and Lynn Carson sat waiting for the service to begin. Bryan was thinking back to the day he had given his daughter up for adoption and he could still feel the pain as fresh today. When Angela had phoned his friend leaving a message to say Anna was in Edinburgh looking for him, all sorts of emotions flooded through him, uppermost was guilt - what would she think of him, a man who could give away his child? Of course, he could never have imagined the reason for her contacting him, but he had to step up and do what any father would do, try to give his daughter the gift of life once again. It hadn't worked out that way, but he wished he had been given the chance to save her...

Angela Johnson sat behind the desk in her office, her next patient due any minute. It wasn't often she allowed anything personal to interrupt her working day but she found herself momentarily thinking of the service about to take place. Angela decided not to attend today, she had done what she could to try and save Olivia's life and thought of it as her penance for not wanting her and the events which occurred after her birth...

The minister came out of the vestry, nodded his acknowledgement to the congregation and signalled to the organist who began playing Olivia's favourite hymn 'Morning Has Broken'....

Matt listened to the music as he waited in the vestry and fought back the threatening tears as he thought about how hard his darling wife had fought for her life after Angela agreed to be the donor. He could still picture Ollie the first time he was allowed into the intensive care ward to see her after the operation, so frail, thin and attached to tubes, wires and machines which were keeping her alive.

Three weeks later he had lost track of how many times they nearly lost her and the amount of hours he sat in the relative's room with Harry and Jean drinking endless cups of dreadful coffee from the vending machine. They always made sure there were two of them there, just in case something happened to Ollie and Matt had left to have a quick shower or buy some sandwiches and decent coffees for them all. Nobody could persuade him to leave the hospital and he insisted on staying around the clock, lying on the floor in a sleeping bag every night in the cold, uncomfortable relative's room. Harry and Jean took it in turn to go and have a shower, grab an hour or two of much needed sleep and also do the food and drinks run. Between the three of them, they could not have prayed or willed their darling girl to live anymore than they had done….

As the hymn came to an end, the verger nodded to Matt and opened the vestry door. After taking a moment or two to compose himself Matt walked out of the vestry and turned to watch as his darling Ollie followed him, smiling and healthy as she carried their six week old son Samuel to the font to be christened. Everyone smiled through tears of joy at the miracle of life, granted to not only Olivia but also to her precious baby boy…….

CHAPTER 45

Alex Mason sat at his desk waiting for his son to appear. An hour ago he left a message with Johnathan's secretary saying he urgently wanted to see him the minute he arrived at the office. He was becoming angrier by the minute, a rare emotion for Alex, however on this occasion it was perfectly understandable. Once he dealt with his son he was taking the rest of the day off to go home and tell his darling wife things that would break her heart, Betty didn't deserve this.

Another forty-five minutes elapsed before Johnathan sauntered into his father's office, dropping down on the well-worn leather chair and propping his crossed feet on the edge of the desk.

Alex looked at his son, then at his feet and waited until Johnathan sighed and removed his feet from the desk. Alex examined his son through new eyes, and thought how smug and arrogant he looked. It was all about looks and possessions with Johnathan, his expensive suit; gold cufflinks; silk tie; gold watch – everything had to be the best. He was shallow and selfish, that he knew, and Alex often wondered how his son had turned out the way he had as both he and his wife were quiet, unassuming people who never judged anyone by their appearance, unlike Johnathan.

Johnathan looked at his father and raised his eyebrows, "You wanted to see me?"

"It's almost midday Johnathan, where the hell have you been?"

"Who got out of bed on the wrong side this morning? I had some business to take care of."

"It seems that you do that too often lately. It might set a good example to our staff if you managed to turn up at the same time as everyone else from now on." Johnathan knew this was an instruction rather than a request and wondered what had got the old man's back up enough to put him in such a bad mood?

Alex sat forward, his hands clasped as he leaned on his desk, and looked directly into his son's eyes wanting to see his reaction when he spoke to him. "I wanted to speak to you about a meeting I had yesterday which concerns you as it happens. I had the pleasure of having afternoon tea with a former employee of ours, I'm sure you will remember her," he paused for a couple of seconds, "Marlene Ross."

Johnathan immediately looked down and rearranged his sitting position but he couldn't disguise the fact the colour was draining from his face. "You remember her don't you, I believe she was your secretary for a couple of years or so?"

Looking very uncomfortable, Johnathan nodded. Alex leaned back in his chair and looked over his glasses at his son's face thinking if he got any paler he would faint. If he had any doubts about the information he had been given, which he didn't, Johnathan's reaction would have quashed them.

"Shall I take it from the colour of you, coupled with your silence, that you already know what this is about?" Alex waited for Johnathan to speak.

"I don't know what you mean father, now I have work to be getting on with so…"

Alex thumped his fist down on his desk, "QUIET!!!" he yelled, "You will sit there and listen to every word I have to say!"

Johnathan looked shocked. Never in his entire life had he seen his father angry, yes he had raised his voice slightly but he had never yelled at him!

"You have deprived a mother of her child and me and your mother of a granddaughter for twenty years! Your mother will be devastated when she hears what a low life her son is, how could you do such a thing to that poor woman?"

"I have no idea what you are talking about," Johnathan shrugged his shoulders thinking to himself there was no proof.

Again his father yelled at him, "DON'T!! I have seen the birth certificate and I've spoken in depth to Marlene and my granddaughter. In fact, it was she who came here to see me as it seems when she contacted you she was threatened with 'consequences' if she dared contact you again! You are despicable and I am ashamed to call you my son!"

"Marlene must have put my name on the birth certificate because she didn't know who got her pregnant. Who knows how many blokes she had to choose from?"

Alex shook his head, "Don't you dare try to blacken that poor woman's name to cover your own tracks. I knew there was something going on between you at the time as other members of staff brought it to my attention. When Marlene left so suddenly you said it was because of personal reasons and although the others might have bought that explanation, I knew something happened between you both, but never did I think for one minute it could be something so serious.

You blackmailed that poor girl into leaving without saying a word, all to cover your own backside! You are a disgrace!"

Johnathan was seething that the office staff had known about their affair, that bitch must have told them! If Avril ever got wind of this, their marriage would be over.

Alex continued, "I have been up all night thinking about this situation very carefully and have decided you should be allowed the chance to redress your past behaviour and compensate both Marlene and her daughter, my granddaughter! You have two options and before you leave this office you will decide which of them you opt for."

"They are?" Johnathan said sarcastically. He was getting fed up with being spoken to like this, it was time the old man retired. Maybe he could do something to speed up his departure, the sooner the better!

"Your first option is to pay Marlene Ross a lump sum, a figure I will decide upon, in an attempt to compensate her for the distress and hardship she has suffered because of your callous and cowardly actions. Thereafter, you will continue to make a monthly deposit to her bank account, money you should have paid all these past years to allow her to keep and raise YOUR child. Instead that poor woman suffered a horrendous ordeal which resulted in her daughter being placed with social services for adoption which broke her heart."

"You can forget it! I'm not going to be blackmailed by her, you or anyone else!" yelled Johnathan.

"Well that's rich coming from you considering you blackmailed Marlene and threatened your own daughter! Of course there is option two?"

"Which is?"

"Option two... well it's much more simple than the first option. You resign with immediate effect and never contact me or your mother again."

Johnathan jumped up and leaned over his father's desk so they were almost nose to nose. "Don't think so old man. It's time you were on your way out! Once I'm finished influencing Ron and the rest of the staff, you, old man, will be out! I got rid of Marlene when she crossed me and I can do the same to you! Nobody gives me an ultimatum, so watch your back father, I'm going to ruin you!"

Alex stood up. He had hoped his son would make the right choice, step up and make recompense for his actions. Johnathan hadn't even asked about his daughter once! Alex walked towards the office door and opened it...

Ron Cook was sitting on the desk in the outer office and his father's secretary was glaring at him and shaking her head. Ron gave Johnathan a wry smile and wagged a finger at him. "You didn't think a smart solicitor such as your father would have a conversation so important without witnesses did you?"

Johnathan looked at him smugly, "Your word against mine, no hard evidence Ron. You old boys need to retire and leave us younger ones to do things the modern way!"

Ron pointed to the intercom with the glowing red light and Johnathan realised they had been listening to every word. "Hearsay old boy, just hearsay!"

Ron opened the small cassette recorder beside the intercom, removed the tape, held it up and smiled at Johnathan. "Time to clear your desk and leave the building sonny boy. You are finished!"

Johnathan stormed out of his father's office and half an hour later, left the building for the last time....

Alex and Ron sat in Alex's office nursing a couple of large brandies and discussed what would happen to Marlene and Christina.

"I have given Marlene a lump sum, although she refused it several times, and that will allow her to enjoy a better quality of life. I have also insisted on paying for her to receive private medical treatment whenever she needs it." Alex shook his head, "Who would have thought all this went on under my nose and I didn't know anything about it. So many wasted years Ron!"

"What about your granddaughter? Do you think she will want to continue seeing you? You couldn't blame her for being wary after the way Johnathan treated herself and her mother."

"Well thankfully Marlene is a lovely woman and luckily Christina takes after her mother and not my son. I've invited them both to the house on Sunday as I know when I go home and explain all this to Betty she'll be desperate to meet Marlene... well, once the shock wears off! I've already introduced her to our granddaughter but hopefully the occasion will be more of a celebration this time!

Neither of us will ever get over the disappointment and shame though! How any child of ours could turn out as vile as Johnathan is truly heartbreaking Ron. I'm hoping that having Christina and Marlene in our lives will help us move forward."

Christina settled in behind the wheel and turned to smile at Marlene. "Are you alright, comfortable enough?"

"Yes love, thank you for asking. I am a bit nervous about meeting Alex's wife, she must be heartbroken at how Johnathan has treated everyone. I was in the wrong too though and should never have been stupid enough to get involved with my boss, a boss who was already engaged to another woman."

"You have nothing to apologise for, he knew exactly what he was doing. He not only lied to you but to his fiancé and he used his position in the company to take advantage of you. He blackmailed and threatened you and also threatened me. He is a vile human being!

I just have to make a quick stop to post a letter and then we can be on our way."

Alex and Betty could not have been more welcoming and it took nearly half an hour for Marlene and Betty to stop crying, Betty repeatedly apologising for the disgraceful way her son had treated both Marlene and Christina. Marlene assured Betty that in no way were her and Alex to blame for their son's actions, eventually getting her to promise not to apologise again!

Once everyone was much calmer and less emotional, they all sat down in the conservatory to have afternoon tea. Betty had gone to a great deal of trouble and had baked scones, a variety of cakes and she made two platefuls of sandwiches.

After they finished eating, Betty asked Marlene if she would tell her what happened after she left her job with her husband's firm and everyone became emotional again as Marlene described the events leading up to Douglas committing the assault. She explained why she had to make the decision to have Christina adopted and as she reached over to squeeze Christina's hand, Betty dissolved into tears again.

Once she recovered, Betty asked about their lives, where they were living and appeared visibly shocked to hear Marlene had lived alone in a tiny rented cottage, in a small village since leaving hospital. Christina had previously explained she now lived in a flat in Edinburgh, not far from the hospital where she worked as an oncology nurse.

Betty voiced her concern that Marlene lived too far away from Christina, but she explained she had chosen to live in the village all those years ago because it was much cheaper and quieter than the city and as rental prices increased over the years, she had no option but to stay there. She quickly added that as Alex had so kindly insisted on giving her a huge amount of money, she would now be looking at moving closer to the city where she could see more of Christina.

Marlene smiled at her daughter, overwhelmed at how lucky she was to have her back in her life and delighted to know she would see her regularly from now on.

Betty looked at Alex, "The cottage dear, we don't use it now and it would be just perfect for Marlene!" Alex nodded at his wife and thought how lucky he had been all those years ago to find a woman who was so kind, caring and loving. He was extremely proud of her!

"There's no need to look for somewhere to live, we have the perfect cottage on the outskirts of Edinburgh. It's just ideal, no stairs; two bedrooms; lovely kitchen with a dining area and a courtyard garden with a small terrace where you can sit out on a sunny morning and enjoy your breakfast! It's fully furnished, but of course we will take out anything you don't want as you'll have your own things, it's yours my dear, please say you'll take it!"

Marlene shook her head, "I couldn't possibly accept your cottage it's too much! Please don't think, for one minute, either of us is looking for money from you. Christina is your granddaughter and we want you to enjoy being grandparents with no strings attached."

It was Alex's turn to speak. "We know that Marlene, we don't think for one minute you are here for money, after all it was me who came looking for you," he smiled and Betty reached out to hold Marlene's hand. "We are delighted to be lucky enough to find you both and we know it doesn't matter to you if we are rich or poor. The fact is we are very comfortable and if we had known about you and Christina you would have been looked after as our family all along.

You are the mother of our granddaughter Marlene and in our eyes that makes you our daughter-in-law, regardless of whether you married our son or not," Betty still held Marlene's hand and she squeezed it gently, her eyes sparkling with more unshed tears. "If we had known twenty years ago what we know now, we would have made sure you were living in a comfortable home with no money worries and that's what we want to do now. I will put the cottage into both your names so you will never have to worry about paying rent and, as our family, it will give us great comfort to know you are safe and secure in your own home.

We have also made some lucrative investment choices over the years and we have transferred one account into your name Marlene and another in Christina's name." Both women gasped and said it was too much and they couldn't accept, but both Alex and Betty refused to discuss it saying it was their pleasure and how happy they were to do something to make their lives easier.

"The accounts provide quite a reasonable monthly income but you can of course withdraw money at anytime. Due to our son's unacceptable behaviour towards you both, we have made some other changes on the financial side of things. I may as well tell you now as we are discussing money that we have already changed our wills. There is to be no argument about what I am going to tell you, it is our decision and it's not up for discussion!" Alex raised his eyebrows and grinned at Marlene and Christina. Betty was also smiling and looked very pleased with herself!

Marlene looked at Christina, shaking her head in wonderment! Christina loved that Marlene looked like a child on Christmas morning finding all the presents she asked for under the tree!

Alex suggested they all have a drink before he continued. "For shock!" he laughed. Marlene needed a brandy, Betty asked for sherry, Christina had lemonade as she was driving and Alex poured himself a malt whiskey. He took some envelopes out of the writing desk and sat down. "Firstly, we set aside some cash a few years ago which is invested and provides quite a good income each month. This was to be given to any grandchildren to help with university fees etc. You, Christina, are our granddaughter and will be our only grandchild so this investment has been transferred into your name to do with as you please. I have also lodged a document with my partner Ron which will prevent Johnathan contesting our new will, which leaves everything including all our investments plus this house, to you Christina." Both Marlene and Christina gasped as the house was obviously worth a fortune!

"I don't know what to say, thank you is just not enough! What about your son, surely he will be very angry about it?" Christina asked.

"We don't want your thanks, although it is appreciated my dear," Alex said. "We just want to enjoy having you and your mother in our lives if you'll let us. As for Johnathan, the will is watertight and I hear he will be moving away from the area soon to avoid any scandal! At the moment his wife does not know what has happened, but I'm quite sure it will not be long before someone puts her in the picture!"

Christina got up and walked over to Alex who had been leaning against the patio door, which led out to the garden. "Of course we want you to be part of our lives," she smiled and hugged him. "I also have to think about my adoptive mum and dad whom I love very much and who have been behind me one hundred per cent in my search for my birth family. They are my family too."

"I totally understand my dear. If it doesn't upset them, we would like to meet them and hopefully they will adopt us all too, as without their loving care, you might not be standing here today!"

Christina turned to look at Marlene who was smiling and nodding. "I would like that too, if they were okay with it."

Christina already knew her mum and dad would be delighted to meet her birth family and she looked at them all grinning widely, "This is one of the best days of my life! My two families are merging into one and I've never been so happy!"

The four people who said their goodbyes that afternoon were each changed in a different way.

Alex had a daughter in law who had been through a horrendous experience, due to his son's disgusting behaviour, but she wasn't bitter. He had a grown up granddaughter who was intelligent, caring and kind, just like her mother and grandmother. His wife's broken heart was starting to repair at the promise of having Marlene and Christina in her life and for that he thanked god.

Betty was immensely grateful to have been given the chance to meet Marlene and her granddaughter. She was full of admiration for the way Marlene had coped with the tragedy and hardship life had thrown at her and she would be immensely proud to introduce her to her friends as her daughter in law. Most of all she was thankful to them for allowing her and Alex into their lives as many others would have refused to have anything to do with them after the way their son had treated them. She was looking forward to getting to know them and spending as much time as possible with them both.

Marlene couldn't believe how her life had changed since Christina and Alex found her. She was very grateful to Alex and Betty for accepting her and her daughter into their lives without any hesitation. She instantly liked them both and was looking forward to spending more time in their company. She had been given a house closer to them and Christina and would never have to worry about paying the bills ever again! Suddenly she found herself with a family after all the years spent alone and she silently thanked Connor and her cousin Jamie as, without them, she may not have had the will to carry on living - she was finally happy again!

Christina had grandparents whom she really liked and who had shown immense kindness to her and Marlene. Her mum and dad would be happy she found her birth family and as Alex had suggested, she knew they would all become a family unit. She had her birth mum back and Marlene's life would change for the better now she had a family around her. How she survived such an ordeal Christina could not imagine, but she deserved to be loved and cared for and that's just what she would do. Alex and Betty would also become a huge part of her life and Marlene's and the future now looked bright for all of them!

As they all waved goodbye, Christina drove along the driveway and onto the road. She smiled secretly to herself, as there was one other thing, which made today just perfect!

On her way to visit her grandparents this morning, she posted a letter and tomorrow morning Johnathan Mason's wife would receive a letter explaining why her husband's family had disowned him and why he would never benefit from his father's success.

Finally, his secret would be out, his wife would know just how he treated people and Johnathan would have to live with the consequences....

She turned and smiled at her mother - yes it had been a perfect day and the future looked bright!

CHAPTER 46

On the drive home Mike and Rachel were chatting about the weekend, her brilliant birthday party and her parents.

"I take it you don't have any siblings?" asked Mike.

"No, we are not a straightforward family, as in mum and dad are not my birth parents."

Mike look surprised, "Tell me?"

"Well my dad was Maggie's brother and when I was three mum, dad and myself were all travelling in the car when it was hit by another vehicle. Mum and dad were killed outright but I got stuck in the foot well and didn't even have a scratch on me. Maggie was my godmother and dad left me in her care, so she and Stuart adopted me."

"That's a sad story, but you are lucky to have such lovely parents in Maggie and Stuart. Did they not want any other children or was one of you enough!" Mike laughed.

"Cheek! Well you must never repeat this…." she looked at Mike and he nodded. "Promise me?"

"I promise, cross my heart."

"Just after I turned fifteen, Maggie sat me down and told me the story I'm about to tell you. She said it was a lesson about teenage sex and what can happen if you have sex, without taking care. She then told me when she was sixteen, she got pregnant and her father banished her to the country to stay with her grandmother until her baby was born. He was going to make arrangements for her baby to be adopted and then she could take up her place at university."

"So what did happen to the baby?"

"It's a really sad story. It was just after New Year and because the house was so remote, way up north past Ullapool, when Maggie went into labour she couldn't make it to the hospital because of a blizzard. Her grandmother delivered Maggie's baby boy and because he was born in her grandparents house, she named him George after her grandfather, my great grandfather!

Her father arranged with social services to take Maggie's baby away as soon as he or she was born, but because they were snowed in, she actually got to spend a few precious days with him, although as soon as the road to the house was cleared, George was taken away leaving Maggie broken hearted. She never spoke to her parents again!"

"You're right, it is a sad story, very sad!"

"Maggie told me she thinks about her baby all the time, especially on his birthday and at Christmas. It must be hard not knowing where your child is, if he is happy and healthy, or even worse what if like my mum and dad something awful has happened to him!"

"I think we need to get off this subject, it's too sad to think about, we need to talk about something else. Did you remember to get your passport, because if we do manage to go skiing you will need it!" he smiled at Rachel as she nodded enthusiastically! They chatted away happily, Mike relaying skiing stories, most of which were amusing at his expense!

A few days later, Mike was sitting in Rachel's flat waiting for her to get changed so they could go out for something to eat and he noticed her passport lying on the coffee table. Being nosey he thought he would have a look at her photo so he could tease her about it, then he noticed her name. It wasn't just Rachel MacIntyre, her middle name was Roberts and when she came into the room he waved her passport at her and joked about her photo. "Where does your middle name come from?"

"Maggie decided it would be nice for me to keep my family surname and added her married name to it."

"So, Maggie's maiden name was Roberts?"

"Of course, same as my dad's."

As Mike drove north, he thought about the past couple of weeks. Ever since the night he saw Rachel's passport, he had been wrestling with his conscience and only last night had come to a decision.

His mum and dad told him from an early age they had adopted him as their baby died due to a heart defect not long after he was born and they couldn't have any other children because mum had to have an operation. He had a fantastic childhood, loved his mum and dad deeply and never wanted to search for his birth parents, he was very happy with the parents he had.

However, when he was about eighteen he did obtain a copy of his original birth certificate, just to have, not for any other reason other than to know the details of his birth. There was nothing under father's name, but his mother's name was Margaret Roberts and from her date of birth she would have been 16 when he was born. He had been named George and was born in January in the parish of Ullapool, Wester Ross.

He knew from his birth certificate and the story Rachel told him that he was Maggie's son, but he had to get her to confirm it and last night he decided to drive up and talk to her.

He wouldn't have made the choice to reveal who he was but if Maggie was his mother, then he was dating his cousin or his stepsister or both? It was all so complicated but he could think of nothing else and although he already knew, he had to tell Maggie.

Maggie opened the door and was surprised to see Mike standing on the doorstep. Her first thought was something had happened to Rachel, but Mike reassured her she was absolutely fine, he just needed to speak to her about something.

Maggie invited him in, made some coffee, put some biscuits on a plate and pulled up a chair at the breakfast table. Her stomach was churning, as there was something different about the way Mike was watching her, he was studying her very intently.

"So Mike what would you like to talk to me about?"

Mike looked into Maggie's eyes, the same green eyes as his. Why had he not noticed her eyes when he was here with Rachel? "If I said to you I was George Roberts, would it mean anything to you?"

Maggie never broke eye contact with him as she replied, "I knew it was you the minute I saw you!" she gave him a faint smile.

"You did?" Mike looked surprised.

"The minute you turned around to face me on the night I met you, it was like looking at Simon all those years ago! You have his hair colour and features but you have my unusual green eyes."

"Simon? He is my father?" Maggie nodded.

"Why is he not on the birth certificate?"

"My father was so angry with me for getting pregnant he never spoke to me, never mind discussed who the father was. He just wanted me whisked away out of sight as quickly as possible to avoid a scandal, which would have hurt both his and my mother's reputations. She was a pharmacist and he a highly respected surgeon who were both disgusted and furious with me for letting them down.

They decided how to deal with the situation, which was to send me to my grandmothers, in the middle of nowhere, until I had you and they arranged for you to be adopted - I had no say about any of it and had to do as I was told."

Mike nodded. "I see. I got a copy of my birth certificate just out of curiosity, but never intended to look for you, however I saw Rachel's passport and saw her middle name was Roberts. I thought you were her birth parents but when we were talking on the way home after her birthday party, she explained about her mother and father's accident and how you adopted her.

She then told me the story of where you had your baby and why you called him George and although she made me promise never to say anything, it was just too much of a coincidence and I couldn't stop thinking about it. I've been going over and over it in my head for a couple of weeks and last night I decided I had to find out the truth and now I know you are my mother, I have to stop seeing Rachel. She is my cousin and maybe somehow my stepsister? It just wouldn't be right to continue in a relationship with each other!"

"I have to admit I have been worrying about the same," said Maggie, "but I couldn't say anything to you, it wouldn't have been right. I did talk it over with Stuart and we thought if you kept seeing Rachel, I would be able to find out more about you over time, such as your birth date. Obviously if you had the same date of birth as George I would have had to talk to you about it." Mike nodded. "So what are you going to do about you and Rachel, technically you are cousins and although you both have the same mother, I've checked and you are not doing anything illegal!"

"We can't stay together, it would be too complicated and I don't think it would be the right thing to do. Before I met Rachel, I was offered a job lecturing in Canada, it's a swap scheme where a Canadian guy takes over my job and vice versa. Because I care so much about her, I postponed making a decision and would probably not have taken the job but this situation changes everything and I've decided to go."

"I'm so sorry Mike, I can't believe this has happened!" Maggie's eyes had filled with tears.

Mike leaned forward and took Maggie's hand. "It's not your fault Maggie, please don't get upset, none of this is your fault. What are the odds that Rachel and I would meet and start dating?"

"Moving to Canada is a drastic choice just to end a relationship!" Her son was holding her hand! She just couldn't believe he was sitting opposite her, but now he was talking about moving to Canada and she was going to loose him all over again!

"I've thought about nothing else since Rachel told me about you and on the drive up here I decided if you confirmed my suspicions, I would take the job. It will be the easiest way to end our relationship, as we can't tell Rachel the truth. I realise she will be upset at first but we can still write to each other and I'm sure in time she will meet someone else. If not, then I will have to invent a girlfriend at my end, but I hope it's the other way round for her sake, I really don't want to hurt her!" Maggie squeezed his hand tightly and slowly shook her head.

"Don't get upset. I think it's for the best, as I said, if I hadn't met Rachel I would have taken the job anyway. If I stay, I would have to break up with her and we would constantly bump into each other, which wouldn't be fair on either of us. It has to be a clean break and it's not often you get a job offer like this - fate is something I've always believed in and in this instance it's been a major factor!" He shrugged his shoulders and gave Maggie a half smile. "Fate that I met Rachel, fate that she was your daughter, fate that I have been offered a job when I needed to move away and of course fate has led to us finding each other again!"

Mike squeezed Maggie's hand and gave her a reassuring smile, "I will tell Rachel I have to take this job to further my career and while I'm away she can concentrate more on her studies. As I said, I will promise to write but eventually our relationship will peter out. She is a very popular girl and before you know it, some other lucky guy will take my place. It's a sacrifice I have to make to protect us all, just as you made a sacrifice for me all those years ago! This has to stay our secret though Maggie?"

Maggie sat back in her chair and sighed. "I don't want to lie to Rachel, but I have to agree this is such an unusual situation and the truth would change all our lives - it's already changed ours. Although I think you and I could handle it, I'm not so sure about Rachel and I couldn't bear our relationship to be spoilt, I love her so much!

I know you said you never had any intention of finding me, but, as I am not going to see you again, I have to take this opportunity to tell you how very sad I am that I will not get the chance to get to know you better. I am so very lucky to have met you and know you've had a good life with loving parents and most of all that you've been happy! It has always worried me that you might be unhappy and your adoptive parents didn't love you enough!"

Mike grinned at Maggie. "You had no option but to do as your father wanted. I have been very happy and love my parents, however, I am also very glad to have met you and now I know where I get my green eyes from!" Mike stood up to put his jacket on and turned to Maggie who was also on her feet. "So it's settled, neither of us will mention this conversation, I will disappear off to Canada and you will be here to make sure Rachel is okay."

Before Mike left, Maggie asked if he would accept something to remember her by and he agreed. She quickly went up to her room and came down carrying her jewellery box. "After you were taken away from me I stayed with my grandmother until I went to university and on the day I left, she gave me this keepsake which I would like you to have." Maggie took a gold watch from the box and handed it to Mike.

"I can't take this Maggie, it was given to you."

"Look at the inscription on the back."

Mike turned the watch over and read, "To my darling George," Mike looked a bit surprised.

"My grandmother gave it to my grandfather, who you were named after, for their golden wedding anniversary. I would like you to have it for two reasons. It was your great grandfather's watch and the inscription was a loving message from his wife, but when you look at the watch, I would like you to know the inscription also applies to you from me," her voice faltered slightly with emotion as she spoke.

Mike was very touched by Maggie's gift, gave her a tight hug, thanked her and put the watch on his wrist. Maggie was also very touched that he immediately wore the watch as she thought he would just put it in his pocket

Maggie walked Mike to the door, gave him a hug and watched as he got into his car, her heart breaking just as it had the day he was taken away from her all those years ago. Mike smiled and gave her a wave as he drove away and as she waved back a sob escaped as she broke down.

As Mike started to drive away knowing he might not see Maggie again, he was surprised to find himself unable to just walk away from her and made a snap decision not to disappear from her life again, she didn't deserve that, he liked her and found himself wanting to have some form of relationship with her. He stopped the car, reversed back to the house and walked back to the door where a tearful Maggie was standing.

"Oh Maggie, please don't be upset!" He gave her a hug and stood back, a bit unsure how to begin. "I find myself unable to walk out of your life again Maggie and I'm not sure how you feel about it, but I would like us to keep in touch. We could write, find out more about each other and keep up to date with our news. I could also send a Christmas card and sign it George and should Rachel ever ask, you could just say it was a friend from your schooldays – there's a bit of truth in there!" Mike smiled at Maggie who couldn't hide her shocked delight!

"Oh Mike, I'm so glad you feel this way, I would never have said anything, but I would have been devastated to loose you again!"

"That's settled then – we may even be able to meet up occasionally, Stuart too, once I'm back from Canada – Rachel would never have to know?"

"Really! I would love that, I can't believe this is happening – you've made me so happy, thank you!"

He kissed her on the cheek, enveloped her in a bear hug, then loosened his hold slightly as he stood back, "I have your address and will write once I'm settled in Canada." He looked down at his wrist. "I will treasure my watch - always. Look after Rachel and write regularly, let's not loose each other again!"

He kissed her on the cheek once more before getting back into his car, waving as turned out of the driveway.

Maggie sat at the breakfast bar and let the tears flow, however they were not unhappy tears. She never thought she would see George again and due to a twist of fate, they had been lucky enough to spend some time with each other! From now on they would keep in touch, of that she was sure - and they were going to meet up when he got back from Canada!

Now she would need to be strong for her daughter, a child who filled her life with love and who, without any realisation, brought her son back into her life! Rachel was about to suffer the hurt of losing her first love and she would need the love and support of her mum and dad.

She would not have the relationship she yearned for with her son, but for her it was enough for them to be able to write to each other and meet up occasionally. For now she was content, knowing he grew up in a happy home and was loved by his adoptive parents - she could at last stop torturing herself.

To know Mike did not resent her for giving him away, released the guilt she carried with her since his birth. It was more than she could ever have hoped for!

She had been blessed with a husband and two beautiful children and for that she would be eternally grateful...

CHAPTER 47

Peter Cameron sat back in his chair and looked at the photographs on his desk. Laura smiled back at him and next to her was a photograph of himself and their son Jack, both happy and smiling on the day Jack married his beautiful Mollie!

However, the photo that stole his heart every time he looked at it was the one of little Sara, his granddaughter, on her first birthday. He filled with pride whenever her name was mentioned and had joined the league of proud granddads who took every opportunity to get her photo out of his wallet and brag about how adorable she was!

He was looking forward to the following day as it was Jack and Mollie's third wedding anniversary and he was spending the weekend babysitting for Sara to allow them a night away in Edinburgh.

Sara was almost two now and he loved nothing more than spending time at the farmhouse with her, Jack and Mollie. He and Sara loved to go out for walks through the wood to the pond, where they fed the ducks. Sara loved to splash in every puddle along the way, squealing with delight when she succeeded in soaking them both! He had just been out to buy her a raincoat and a new pair of bright red wellington boots for their walk tomorrow and he knew Sara would love her wellies as her mummy had a matching pair!

Peter also bought a new picture storybook for Sara about a family of ducks, 'The Quacker Family', they would read it at bedtime tomorrow night – Sara just loved ducks!

He took a deep relaxing breath and leant back in his chair. He was finally happy again, content with life and blessed with a close relationship with his son and his family.

There was only one person missing from his life, his Laura, but she would always live on in his heart, a heart that was full of joy and no longer broken….